IN SEARCH
OF MERCY

IN SEARCH OF MERCY

MICHAEL AYOOB

MINOTAUR BOOKS

A THOMAS DUNNE BOOK

NEW YORK

This is a work of fiction. All of the characters, organizations, and events portrayed in this novel are either products of the author's imagination or are used fictitiously.

A THOMAS DUNNE BOOK FOR MINOTAUR BOOKS.
An imprint of St. Martin's Publishing Group.

www.thomasdunnebooks.com
www.minotaurbooks.com

ISBN 978-0-312-64492-5

First Edition: October 2010

10 9 8 7 6 5 4 3 2 1

To Mom, Dad, and my sister Rachel

Acknowledgments

I've been blessed with no shortage of supportive friends, teachers, and family members. For the sake of brevity, however, I'll focus on those who helped me through this particular book. Whether they read the rough drafts, offered encouragement and advice, or just endured my moods, I couldn't have made it this far without them:

Beth Barrows Elliot; Jane Bernstein; Kalisha Brown; Seth Burdick; Brad Crutchfield; Rick Easton and his parents Pat and Dick; Mike Gartland; Joe Guzzo; Maureen Howard; Sarah Labarge; Brian Maloney; Brendan McLaughlin; William J. Moner; Patrick Mullen; Caroline Murnane; Brad Powell; Kevin Ruppenthal; Ger Tonti.

Also, thanks to Ruth Cavin, Gar Anthony Haywood, Christina MacDonald, Toni Plummer, and everyone else at Minotaur Books/St. Martin's Press who brought my words to your hands.

And thanks to Amber, who told me what I needed to hear when I didn't want to hear it.

IN SEARCH
OF MERCY

1

I played for some bad crowds, but man, that last one . . . A couple hundred drunks banging on the glass, chins flapping with beer fat. Glazed eyes beaming hatred at me and Time itself. I was just a Falcon goalie blanking their Blizzard kids, but their beef with Time ran deeper. Time yanked them out of high school and dumped their bloated asses on those bleachers. It left them impotent, screaming at their kids to hit somebody. Hurt somebody, cripple somebody if you have to, as long as you win.

"Goalllll-chick, Goalllll-chick," they chanted dirgelike during every lull because my last name is Bolzjak. "Goalchick" kind of rhymed with it, and more importantly, "Goalchick" let me know I was a long-haired fag. It was that kind of crowd, that kind of vibe. Pennsylvania state championship, nine minutes left, tied 0–0, and you just knew things wouldn't end peaceably.

The ref went down, tangled in Falcons and Blizzards. A guy in the stands screamed, "Get off your knees, ref, you're blowing the game!" so loud the ref heard him. So the ref got up looking for the guy and missed a high-stick to a Falcon. A crush of noise came down from the bleachers, boos mostly, quaking Cooper

Rink to the rebar in its concrete bones. The glass panes around the ice swayed more than glass panes ever should.

The Blizzards came charging back with a two-on-one. Left passed to Right and juked my defenseman. Pass back to Left. Shot.

I took it in the chest, let the puck drop in my glove. Even did the old Statue of Liberty, raising my glove high to rile the Falcon fans. And it worked; they leapt up and screamed themselves hoarse, though I still didn't see Mom or Dad anywhere. It felt weird to play to a crowd without them, weird to see strangers in their usual spot. But I couldn't afford to think about it, not with eight minutes left.

The ref dropped the puck for a face-off. My guy clacked sticks with their guy, and the puck rolled out to the far end.

Something white appeared against the glass to my right. I looked over to a poster of a Falcon goalie strapped in an electric chair. Double quotes bracketed his hands and feet to show that he was shaking. Smoke puffs rose from his smoldering eye sockets. The scorekeeper's light hung over his head, glowing red with the same current that sizzled his body. FIRE IT UP! read block letters across the bottom. I couldn't tell if the artist used paint or Magic Markers, but damn.

The ref whistled the play dead, and everybody stopped all confused. Coach waved us to the bench, looking grim in his fudge-colored suit. Last time he wore that thing was the last time he coached a championship. Judging by the polyester of it, Coach hadn't seen a championship since the Carter era. Nor had he modified his Caesar haircut since then, nor shaved his gray mustache that twitched when he talked.

Our team captain, Durdovitch, pushed his way through to get closest to Coach. Standing six foot five and weighing over two hundred pounds, Durdovitch was a tower of anger. He kept track

2

of the concussions he doled out by stenciling little skulls on his locker. At last count, he was up to six. "Coach," he said, "if that Timonon kid touches me one more time, I'm gonna fuck him up. You see what he did? That was a flagrant fuckin' cross-check."

Then the ref came over and said, "Sorry about the stop, but we got a problem with Larky's audio. They tried everything upstairs, but they still can't get it up. They want to patch him into the rink's PA. We're not crazy about the idea, but if both teams agree to it, we'll go ahead. Ropersdale's okay with it, so it's your call, Coach."

We all looked to Coach, having no idea what the ref was talking about.

Coach said, "Kip Larky's here, guys. I didn't want to tell you because we didn't need the distraction. He's broadcasting this on public access and calling the game himself. Personally, I think he's a sleazy hack looking to ham it up and pad his demo reel."

But the Falcons only heard "Kip Larky," who was Pittsburgh's leading high school sports reporter, and "broadcast," and it was all let's go, let's play, awesome, cool, let's go, go, go. I sensed that Coach hated the idea. He looked right at me and said, "If it's gonna be a distraction, forget it. We won't do it." Looked at me like he knew Mom and Dad weren't there, like he'd been watching me watch the stands.

The other guys looked at me, too, but not real friendly, like I was gonna veto something fun. We'd already had some tension—they still didn't like that *Post* article that called me a phenom. Dexter Bolzjak, savior of Pittsburgh high school hockey—and now this. Me the phenom jeopardizing their big TV break.

"No, it's cool," I said. "All cool. Let's go."

The PA booth overlooked the ice from behind my net, a cubicle walled off with glass. On non-hockey nights, the staffers used it

3

to pipe in Top 40 music or announce discounts at the snack bar. But when I settled back in net, I saw Kip Larky up there, wearing his trademark white shirt and pink suspenders. His scalp shone through his hair plugs, just like on TV.

"Hell-ooooooo, ladies and gentlemen, this is WPIT's Kip Larky broadcasting from historic Cooper Rink! Smile, because tonight you're live on public access!"

His voice boomed out over the PA, and the crowd lapped it up.

"We got ourselves a real blockrocker here, a clash of the titans. Rob 'Da Bomb' Bomley in goal for the Ropersdale Blizzards versus Dexter 'The X-Factor' Bolzjak of the Truman Falcons. Both have been near perfect throughout these playoffs, but tonight only one can be a champion. The other a mere footnote. Forever remembered as a loser, if remembered at all."

I rolled my head around, crackled the tendons in my neck. Holding up okay there. Crouched, leaned forward. My knees were numb, but I could still trust them to move. Sweat soaked through my pads, kept dripping to my lips. It tasted no worse than warm beer. Took a fresh grip on my stick, and once again I was a fortress. An icon. I owned that ice, every divot and scratch.

Couldn't help it, I looked up to the bleachers again. Still no Mom and Dad, but close to the glass was a girl staring at me. Not screaming or clapping, not even blinking, just sitting there perfectly still and pretty. She had bloodred hair that looked natural with her pale skin, green eyes that could have lured mine from the game. I refocused but noted her position.

The Blizzards won the face-off, and back they came, crashing my space.

"The Blizzards set up a two-on-two. And oh, look at the move Torkle just put on Kelly! He's got a lane! Shot!

4

"Save, Bolzjak!

"Rebound—shot! Save, Bolzjak!

"A tussle around the net! They're scraping for the rebound. It rolls to Winchel—stolen! Stolen by Torkle! He backhands it!

"Save, Bolzjak! Off the blocker! Ladies and gentlemen, this is THE Dexter Bolzjak! He's a juggernaut out there on the ice!"

Kelly cleared the puck, and our fans went half past apeshit. Screaming their throats to pulp, waving green-and-white Falcons towels. Their energy boosted mine if you could believe it. Call it adrenaline or confidence, but my whole body quickened. My knees felt loose, limbs more limber, and the puck looked like a spare tire to my eyes.

The other Falcons caught the same surge. They churned a step harder, passes clicking from blade to blade as they skated and blurred to pure flowing motion. If I hadn't known what those kids were like in the locker room, I would've sworn I was seeing poetry.

The Blizzard defenders backpedaled. Durdovitch forced the puck between them and went straight for Bomley, and even Da Bomb shrunk back from two hundred pounds closing fast.

"But Timonon hooks Durdovitch from behind! Durdovitch can't keep the puck, and the Blizzards will steal it. No whistle. There's no whistle on the play. Boy, I can't believe there's no call. Did Timonon get away with— Oh my God! Oh my God! Durdovitch just whacked Timonon in the face!"

Timonon crumpled to the ice. The Blizzard fans blew out their throats screaming and booing, none of them knowing that Durdovitch got off on it. He told me himself he loved it, said booing was the best sound he'd ever heard besides his Glock.

The ref doubled over blowing his whistle, and the linesman

grabbed Durdovitch. But there was no fight to break up. Durdo-vitch seated himself in the penalty box, surrounded by glass and raging Blizzard fans. He showed neither fear nor remorse, much like his idol Mike Tyson.

"Disastrous for Truman High. Absolutely disastrous. Just when they really needed their captain to step up and show some maturity. That'll be a five-minute major for fighting."

Coach hung his head and aged a decade. Meanwhile the ref tried to gather everybody for the face-off, but it was no use. Pissed fans threw a few bags of popcorn on the ice. Before the linesman could even summon the staffers, everybody was looking at the penalty box.

Durdovitch was on his feet, choking the box's water bottle with both hands, spraying a geyser over the glass. His target, a massive Blizzard fan, was beating on the glass with obese fists. Red-faced and cursing as the water showered him and his blond buzz cut.

The glass could not contain the fan's girth or wrath. It shattered in a mess of crystal pebbles, and he teetered on the drop-off. His lard sac hung over the edge, pulling him forward despite his arms' desperate flapping.

"Oh my God, did you see that?! A fan has fallen into the penalty box! Yes, into the box! Somebody better get him out of there. Is he all right? What's this? Durdovitch appears to be— Somebody get that guy out of there!"

Durdovitch's fist cocking back and plunging, that's all I saw at first. Then, through the commotion, Durdovitch pulling the guy up by his jersey. Then pulling the jersey over the guy's head, exposing his tits and gut. And then Durdovitch hammering away. He finally got to be Tyson, and it was like watching Tyson go off on a manatee. You could hear each thwack, see the guy's flab fly in all directions. Flab undulating with every blow.

The crowd loved it, even the Blizzard fans. They disowned that guy the second he broke through the glass, and they cheered every punch as loud as the Falcon fans. Players on both teams laughed. Even the linesman was smirking as he tried to break it up. In fact, the whole building seemed entertained except for a little blond kid standing on the drop-off's edge, looking down into the box. I couldn't tell if he was screaming or crying.

Larky gauged the crowd and piled on, *"A left! A right! Another right! A body blow! But how could you miss that body? Upstairs now! To the head! Left hook! Uppercut! Down goes Fatso! Down goes Fatso! Somebody call Greenpeace and save the whale!"*

In the midst of all this, I looked at her again, and sure enough she was looking back at me. The girl with the ghostly skin and haunting gaze. She undid the top button of her denim jacket, then reached down to the next. Eyes never leaving mine, unbuttoning button after button.

Coach screamed at me to wake up, get my ass to the bench. He'd been waving me over, and the other Falcons were waiting. After all, the delay functioned like a free time-out.

Durdovitch approached the bench with me. The linesman and ref flanked him like bailiffs, each holding an arm. "You saw that, Coach. He was gonna attack me. I had to do something."

"Game misconduct, Durdy. You're done. Ejected."

"But, Coach—"

"See you downstairs."

"But, Coach, can I say just one thing. Please? As team captain?"

"Make it quick."

Durdovitch surveyed us, his troops. The bench, his defensemen, his fellow forwards. "We worked our asses off to get here. Most of us for four years. I wish I could be out there with you, but

7

you saw how they screwed me. It's okay, though, because we got a phenom in goal." He yanked his hand from the linesman and slapped his clump of bloody knuckles on my shoulder. "We know you won't fuck it up, Bolzjak."

The Falcon fans gave him a standing ovation as he skated off. The Blizzard fans booed, but probably not as much as Durdovitch wanted, and the staffers installed a new pane. Or swept the crystals out of the penalty box. Or helped the EMTs load the battered fan onto a stretcher while the crowd sang the "Hey, hey-ey, good-bye" song.

Coach said, "Okay, it's simple, and it's what I've said all along. We're a team. No matter what happens, it comes down to what we do as a team. Forget Durdy. Get him out of your heads. You have to win without him, and that means killing this penalty. Give them nothing. No room to skate, no room to pass. Shut down the lanes, and watch Torkle. He's been smoking you guys all night."

I started back to my net, but Coach reached over and grabbed me. Leaning in close so nobody else could hear, he said, "Hey. You okay? Something on your mind?"

They didn't show, I wanted to say. Mom didn't show. Dad didn't show. They didn't show, and it's left a gaping hole in my game. This wasn't supposed to happen; I wasn't supposed to care. But of course I couldn't say such a thing at such a time. It would've made me look weak.

So I said, "Yeah. Winning's on my mind. What else you want?"

Coach's mustache twitched up into a half smile. He gave me a shove and a get outta here.

Finally the ref resumed the game. Six minutes left, and we'd be short-handed for five. The Blizzards won the face-off and crossed the blue line. Instead of shooting, they took positions in my zone. My guys fell back, trying to cover.

8

The Blizzards edged in toward me. Right Blizzard tipped it to Left, who faked a shot then shot. The puck thunked off my leg, rebounded past my catcher to Kelly. He wristed it all the way back to Bomley, and the Blizzards had to retreat.

The girl touched her fingertips to her collar, slid them down along her chest. Slowly, artfully slowly, she opened her jacket, revealing a white T-shirt that read GOALCHICK in black letters. The "O" and second "C" rung around her nipples. Then she smiled all cutesy and blew me a kiss.

That settled that. No way would I look in her direction again, the sadistic bitch. And you'd have to be sadistic to make a shirt like that, let alone wear it. I swear I had nothing against the good people of Ropersdale, PA, prior to that night. Nothing, but man, they came heavy with that Goalchick shit.

But you know what? It didn't matter. Screw her, I thought, I'll show her. And as for Mom and Dad, I shook that off, too. I knew—just knew—they were in the building somewhere. And when it was over, and we won, I knew they'd be the first to congratulate me, and they'd have some funny reason for not being in their usual place. Like Larky said, I was a juggernaut. And juggernauts don't sweat chants or T-shirts or lack of support. They just crush stuff.

Back came the Blizzards. Center dumped it off to Left. Winchel tried to check him but missed, slammed into the boards. Left ripped off a shot, and ding! The sweetest sound in hockey.

"Off the post! It hit the post! Bolzjak scrambles to cover it, but Heenan gets to it first! Heenan shoots! Off Bolzjak's skate! It's still loose! Knocked away by Bolzjak, and the Falcons will clear.

"Boy, I don't know. Bolzjak looked a little rattled on that last attack. I think the Blizzards might be getting to him now. He didn't seem very focused there."

9

"Goalllll-chick, Goalllll-chick," they chanted, louder than before.

Back came the Blizzards again, unrelenting, with ticktack passes. Left to Right to Center.

"Shot! Save, Bolzjak!

"Rebound! Shot!

"Saaaaave, Bolzjak! And the Falcons will clear.

"No, wait! Torkle kept it in at the point. Torkle goes to pass—no, he doesn't! He just burned past Kelly and wrists it!"

I dropped to my knees, and I knew by the roar.

"Scoooooore! Oh, Lord, what a score! Right between Bolzjak's legs!"

The Blizzards mobbed Torkle.

I dug the puck out of my net, glanced up at the scorekeeper's light. The bulb glowed red like a bloody cherry.

The Falcons kept their distance from me, and I ignored them anyway. Just to make a point, I reset like nothing happened. Got back in my crouch, rolled my head around to work out the kinks. My way of saying, let's go. We got five minutes left. Are we gonna show up tonight or what?

The ref dropped the puck at center ice. Conlan won the draw, and the other Falcons plowed ahead, knocking a Blizzard on his butt. The puck ended up in the far corner, caught in a scrum of blades.

So with the play down at the other end, I did a bad thing. Call it a moment of weakness, but I looked her way again, the girl with the red hair and ghostly skin. Thought I could sneak a glance, but she was already watching me. A skeleton sat to her left, a witch to her right. Behind her, three zombies with rotting skin. In front of her, a green-faced ghoul holding a scythe. A blond girl with a

10

gashed throat and blood on her white bathrobe. An ape holding a bloody straight razor. All of them looking right at me, all laughing.

Next thing I knew, three Blizzards came rushing into my zone. The crowd rose to its collective feet, striking up the "Goalllll-chick" yet again. And I'm thinking—maybe that was the problem—I'm thinking about that chant. That fat guy's bloody face, his little kid seeing him get pummeled. That I just saw monsters in the stands. And I'm thinking it's time to stop. I don't want to be here anymore. I don't want to be doing this. Playing this game was a mistake, and I want it to stop.

"Heenan on the wheel and deal. He'll dump it behind the net. De Felice gets there first. De Felice muscles it past the Falcon defender. Bolzjak—what's Bolzjak doing? He's not even looking in the right direction!

"De Felice centers it! Shot, Timonon! Deflected!

"Shot, Heenan!

"Yes! Yes! Oh, God, yes!"

I stayed facedown for what felt like a minute.

"Pussy," said a passing Falcon.

The redhead laughed and clapped, surrounded by humans again, clapped and laughed. My right eye twitched. Not like Coach's mustache, but uncontrollably, like the nerves in my face were electrified. Sizzling from the inside out like the poster said. But no way would I lift my mask to rub my eye. Everybody would think I was crying.

"Somebody get Bolzjak a cane and a guide dog. That was pitiful. He looks like a corpse out there, twitching under its own autopsy."

That was all the shtick I could take. In fact, I took off my mask, turned around, and told Larky to shut the fuck up. Screamed it, really.

"Oh, now he seems to be saying something to me. What, Dexter? I can't hear you, son. But I saw you suck on that last shot. We all saw you suck on that last shot!"

Okay, fine. Never mind, I thought, and reset my stance. By then I didn't care what the crowd was doing or chanting. Forget the score, forget Larky. Forget the sadistic redheaded bitch and her Goalchick T-shirt. Forget the monsters and Marvin and Samantha Bolzjak. From now on, this was for pride and nothing less than my balls. And I was not leaving the ice without my balls.

The ref dropped the puck at center ice. Somehow it found Torkle, who barreled through everybody on a breakaway. Loping on ahead, picking up speed, stirring a roar in his wake.

He stutter-chopped the blade around the puck, then cocked for a shot. I shrunk back with the fake, crossbar touching my nape. Stutter-chop, stutter-chop, and—

"Scooooooore!

"Three—nothing, Blizzards! Torkle's second of the night! Don't get up, Bolzjak. Your money's on the nightstand!

"Ladies and gentlemen, we are witnessing the Chernobyl of high school hockey. Bolzjak has given up three goals in less than a minute, a state championship record. Exposure. That's what we're seeing here. A false talent, stripped of the will to win, laid naked on the ice and withering before you."

Eyes closed, I could still see the Blizzards high-fiving Torkle. The Falcons spitting and cursing. The redhead laughing so hard she cried, mascara pooling around her eyes and dripping down her cheeks in black streams.

"Your coach wants to see you," the ref said.

Falcons lingered around the bench, some staring at me like I'd fondled their kid sisters. Coach stood there, arms crossed, trying to stay poised. But there was hurt in his eyes, and I could barely stand to look at him.

"I'm putting Meekham in," he said, and handed me a bunch of keys. "We'll talk later tonight. In the meantime, take these and go. The green Chevette by the Dumpster. I'm not letting you in that locker room with Durdy. Not till he calms down. So go kill an hour. Give me time to talk to him."

"You serious?" I said, but his face was answer enough.

That was one shameful skate. Past all the other players I went, past the stands and everybody staring, all the way to the Blizzard net before anybody realized I was leaving. The crowd didn't know what to do, torn between booing a loser who blew it and cheering a loser who tried his best. Even Larky said nothing as I knocked on the glass for a staffer to let me out.

But then some guy screamed, "Go home, you fuckin' faggot!" and a rain of random shit came pouring down with the boos. Cups, nachos, pretzels. Crouching for cover, a staffer got pelted with a half-eaten corn dog as he opened the door.

I waddled past the food court, my blades clicking on the concrete, past the lockers and the rental skate booth. Staffers smirked at me as I wedged through the turnstile. The lady in the ticket booth glanced up from her tabloid, yawned, went back to her Tom Cruise and Michael Jackson.

And that was how I left Cooper Rink. With all the boos, Goalchick chants, Larky, the redhead, the Falcons, the Blizzards, the lack of Marvin and Samantha Bolzjak, and everything else festering behind me.

We all need a place of escape, I think. A nook in the planet where nobody would follow us or try to find us. Someplace quiet to collect our thoughts and junk the clutter, a haven no matter how rough things happen to get.

Old Watermill Road served that purpose for me. I'd found it coming home from my first practice at Cooper Rink. I didn't know the area and ended up lost in a maze of lookalike suburban streets. If nothing else, Old Watermill looked different. It was a strip of scarred mud, too narrow for two cars to pass, smothered with woods and darkness.

You couldn't take it fast, not with its curves and drop-offs. Nobody ever gave it guardrails; it still had wormwood posts strung with rusty cables. You could even see a spot where somebody rushed it, a gap where the posts were broken. Step to the edge of the drop-off, look down, and you'll see burnt scrap wrapped around a trunk. And you can't help but wonder if the body's still there, thrown from the wreck, left in a gulch for the maggots and rats.

But stay with the road, respect its age, and it widens and brightens and brings you to Willet, PA. Proud home of Duchess, the county's blue-ribbon pig. From there it hits the highway, which I'd take back to Pittsburgh, arriving home in time for homework. Old Watermill made for a great cooldown, and I drove it after every practice or game.

The last one was no different, only I used Coach's car instead of Dad's. Bits of Chevette clinked off with every bump and scrape. My gear knocked around the backseat. Coach had left a mix tape in his stereo, a collection of every '70s rock band featuring a white guy with an Afro. I let it play, for no amount of Styx, Journey, or Foghat could faze me at that point.

Everything from the rink still blared in my head. Goalchick Goalchick *Scooooooore!* Not my fault, couldn't be my fault. The girl's eyes and the Goalchick on her chest, I couldn't suck that bad. I've never sucked that bad. *Scooooooore!* You don't go from

14

phenom to fuckup that fast, but God, that fat guy's face all fractured and smashed right in front of his kid. Did I really bet my balls on that last one? *Scooooooore!* A hole in my game, not my fault. Mom and Dad's fault, not mine, a hole in my game. Yeah, let's not forget that. Where were they, what excuse could they have for skipping the state championship, the night I got *stripped of the will to win* defined?

And so it blared till I saw the Ford Taurus up ahead. That was weird enough; I never once came across another car on Old Watermill. Even weirder, it straddled the edge of the road. Lights out, engine off. Leaves screened the passenger's side. The driver's door hung open and blocked the way.

Pulling up behind it, I cut the music and honked. Nothing moved. Not in the Taurus, not in the woods. No sound, only stillness.

Honked again. Heard nothing but the nasal rattle of the Chevette, and I didn't like the feeling I was getting. People don't just leave cars half off the road, doors open, for no reason. It felt wrong enough, off enough, that I thought about turning around.

But I couldn't, and nobody else could. Old Watermill was too narrow. Any attempt, and I would've ended up as stuck as the Taurus. I rolled down the window, said yo, what up, and still nobody answered. If I wanted to go anywhere, I'd have to get out and close the door myself.

So I walked over in my socks, hoping not to step on glass. The Chevette's high beams painted the road pale and lunar, the tree trunks like pillars of chalk. I got to the door, and my hand froze on the handle.

A high-heeled shoe lay on the dash. Money, makeup, coupons, and a wrapped tampon littered the front seats. On the hood was a ripped-open purse, a white blouse on the windshield.

15

That feeling I didn't like, it was screaming to leave. But I didn't leave. I had to keep looking, had to see what else was there. I went around to the front of the Taurus, and that's where I found the woman facedown. Dirt and twigs stuck to her naked back, Pants pulled down to her ankles, panties down to her knees. She wasn't moving, wasn't breathing.

I'm whispering, Oh God no. Please God no, and I admit I was shaking. Chilled to my guts, shivering but itching with sweat.

Still I knelt down next to her and touched her shoulder. She felt hard and smooth, too smooth to be human. Smooth like plastic, and I knew when I touched her hair, knew before I dared to tug it. The wig slipped right off her head, left me holding a black mop of curls.

The woods rustled behind me. Nope, never got a look at him. Before I could turn around, the fucker shoved me down. He dropped all his weight on my back, popped my lungs. And jabbed something to my neck, something with a point.

"Scream and I'll stab you. Struggle and I'll stab you. Cross your hands behind your back."

He ripped duct tape from its roll, wrapped it around my wrists. But not too tight, not enough to cut off circulation. And for all the overload in my head, one thing was clear: the fucker knew what he was doing. He was skilled at this shit.

"This ain't the usual car. Where's the usual car?"

I couldn't speak, still wheezing from the slam. So he yanked my ponytail, jerked back my chin. Then held the knife so I saw the blade, lowered it to my throat.

"Where is the usual car?"

"The rink. Coach lent me his."

"Open your mouth."

He kept the blade steady with one hand. With the other, he

16

stuffed a hairy lump in my mouth. I tasted a steel wool scouring pad, the kind with blue soap flecked in its wires. He ripped more duct tape from its roll, pasted it over my mouth.

"Don't cry," he said. "You were loved once, I'm sure."

That's when that night went really bad, down to a place I'm never going again. And that's all you need to know besides this: it happened eight years ago, April '93, and I don't dwell on it. Time has not stopped, and I have managed. In fact, I've had no reason whatsoever to think about that night, ever.

At all.

Till today, maybe, when a pretty strange thing happens at lunch.

2

So I'm eating at the Biggies down at the Strip, facing the front window. Positioned so I can see everybody who comes in before they come in, and that's key. Because if I don't like the looks of somebody, I'm gone. Sorry, but I'm not sitting around, ass out, asking to get jacked. Not again, and that's not negotiable.

The problem is, when you sit by the front window, other customers hover over you when the line backs up. Sometimes they even touch you, which means stress.

Like for instance, the mom and two kids who brush past me. Mom's squeezing a kid's wrist in each fist, yanking them along as the line moves. One of the kids, a girl maybe eight years old, starts to cry. Mom whips her around, makes the beads in the kid's hair click like an abacus, and says, "Shut up, or I'll smack you upside the head." The kid stiffens like everybody else in earshot.

Plus the mom is black while most of the place is white. So there's added tension. Lots of averted eyes and timid glances, like the surrounding white folk want to comment but won't while mom glares around at them, everybody braced for escalation. And maybe that's a little sample of Pittsburgh, a town where race relations still resemble the '60s. And I mean the 1860s.

But the mom moves on, and crowding me next is a guy with a mullet and a Steelers tank top, showing off his inflated arms. A slinky chick with low-cut jeans and half a T-shirt stands beside him. Her hair's an elaborate mass of blond and brown strands, piled high and held together with lacquer. Lots of guys would be proud to have a girl like her, but her guy keeps looking around like he's trying to catch somebody ogling her. Like he's waiting for a reason to get in somebody's face.

Then they move on, too, one step closer to the register and an old lady in a red-and-yellow Biggies uniform. Granny seems afraid of the register as she hits its buttons. Here's a woman who survived the Depression and World War II and who knows what else, and she's spending her last days ringing up Biggies orders with trembling hands.

It doesn't pay to think about these things, let alone care. Cool robotic detachment is my policy. And that might sound funny, but the air's thick with anger in this city. A hostile chill that eats away at your skin if you let it, gets under your nails and down to the roots of your teeth. So you stay apart, and you keep looking for the fuckers because they're always out there, just waiting for the chance to jump you.

But regardless, I'm eating some greasy fries and smelling the stink of my fingers. Literally they stink because I've been handling onions at Marchicomo's produce warehouse all day, sorting the rotten from the decent. Like I said, I've managed. In fact, I got two jobs, and the warehouse thing is Job 2. It pays the rent and erodes the soul, but things could always be worse, I guess. Could be elderly and working at Biggies. Could be a junkie. Could be homeless.

And speaking of misfortune, a bum walks into the place. I can already tell this guy will impact the scene as it were. Some people just have an aura about them, and his is a mist of self-made fumes. Like how Dracula always makes his entrance in a fog, the bum travels in a cloud of BO and cigar smoke.

He looks about seventy, bald except for a fringe of white hair around the back of his head. Big brown eyes set far apart and bloodshot. Overgrown nose hairs in need of a snip. By the blots and crust on his tan jacket, he might've slept on a park bench while birds took turns shitting on him. Or maybe he got smashed and passed out on a bed of back-alley garbage, God only knows.

The bum staggers toward the line, sees the two little girls staring at him. So he smiles and waves hi, which prompts mom to yank the girls' wrists again, saying, "Don't you look at him!"

"That's it, lady, hit the kid!" the bum says, and applauds. "Who wants to see the lady hit the kid?"

Now everybody's staring at him. But he moves on, oblivious to the attention he's attracting. Trying to cut through the line, he grazes the chick with the elaborate hair.

"It touched me!" she says, lips scrunched with disgust. "It touched me!"

Her boyfriend steps in, thrusts his chest out at the bum. "Keep moving, old man. You don't want a piece of this."

"Hey, whoa, Mr. Steely Tits, I'm moving. Don't want no piece of you. But I wouldn't pass on a piece of that," the bum says, and winks at the girlfriend.

"Just keep moving," the boyfriend says, and rests a hand on his girl's back.

I'm watching this and trying not to laugh. Then the bum looks right at me, like I'm part of this scene, and comes staggering over. Just what I need.

"Hey, kid. I know you from somewhere, don't I?"

"No. Don't think so."

"Yeah, I do. I seen you working over at Marchicomo's. Aren't you Marv Bolzjak's kid?"

Fuckin' Pittsburgh, man. It's a small, small town. Live here long enough, and everybody knows you or your name or someone in your family. But what am I gonna do, lie? I admit that yes, I am Marv Bolzjak's twenty-five-year-old kid.

The bum takes that as a cue to join me. I'm trying to place him, and I can't. Maybe I've seen him before, but it's not like I go around studying bums. This one pulls out a wallet, of all things, and tosses a bill on the table. "No wonder you look like hell," he says. "Take that, go get happy. Get yourself a girl and some drinks."

I pick up the bill to give it back, but it's a hundred. That's half a week's pay and not so easy to turn down.

The Biggies middle-aged manager comes over. His clip-on tie hangs crooked, his cheeks pockmarked like they'd been pressed to a waffle iron. He puts his hands on his hips, all authority in his white shirt, and says, "How many times I gotta kick you outta here, Lou?"

"He's not bothering anybody," I say. "In fact, I'm buying him lunch. Tell him what you want, Lou."

Lou slurs something about Biggie Meal #7. I pocket the hundred and hand the manager my own crumpled five. "Keep the change, Slick."

"Real cute. Don't get too comfy, cause I'm making this to go. You hear me? To go!"

Once he leaves, I turn back to Lou. "So, you wanna tell me who you are?"

"Lou Kashon, best salesman in the Strip! Don't believe me, do you?"

No, I can't believe the bum could sell anybody anything. But

21

I do know the name. Kashon's is another produce wholesaler, like Marchicomo's. A name painted on another warehouse a few blocks from mine. And whenever anybody at Marchicomo's mentions the Kashons, they tend to call them A-rabs, camelfuckers, ragheads.

Lou digs into his jacket pocket, deposits a mess of paper on the table. No money this time, but some numbers slips, a few tickets from the Wheeling dog track, a police citation, and pink receipts with a Kashon logo, meaning the name ELIAS KASHON INC. between two cornucopias. Only these receipts interest Lou. He taps a blackened nail on their scribble, saying, "See that? I moved five bins of melons today! Five! And four pallets of greens! Collard, kale, mustard, turnip. I'm talking *California* greens, kid."

The manager returns with the food. He drops the bag right on my fries and says, "Yep, that's our Lou. The legend himself. The wheeler-dealer. Plays his cards so close to the vest, he hasn't changed the vest in twenty years. Now get him the hell outta here."

If you look at a map of Pittsburgh, you'll see a city defined by rivers. The Allegheny curves down from the north, the Monongahela snakes up from the south. They meet at a sharp angle, which does two things: (1) forms the Ohio, which flows out west till it hits the Mississippi, and (2) pretty much divides Pittsburgh into three parts. Everything above the Allegheny and Ohio is North Something, everything under the Mon and Ohio is South Something. In the middle lies the city's heart, a triangular wedge of land that narrows to a point where the rivers meet. Near that point is the Strip District, a slender stretch along the Allegheny. Its main arteries—Smallman Street, Penn Avenue, and Liberty Avenue—parallel the river while Eleventh through Thirty-third streets run crosswise.

Off the map and on the ground, the Strip packs its action

between Sixteenth and Twenty-second. Wholey's Fish Market, Sambok Oriental Foods, and Parma Sausage cluster along Penn near Seventeenth. On Eighteenth is Primanti's, a joint famous for loading its sandwiches full of fries and coleslaw; call it Pittsburgh's answer to the Philly cheesesteak. Farther up on Penn are dueling Italian delis, Sunseri's and Penn Mac, along with Enrico Biscotti, Fortune's Coffee, and the My Ngoc restaurant. Vendors line the sidewalks hawking CDs, cheap toys, and used books. Shish kebabs sizzle on grills, floating pork and chicken smells that give way to roasting peanuts and falafels.

I'll admit the Strip's all right. It offers lots of honest, unprocessed food. It seems like every other business has been there forever and stays family-owned, keeping names like Stamoolis and Hermanowski. And its mini-groceries, cafes, diners, and junk shops make you feel like a traitor for shopping anywhere else, especially anywhere corporate and chainlike.

Even so, there's still one place I dread walking past, a store that hogs most of Penn's 1800 block. That would be the Steel City Novelty Co., its sole proprietor Mr. Marvin Bolzjak. I pass it damn near every workday, and I never stop in. I don't even look in. I'm sure he's seen me countless times, but remember: cool robotic detachment. Keep walking.

Besides, I know the place and the man better than anyone. I could literally walk in there blindfolded and find the noisemakers and cherry bombs, the joybuzzers and rubber spiders. X-ray glasses, magic eight balls. Cardboard stand-ups of the Clintons, Captain Kirk, and Batman. I could go to the section where the store turns pious and pick out the plastic rosary beads and laminated photos of the Pope. I could even walk the party supply aisle and tell you the colors of the plates, cups, and napkins by where they sit on the shelf.

As for the man himself, look, I don't hate him. I don't even dislike him. It's not that he no-showed the game, which, one could argue, was a factor in things going down like they did. I don't blame him for that so much anymore. It's more that he wouldn't fight when Mom bailed. He never fought to keep her, never defended himself against the tons of shit she talked. Instead he retreated and hid there behind the counter of his humble little shop, peddling gags and trinkets.

I'm sure his take on me ain't pretty, either. He put me up after high school, did what he could to support me through college. So he was kind of upset when I dropped out midway through. Never screamed or got downright pissed—never fought—but you could tell it gutted him. He kept saying I'd go back, reassuring himself more than anything. He even got me the job at Marchicomo's to keep me "engaged" till I went back. Only I never did. Instead I moved out of his house and never took another class. And that was six years ago already.

So it's awkward enough to pass that window on a normal day. After getting kicked out of Biggies, though, I got Lou with me. I'm not thrilled with all of Penn seeing us together to begin with. But then he's gotta stop right in front of Steel City and wave, saying, "Hey, Marv!"

Don't even pause, just keep walking.

"You're not gonna say hi to your old man?" Lou says, hurrying to catch up. "Marv's good people. What's your problem with Marv?"

At that point, I stop and say, "Dude, I don't know you. And I don't think I owe you an explanation."

That brushes him off the plate, and we walk awhile in silence. By the time we get to Marchicomo's on the corner of Twenty-first, I'm thinking I might've been a dick. We end up lingering by the side door, both knowing there's something more to say than bye.

I pull the hundred from my pocket. "Look, I can't take this. Thanks, but I can't."

Lou smiles, showing brown teeth. "Ah, take it. I got enough. That's nothing but walkin-around money."

I'm staring at this guy, this total fuckin' bum talking about his surplus funds. But then he leans in closer and says, "Between me and you, there's a lot more where that came from. I know Sal Marchicomo. He's okay for a dago, but he don't pay. Me, I could pay you double what you're making here."

"Doing what?"

"Stop over at Kashon's sometime. I'll tell you about it, Hockey Star," Lou says, and shambles off on Twenty-first toward Small-man and the river. Leaves me standing there, stunned and holding his hundred.

Back in the warehouse, I find the other guys doing the usual. Going in and out of the cooler, knocking aside the plastic flaps that curtain its entrance. In with an empty dolly, out with a load of boxes. Dumping the boxes onto worktables, discarding the rot—slimy lettuce, oozing cukes, lemons with green powder for skin—arranging the passable produce on Styrofoam trays. Shrink-wrapping the trays. Stocking them on the racks outside and store shelves next door.

The guys also bullshit and rip on each other, distracted enough that I return to my corner unnoticed. My table's covered with onions, just like I left it. I'm supposed to separate the solids from the softies, the dry from the sopping, and repackage fifty-pound sacks into ten-pound plastic bags. Poke holes in the bags with a nail so the onions can breathe. Then stock and repeat.

But there's trouble once I start. A dizziness creeps up on me. It's barely noticeable at first, but gets worse fast, and soon I'm caught in a spinaround. It's like the moment when being drunk stops being fun, when happy-smashed becomes oh shit I overdid it. When the room spins however still you try to sit, and you have to start plotting a quick route to the toilet.

I can fight it off if I focus hard enough, so I toss some onions in a bag and grab more. Toss and grab, toss and grab, rustling through papery skins. My head's swimming, but I'm hanging in till I grab one that squishes in my grip.

The onion spurts juice all over, creams my hand with pearly gunk. And there goes my focus. Now the walls speed around at a sickening clip. The guys' voices stay normal, but their faces smear to mush. Mine starts itching all over, all around my eyes, and I duck in the big fridge before anyone sees me struggle.

The cooler's a long space confined by pallets and crates, its walls plated with metal. A fluorescent tube fizzes overhead, providing twilight. Way in the back, I find a box of broccoli packed with crushed ice. I grab some and wipe the crap off my hand, but the spinning doesn't stop. Plus my face goes from itch to burn no matter how much wetness I slap on. Finally I scoop out a double handful of ice and bury my face in it.

That's when the fuckers come busting in, armed with fragments of that night: the dummy facedown by the front of the car. My hand on her naked shoulder, touching her hair. And it all came off, just slid right off her bald head. My fingers in a black mop of curls, then the shove. Knocked me down before I turned around. Told me to get in the trunk. And I wasn't gonna fight his knife, even if I wasn't hand-tied and gagging on a pad of wires.

Stop, I'm telling myself. Stop it already. And the spinning has stopped, the itch scratched. I know it was all in my head all along. Rooms don't magically spin, and I don't have a skin condition, I know.

But here's what else I know. I got four fuckers after me at all times. Not physically, at least till they get paroled. But mentally, yes. Psychically, yeah. I never know when the room might spin, and when it does, it's like they're huffing and puffing and blowing my brains in.

So I work to prevent that, even if the work is secret. Even now, anyone would look at me and see a guy crouched in a dark, cramped cooler. Dripping wet hands on his face for some reason, taking deep breaths, shivering. But what I'm really doing is building shelters with straw, sticks, bricks—whatever's on hand, whatever I can scrape together before the next attack.

Secret or not, it's hard and constant work. It doesn't pay, but it keeps me sane. In fact, I think of it as Job 1.

3

I come home to my corner of the basement, drop onto my cot. Judd and his mom let me stay here for a couple hundred bucks a month. It's nothing spectacular—my clothes in piles on the floor, some books left over from the Erin thing, a picture of Vampirella stuck to the wall by a few *Far Side* cartoons—but it serves its purpose. It gives me a place to crash unhassled by the sun. If I sneak a couple of Judd's mom's pills from upstairs, I can pass a whole weekend knocked out on the cot, easy.

I'm rarely alone, though. Jeepers, my black-and-gray tabby, haunts the place. If he's not squatting in his litter or eating, he's sleeping alongside me. I adopted him from a shelter that would've killed him, and he gives me a friendly presence in return. We are two old souls who don't need to speak to understand each other, bonded by a passion for doing nothing.

Then there's Judd, who I've known since junior high. We used to hang at my house after school, unsupervised, watching slasher movies till my parents came home from work. These days, Judd makes his own movies on a computer rig that takes up half the basement.

He calls it the Wall of Justice, or just the Wall for short. From what I can see, he's got about eight hard drives stacked to the ceiling, three videocassette players—VHS, 3⁄4 inch, Beta—decoders, videodisc burners and players, a video-editing shuttle, and two video monitors on either side of a huge computer screen. Plus more slabs of black plastic on the floor doing God knows what besides humming and burning LEDs. And a shitload of tapes and discs everywhere, spilling over from a packed file cabinet.

Judd spends most of his day at the Wall, hurting celebrities. Usually beautiful people, like actresses and models. He begins with his archive of ultraviolent movie or news footage, then goes to his archive of celebrity footage. Then, with illegal software and meticulous frame-by-frame alterations, Judd merges one into the other; he inserts celebrities into ultraviolent worlds.

Like for instance, this Sandra Bullock project he's working on. There's a dark alleyway on the computer screen. Judd types, leans back in his chair, and lets the footage roll. Dark alleyway. Cut to Bullock, sweetheart star of romantic comedies, walking and looking worried. A ski-masked figure jumps out of the shadows with a crowbar and swings at her. Cut to a close-up of the crowbar connecting, cracking Bullock's cheekbone. Her head whips around, neck snaps. And she drops, probably dead.

"Almost," Judd says to himself, and pauses the video. "But I'm still not getting that *thwack*."

In the worlds of Judd's projects, a random socialite slaps Audrey Hepburn in the face, sending her cigarette holder flying. The Tin Man goes apeshit and slams his axe into Judy Garland's back. The Virgin Mary finally loses her temper over Madonna's shenanigans, descends to Earth, and tackles Ms. Ciccone through a plate-glass window.

But don't call Judd a misogynist. He devotes equal time to his male-centered projects, though his men aren't beautiful so much as decent or tough. So, after drawling his homespun wisdom on the war in Vietnam, Tom "Forrest Gump" Hanks gets his teeth kicked in by the Hell's Angels. John Wayne screams like a sissy when a Comanche brands his crotch with a white-hot cattle prod. Jimmy Stewart chooses his wonderful life over suicide on that snowy Christmas Eve. As he runs home to his family, screeching season's greetings to all of Bedford Falls, he blindly enters a gangster movie. A vintage car pulls up beside him. Tommy guns poke out the windows, barrels blazing, ripping Stewart to a heap of smoldering pulp.

When Judd's feeling artistic, he'll refer to himself as a collagist. He'll talk about taking images—tools of the Corporate Media Power Structure—and turning them into weapons, firing them right into the guts of The Machine. He's undermining an oppressor, subverting convention, fucking the hierarchy, all real punk. If you suggest that he's really just stealing other people's work, mashing it up, and calling it his own, he'll say he's doing the same thing rappers and hip-hop producers do. And can you deny that hip-hop's a valid art form? If you suggest that he gets off on violence and helps others do the same, he'll say the world's a violent place. He's just reflecting reality, and it would be dishonest of him—cowardly, even—to do otherwise.

When Judd's feeling businesslike, he'll refer to himself as a culture-surgeon. And it does seem like he's on call. His cell phone's always ringing, e-mail always beeping. Adults of all backgrounds and tax brackets seek him out, all willing to pay for his service. Judd even has his own Hippocratic oath. He won't use children, living politicians, or rape. Nor will he do work that attacks a specific racial, ethnic, or religious group. Sorry, but that kind of thing attracts unwanted attention, brings on heat he doesn't need.

He looks back at me, Bullock laid out behind him. "You okay? I can draw the curtain if you want."

The curtain is a bedsheet hung on a line between the Wall and my cot. I'll say this for Judd: he's considerate enough to think his work might hurt me. But I tell him no, don't worry about it. It's all movie violence, and I've been stone to that since we were kids. Even the news footage he uses looks like a movie. And if he wasn't always offering to shield me from his work, none of it would remind me of that night. The difference between seeing thwacks on a screen and getting thwacked yourself is really that basic.

I never say that to Judd, though, because then he'll get curious and expect details. He read the papers, I'm sure. He knows there were four: one with the knife in the woods, three waiting in the garage with a video camera. He saw the word "molested" in print like everybody else. And of course he knows it was taped, and the tape was confiscated by cops, analyzed by lawyers, filed as evidence, locked in a locker. That doesn't mean Judd or anybody else is entitled to first-person details from me. And neither Judd nor anybody else should think I dwell on that night. Because I don't, and Job 1 dictates I don't.

Besides, Judd admires me for "surviving some sick, brutal shit" while he only plays with pixels, manipulates bits and bytes. He even called me "hard core" once with awe in his voice. You take status where you can get it, I guess. So why should I squander it with a bunch of details?

Judd leans aside so I can see the whole screen, the paused Bullock splattered on the pavement. "Can I get your honest opinion on something? Once she's laying there like that, should I make her nipples poke up against her blouse?"

"That might be overdoing it."

"Gotcha. Don't wanna overdo it."

He types, and the sequence loops back to the start. Dark alleyway. Sandra Bullock, sweetheart star of romantic comedies, walking and looking worried. A ski-masked figure jumps out of the shadows with a crowbar . . .

Judd watches, light reflecting off his blocky glasses. He doesn't blink at the moment of impact but shakes his head no. Still not satisfied. Still not getting that thwack.

The next morning Judd lets me borrow his car, so I get to Smallman Street early and luck into a parking spot. Better yet, I'm right where I want to be. Semi-hidden among other vehicles near the corner of Twenty-second, facing Kashon's.

You might even call this a stakeout. I'm reclined and working on a Biggie Breakfast and coffee. Not spying, exactly, just preferring to remain inconspicuous while I happen to observe the warehouse. And man, is it a sight out of Time. It's one of maybe ten produce wholesalers left in the Strip, a place that used to have a hundred.

To hear the old-timers talk, Smallman enjoyed a monster boom back in the early 1900s. Railyards filled the space between street and river, and a constant parade of trains rolled in with produce from across the country. Wholesalers turned Smallman into a food-distribution bazaar, buying trading haggling auctioning the stuff right off the boxcars. The Pennsylvania Railroad even built a hulking terminal that stretched from Sixteenth to Twenty-first, leasing it as warehouse space while extra business spilled over to Penn.

Then it all kind of died after World War II. Big grocery chains muscled in and took control of distribution, buying direct from the farms and cutting out the wholesalers. And the railyards emptied out as trucking replaced trains. So the terminal's still there, but the Pennsylvania's gone. Artsy boutiques rent the space as much as anything food-related; what used to be the railroad's office is now the Society for Contemporary Crafts. Likewise, nightclubs, galleries, and lofts occupy the blocks across the street.

Call it gentrification or transition. A loss of local color or the way of the world. Whatever it is, Kashon's sits alone and apart from the change. The warehouse doesn't even face Smallman at a right angle but slants on a diagonal, situated along the forgotten rails. Almost all the old yards have been ripped out or paved to make parking lots, but you can still see metal slivers in the ground around Kashon's, exposed in patches where the asphalt gapes. Even a few broken-down boxcars linger behind the building, with God knows what living in them.

Meanwhile the building itself decays. The mortar between its bricks has worn away, leaving walls you could topple with a sledge. The loading dock's edge has crumbled to pebbles. And the painted-on banner—ELIAS KASHON INC. between two cornucopias, like the logo on Lou's receipts—flakes off in scales, one wirebrush away from being erased.

A maroon Buick pulls up to the warehouse, an old black guy at the wheel. Lou steps out of the passenger side, and the Buick departs. Lou looks unsure of where he is, clutching a bottle in a brown bag. Hits the sauce at a quarter to eight A.M. Wipes his coat sleeve across his mouth, climbs the steps to the platform. Then fumbles around with his keys, trying three different ones between swigs. But he still can't find the right one.

This continues for a few minutes, till a boat of a black Cadillac cruises in. Another old guy gets out. He looks kind of like Lou but clean, with a mustache and enough hair to comb over. Pants hiked high, showing off his loafers. He takes out his own keys and opens up the place. Then, looking around like he's worried about being seen, the old man ushers Lou in.

I'm watching this, thinking, Christ, Lou, you stagger into this dump every day, so lit you can't even let yourself in, and you're gonna throw money at me? Who are you to offer me a job? Who are you to mention my dad and call me "Hockey Star" like you know me? Who are you, period?

Next thing I know, thud-thud-thud on the window. A fist rapping the glass by my head. I flinch and spill coffee all over.

Jerillo from work's standing there, holding an unlit smoke.

I open the door, say, "Dude, what the fuck?!"

"Well, shit, I saw you there, thought I'd get a light. You're one nervous person, you know that?"

I punch in the dashboard lighter. We stare at it, waiting for it to pop back out. Two guys with nothing else to say.

Marchicomo's sits on the corner of Penn and Twenty-first, on the bus line and right in the Strip's concentrated bustle. Every morning, we set up a farmer's market on the sidewalk, our racks and tables slowing the foot traffic even more. The building itself contains both a grocery store and the warehouse where me and my coworkers prep the produce. Marchicomo's fills wholesale orders, too, but does most of its business in retail. Keeping the shelves and racks stocked is the thing.

Between the sidewalk, the store, and the wholesale, Marchicomo's seems to do okay. One area where it fails, though, is the wicker department. For some unknown reason, Sal has the whole basement crammed with wicker stuff—tables, chairs, love seats, baskets, mirror frames, and assorted et ceteras. But I've never seen a customer buy a single scrap of wicker. In fact, nobody ever goes downstairs besides Sal's crew. Usually to use the Employees Only restroom, sometimes to smoke a joint.

So when I go down to wash the sticky coffee off my hands,

it's kind of a shock to find a woman sitting on a love seat. She's alone and smoking, even though every wall has a No Smoking sign, and not doing much else. Just sitting, smoking, and thinking.

Then she looks at me with these green eyes. I'll admit I'm transfixed. She might have been a model at one time, maybe when she was a teen. Now pushing thirty, she has a slightly tired look but striking all the same. Dark, parted hair, shoulder length and shiny. Clothes fit for a boardroom: black pantsuit with pinstripes, sky blue shirt.

I buy some time at the sink, thinking, Here's a chick who exudes class. Clearly I have no business talking to her. And yet I feel a duty to let her know she didn't just stare me down, intimidate me like she intimidates a hundred guys a day. Doing anything less would seem weak.

Upon exiting the bathroom, then, I say, "Excuse me. Need help with anything?"

"That depends. What are you good for?"

"I, uh . . . I don't know, I—"

"Next," she says.

And that's it. Next. As in, you're done. Go away.

So I'm standing there looking stupid. And she's sitting there, smoking, looking past me like I don't exist. I think she's joking at first, but no. Never hints at a smile.

"Excuse me? Did you—"

"I said, 'Next.'"

"You can't tell me to leave. I work here."

"Then go do some work."

"Ma'am, I'm not doing anything just because you tell me to. I don't care how good you look."

That brings back her stare. She gets up and walks over, shoes

35

clickclocking on the floor. Of course I'm all spiked nerves inside. I know I've never seen a woman like her before, and yet she's standing right there, close enough to kiss.

"What do you think of me?" she says. "Come on, gut reaction. Don't parse it, just say it."

"Ma'am, I don't know you or what you're doing here or what—"

"Stop with the ma'am crap. Come on. Say what you think."

"I think you're miserable. One well-dressed, miserable professional with a pretty face and ugly attitude."

"Boy, nothing gets past you, does it?"

"Oh, I've let some things slip by."

She looks me over, no doubt formulating a response, when someone comes thumping down the steps. It's Sal Marchicomo himself. His presence makes us step back from each other.

Sal is a short man who wears his shirts unbuttoned too far down, showing off gold chains and gray chest hair. He also takes pride in his tan, always traveling to some beach somewhere to maintain his orangeness. If you cross him, look out: I've seen him berate customers and coworkers to tears. But for the most part, he's easy to get along with. Even if he won't stop yapping about the supposed greatness of Reagan.

So he sees us and says, "Genevieve! There she is! What do you think of your new manager, Bolzjak?"

"I go by Gen," she says, offering her hand and a smile that scorches me down to dust.

I can barely mumble my name or lift my hand.

"Did she tell you she's finishing her business master's at Carnegie Mellon? That program's number three in the *world*, so you better listen to her. Hell, *I* better listen to her."

"Yes, we were just discussing school," Gen says, still beaming at me. "And where did you graduate from, Dexter?"

There's a silence. And I'm standing there, taking it. Staying calm, but taking it.

"Well, then. See you upstairs, Sal," she says, and clickclocks away.

Sal comes over and says, "She's something, ain't she? I'm not fooling myself, Bolzjak. I know she won't last long. The second she gets another offer—shoom! Out the door. But ain't nothing wrong with having her around till then. Not a girl like that."

So considering how my workday started, you might understand why I bailed early. Skipped my lunch break, went back to the car, and just sat there for a while. Face in my hands, in no hurry to hit the rush-hour traffic. Call it a "This Is Your Life" moment, when all you can do is take a few breaths and see your situation for what it is.

I'm doing that, then. Sitting, trying to relegate this Gen to a place of no importance where she belongs. Trying to stop replaying our encounter over and over, stop thinking of all the comebacks I could've made but didn't. And maybe I'm just being petty, but I have to wonder how she ended up here if she's such hot shit. She's getting a master's from the number three program in the world, and they can't set her up with anything better than Marchicomo's?

But never mind, there's movement across the street. The wooden door of Kashon's slides open, and Lou emerges. He steps onto the dock and looks right in my direction. No mistaking it, he sees me. He waves, even, and I wave back.

Then he waves me over, beckoning me to go there. I'm like, no. First of all, I'm tired. Second of all, what do I look like, some douche who takes orders from bums? Third, nothing's stopping him from coming to me.

Sure enough, he comes shambling down the steps. I roll down

the window as he approaches, putrid fumes and all. "Hey, kid. You think about what I said?"

"Yeah. There's just one problem. I still don't know what I'm thinking about."

"Give me a lift home, I'll tell you."

"This job's got nothing to do with produce, does it?"

"Not a thing. And I'll tell you what else." Lou darts his eyes from me to Kashon's and back. "It's not something I'm gonna talk about in the open."

"Let's get something straight. Whatever it is, it's not gonna involve any kind of physical contact between me and you. Understand? I don't do that shit. And nothing illegal, either. I'm not hurting anybody or stealing anything. I'm a peaceful man. I live a quiet life."

"You giving me a lift or not?"

Fine. I reach over, unlock the passenger door. As Lou makes his way around the hood, there's movement at Kashon's again. The other old guy, the one with the black Caddy, walks out to the dock. He looks around, spots me and Lou. Doesn't do or say anything, just stands there watching us.

"I think that guy wants something."

"Ah, that's just Eugene. My brother. Piss on him. Let's go."

I pull out onto Smallman and drift past Kashon's. Eugene glares as we pass. I have no idea what his problem is, where I'm going, or what I'm doing. But Lou eases back in his seat, relaxed and croaking the occasional direction. His confidence, more than all his walkin-around money, is what keeps me curious. It's like he's got something brewing just for me, and he knows it's killer.

4

It turns out that we live in neighboring hoods. Judd's house is in Beechview, Lou's place is in Brookline. Beechview lies along one side of West Liberty Avenue, a main road south of the Mon, Brookline along the other. And that's about the only difference between them.

Populationwise, they're both old and mostly white. You'll find lots of bingos and senior centers, see lots of gray hair and frail, tottering bodies. And plenty of FOR SALE or FOR RENT signs as the old folks die or move on to assisted living. Beechview's getting a little more Latin to fill the vacuum, and Brookline's getting a little more black, and now the white folk are grumbling and getting nervous.

More cops live here than anywhere else in Pittsburgh, and yet there's a lot of junkies and drugs. Always has been, along with kids drinking in the parks and picking fights. If you walk around Brookline or Beechview looking even remotely gay, it's only a matter of time till you get jumped. Even if you're just a guy with long hair, there's a decent chance you'll get fucked with, as I learned firsthand. These hoods are kind of retro that way.

Lou lives on Wellsbrook, a classic Brookline side street. Which means it's hilly, paved with cobblestones, and squeezed narrow by parallel parking. His house sits upon a small rise, screened from the street by a maple tree. Two stories tall, white brick with a big picture window on the ground floor. I'd place it in the 1920s and call it a tribute to old-fashioned craftsmanship, at least till I follow Lou up to the porch.

Only then can you see the rot. About half the porch has collapsed, its planks buckled under the weight of a cedar glider. The bulky rocker remains stuck in its hole, not going anywhere anytime soon, weathered and collecting dead leaves.

Lou looks down at it and says, "Yeah. Heh heh. Been meaning to paint that."

Then he opens the door. The smell's the first thing to hit me: the odor of old paper trapped in stale air. And old paper's the next thing to hit me, literally. One foot in the place, and I bump into a stack of *The Pittsburgh Press,* which hasn't been around for ten years. Headline: DC MAYOR BARRY CAUGHT ON TAPE, SMOKING CRACK.

Past that, there's nothing but more stacks of newspapers. Waist-high, chin-high, some piled to the ceiling, all yellowing. The stacks cramp the hallway to a path just wide enough for Lou, but I have to sidestep to move. And I have to move carefully, since one touch might cause an avalanche of ancient news.

I pass a living room packed with electronic junk. I mean mountains of plug-in relics: burned-out TVs with rabbit ears and aerial antennas; busted-up cabinet radios, pocket radios, clock radios; VCRs stripped of their casings; turntables with cracked records; typewriters and calculators with missing keys. No computers, though; all this junk predates the PC.

And it's all covered with dust. A thick, gritty layer of the stuff you could ball up and throw like snow. Dust swims in the light coming through the picture window, settles on the floor in clumps, mingles with the ceiling's cobwebs.

I continue on the path and end up in the kitchen. Lou's hunched over a table crowded with Jack Daniel's bottles and bakery boxes, eating cake with his hands. Smashed dishes fill the sink, shards of glass and ceramic blanket the countertop. Near the fridge sits a litter box that hasn't been scooped in a month. Flies zip from the litter to the crumbs on the table to Lou's face as he eats.

"Want some?" he says with a mouthful of cake.

"No thanks."

"You sure? I got some lemon meringue somewhere. That's good stuff, that lemon meringue."

"No thanks. Really. Look, I should get going."

"Hey, hold on, kid. I need a favor." Lou gets up, opens the freezer. Takes out a bakery box and hands it to me. "Could you bury that?"

"This is the job?"

"Nah. Just a favor."

So I lift the lid. And when I see what's in that box, I drop it with a "Jesus!"

A dead cat lands at my feet. A chunk of skin's been ripped from her throat, blood crusted brown on calico fur. One of her eyeballs dangles out of her head. The other stares at forever, her teeth bared in a frozen hiss.

"Poor Sally. She's a good kitty, but them rats finally paid her back. Been meaning to bury her." Lou takes out his wallet, puts a hundred on the table. "There's a shovel on the back porch. Anywhere in the yard would be good."

"Dude, you're fuckin' sick."

He takes out another hundred, slaps it down on the first. Gives me a look that says, "There. Do something with that."

41

"You need help. Serious psychiatric help. And some kind of social worker."

"Don't tell me what I need! If you can't do this one little thing, then you don't got the balls for the big job."

"Oh, yeah? What's that, Lou? Scooping the litter? Open your eyes, man. Take a whiff. Humans don't live like this. Apes in the zoo don't live like this."

"Kid, I can't lift the fuckin' shovel. Okay? You're right, I'm sick, but not like you think. Now you gonna bury Sally or not?"

He can't look me in the eye. I'll admit I feel a little bad for him, to come out and say what he just said. And again I'm thinking I might've been a dick. So then I can't look at him, either, and end up staring at the money on the table.

Lou takes this as a hint and opens his wallet again. But I stop him by picking up the box. Now our eyes meet, and we share a silence. An understanding that some give-and-take's going on.

Regardless, I can't let him think I'm a pushover. I glance at the money and say, "I'll pick that up when I'm done."

"Come upstairs when you're done. I got something else to show you," he says, and claws into the cake, ignoring the flies on the icing.

At least there's air outside, air and elbow room. Not that I'm thrilled with the task at hand, but it does feel good to do something physical. It's a release like any other exercise, and I'm digging at a decent pace. The hole's about a foot deep, the mound of dirt growing beside the bakery box.

Every so often, I pause to monitor my surroundings. Lou's yard is barren aside from some sparse, anemic grass. A walkway leads to a heap of cement-block rubble, the remains of a garage that used to face the back alley. Beyond the alley are more yards

42

and houses, which means lots of windows and the potential for spying eyes.

Still I'm digging and getting near done when the neighbor's back door opens. This girl walks out cradling a laptop computer, stops a few feet away. Lingering, silently demanding attention.

I'm not great with ages, but I'd guess she's about fourteen. She's a cute kid, chubby with baby-fat cheeks and a belly sticking out of her T-shirt. She wears bell-bottoms with a sunflower patch near the knee. A nose ring, raccoon makeup around her brown eyes, brown hair down to her waist. The most adult thing about her is the unsubtle gaze she's giving me. But I mean, come on. She's about fourteen, for God's sake.

"Hey, whatcha burying?" she says.

"Your neighbor's cat."

"Sally? Aw, no! That sucks! Poor Mr. Kashon. I bet he's crushed."

"So you know this guy?"

"I run errands for him sometimes. Pick up groceries and stuff."

"He tips pretty well, huh?"

"A little. Nothing that great. But guess what. I gotta get a bunch of people's names for this homework I'm doing. I saw you digging out here, thought I'd get yours. Mine's Francesca, by the way. Francesca Kusokovena."

I give her my name, then, spelling it out for the good of her homework. She thanks me and retreats to steps notched in the slope of her yard. Sitting yoga style, Francesca flips open her laptop and starts typing. And I resume digging, making a point to face her. Yes, I realize she's just a kid, but I don't need her or anybody else watching me from behind.

And that's all that happens for the next few minutes. I dig, she types and reads. Occasionally she whispers what sounds like

Holy Crap or Oh My God. Then she comes hurrying back over, laptop and all.

"You're Dexter Bolzjak the hockey goalie? You gotta let me use you!"

"Excuse me?"

"My homework. I have to write a bio on someone I met. And I just found a ton of stuff on you. Way more than anybody else I tried. And some of it's *crazy*! Were you really kidnapped? Those articles say you were kidnapped."

"Whoa. Back up a second. You just said you wanted my name. You didn't say anything about writing a bio."

"Well, *hello*. There's this search engine called Google. You live in a cave or something? Everybody's been using it for like two years now. You don't just give people your name without getting Googled."

"So you put my name in this thing, and it pulls up anything anyone's ever written about me? That's pretty oppressive, isn't it?"

"It's more than impressive. It's awesome!"

While she goes on, then, gushing her love for Google, I can feel something go wrong inside. It's the dizziness coming on, as patient and uncaring as ever. And the more I stand there trying to look unbothered, the worse it gets. Francesca's yard blurs to streaks of green. So I look at her face, but her mouth stretches a meter wide, her eyes melt to syrup. Then my own face starts itching like mosquito bites, and I remember Job 1: focus, don't spin, focus.

I lodge the box in the hole and rake dirt onto it, moving hard to slip the spinaround. Once I'm okay to speak, I say, "Sorry, but no to the bio. Why don't you use Mr. Kashon? Find out how he ended up like he did. I'm sure it's a better story than mine."

"But he's just a weird old guy who smells. Don't get me wrong.

Mr. Kashon's nice. But he's typical. Old people act weird and smell funny. It's their nature. But you were booby-trapped and kidnapped."

"Yeah, I know. I was there."

"Which is why you gotta let me use you. Pleeeeease!"

I push the last of the dirt back into place and thump it down with the flat side of the blade. Pretty hard. Then again, harder, for emphasis. And again just because.

Francesca gets the point but isn't intimidated. She stops talking but doesn't back off. Instead she reverts back to the unsubtle gaze, her mouth open just a little. Enough that I can see one of her teeth growing high in the gum like a fang. I wonder what it would be like to kiss such a mouth, whether that fang could cut my tongue. And that's when I know it's high time to get away from this kid.

I head back to the house, and she says, "Hey, wait! Shouldn't we have a moment of silence or something?" Getting no answer, she starts to say something else as I shut the door.

Old magazines and paperbacks crowd the steps. *Popular Science* asks if Man will set foot on Mars by 1988. *National Geographic* invites you to explore Olympic host Sarajevo. Mike Hammer decays alongside Perry Mason and Flash Gordon. I reach a landing with a stained-glass window, a rose pattern that might be pretty if you could ignore the cracks in the walls around it. The gaps in the plaster, the exposed brickwork seeping with air. Then up to the second-story hallway, past two closed doors till I find an open one.

I guess you could call it a bedroom. Lou's lying on a ratty mattress on the floor, still wearing his jacket and shoes. There's a dresser with a scratched-up mirror. A hardwood floor carpeted with cigar stubs, programs for the Wheeling dog track, bits of fallen ceiling. A window smoked gray with filth.

"Hey, kid, check the bottom dresser drawer. Go on, look."

"I swear to God, Lou, if you got another dead thing in here . . ." I crouch down and open the drawer. And once I see what's in it, it takes me a minute to blink.

It's not just money; it's a ton of money. Mostly hundreds, but with a lot of fifties and five hundreds mixed in. A drawer so deep with cash, I reach down to my elbow and just sift my fingers through it. Scoop out a handful and feel the grime, the crinkles, the crisps. Then scoop out another with both hands and press my face to it, breathing the worth.

"Yeah, heh heh. Feels good, doesn't it?" Lou says.

His voice triggers something ugly in me, thoughts that race across my mind before I can stop them. I look at Lou and see a scheming, money-grubbing Arab posing as a bum. A raghead, a camelfucker, just like the guys at Marchicomo's say. And what's he doing hoarding all this cash while his house falls apart? While a hardworking guy like me lives in a basement? I even think about him kicking it. He's old and sick, isn't he? How much longer can he last, and what good's all this money gonna do him at this point?

I shut the drawer, my hands shaking. "That's a lot of money."

"Ah, I had a couple good runs at the track. Played the dogs till I got sick."

"Come on, Lou. Nobody wins this kind of cash at the dog track."

"Ask 'em if you don't believe me. They know me there. They'll tell you." He sits up with a grunt and says, "Anyways, it's all yours if you do something for me. I need you to find someone. You ever heard of Mercy Carnahan?"

"Wasn't she a movie star? I thought she was dead."

"She ain't dead; she disappeared."

"So that's the big job. Who else you want me to find? Bigfoot? Puff the Magic Dragon?"

"If it was easy, I wouldn't pay you to do it. And if I wasn't sick, I'd do it myself."

"Okay, then. Why don't you hire a detective? Someone who'd know how to find her. Or better yet, go to a doctor."

"Cause I'm asking you. I want you to do this, and I got my reasons."

"Like what? I mean, of all people, why me?"

"Kid, I don't feel good, and I'm not spelling everything out for you. You saw the money, and you know what I want. Nobody's making you do a damn thing."

"Then I guess I'll have to think about it."

"Think about it. And I'll tell you what else. Her real name's Agnes Zagbroski. When you find her, tell her I want to see her. She'll remember me."

Lou lies back down, rolls over. I'm still standing there when he starts snoring. So there's me, him who's asleep and nuts to begin with, and all that money. And don't think I'm not tempted to sneak over and grab some. It's not like Lou would even notice a difference.

But as much as I want to, I can't. Call it conscience or a code, or maybe pity. I just know that I need to get out of here. This dusty air's thick with sickness, whether from Lou or the lure of the money, and I can only inhale so much.

5

I wake up later that night to see Judd doctoring a car commercial. On the computer screen is a silver sports coupe cruising down a country road. A sexy chick's at the wheel, blaring a song on her stereo. I think the band is T. Rex, if countless hours of classic rock radio have taught me anything. Heavy '70s guitar sound, lyrics about being your toy, your twentieth-century boy.

Cut to a pair of guys driving the same car on Highway 1, surfboards strapped to the roof, bobbing their heads to the same song.

Cut to an attractive man and woman dressed for the clubs—same car, same song—driving the night-lit streets of a big city with no traffic.

Cut back to the girl, shown only from the mouth down. She licks her lips while the camera ogles her perky tits in a tight pink T-shirt. So far this is a real car commercial; I've seen it on TV myself.

But then a train whistle shrieks, and the T. Rex stops.

Cut to the girl's coupe approaching a railroad crossing. A locomotive happens to come barreling down at that exact moment, and smash: a glass and plastic explosion. The coupe rolls over and over, crumpled to scrap. The train thunders on with no regard.

"Oh, yeah! Lick those lips, baby. Lick 'em now!" Judd says.

"Hey, you know a lot about old movies, right?"

He flinches, startled that I'm awake, and pauses the video. "How old? Like pre–*Star Wars*?"

"Like black-and-white stuff."

"It hurts my eyes to look at that shit. I use it when they ask for it, but I don't seek it out."

"Then I guess you don't know much about Mercy Carnahan."

"I know she was hot. I'd fist her if we were back in the forties or whenever."

"Is she still alive?"

"That's a good question. I think she's the one who disappeared. But there's the one who OD'd, the one who went nuts, the one who went nuts and OD'd, the one who beat her kids, the one who died in a car wreck, the one who drowned, the one who was anorexic, the one who got fat and drunk and married twenty guys. It gets hard to keep track of them all."

"Did you ever, you know . . ."

"Use her? No, nobody's ever asked. You want me to?"

"No, no. I'm just saying. Her name came up at work, and nobody knew if she's still alive."

"Then look her up. I'm sure there's a ton of fan sites on her. It's all yours if you want it. I'm fried for today," Judd says, and plods upstairs in his saggy gray sweats.

I wheel up to the Wall, go to one of the oldfangled search engines I know, and type Mercy's name. The computer pulls up a list of links, the first 10 matches of 1,274,000. Assuming it makes sense to start at the top, I move the cursor to the number-one link, called The Temple of Mercy, and click the mouse button.

The screen flashes. A red curtain appears, then parts to reveal a black-and-white photo of Ms. Carnahan.

Let me just say this. I've never been into actresses. There's just too much media shoving them in my face all the time, even for somebody who "lives in a cave" like I do. Too many magazines, celebrity-obsessed TV shows and cable channels, gossip Web sites. Seems like I'm always seeing too much of the latest Hot Young Things without seeing their movies, which probably suck to begin with. Not that it matters. These plastic, vapid chicks usually wash up in five minutes anyway, clearing the red carpet for the next crop of Hotter Younger Things.

Nor do I see the appeal of old-time Hollywood icons. It always seemed sad and ghoulish to lust for women who were considered hot decades ago but are now dead or near-dead. To me, they're names more than faces—Greta Garbo, Marlene Dietrich, Grace Kelly, Rita Hayworth, Brigitte Bardot, and so on—and I couldn't pick any of them out of a photo lineup.

That said, this Mercy person's a stunner. She commands the camera with her eyes, so bright they must be blue; beckons with arched brows and the hint of a smile. She wears a dark dress and dark gloves. Stands with one foot on the floor, the other hiked up on a chair, displaying a generous stretch of leg. Black bangs and straight hair frame her pale face. Her beauty is gothic, vampirelike. In fact, after checking the picture on my wall, I wouldn't be surprised if the creators of Vampirella modeled her after Mercy.

More links along the bottom of the screen: <u>Biography</u>, <u>Filmography</u>, <u>Video</u>, <u>Photo Gallery</u>, <u>Resources</u>, <u>Contributors</u>. I click on <u>Biography</u>, and the screen flashes. Mercy reappears on the left, leering at a block of text to the right. She touches one gloved fingertip to her mouth, pinching the satin with her teeth. I try to ignore that and focus on the text, which reads as follows.

Today most people know Mercy Carnahan as the tough-talking, velvety beauty who ignited film noirs like It Takes a Devil and The Damned Don't Love with her sultry screen presence. She may be equally famous for abruptly ending her career, becoming so reclusive that no one has located her, alive or dead, since 1958. A number of Mercy biographies have been written [see Resources], and here I hope to summarize their findings and my own research, providing insight into her mysterious life.

THE LITTLE DANCING DYNAMO

Joseph Zagbroski and Frida Ullufsen emigrated to America from Poland and Sweden, respectively. They met aboard a New York–bound steamer in 1922 and married later that same year. With loans from Joseph's relatives, the couple settled on a small farm in Harmony, Pennsylvania, a village about thirty miles north of Pittsburgh.

Soon their marriage suffered a heavy strain as Frida lost two children in two years. A daughter arrived stillborn in 1923, and a son succumbed to pneumonia just hours after his birth in 1925. Already known to have a volatile, tempestuous side, Frida withdrew into a severe depression and remained bedridden for months. Nevertheless, she gave birth to a girl, Agnes, on December 8, 1926.

Within six months, Frida nearly drowned the child in a brook behind the farmhouse. We biographers continue to debate the cause of this incident. Most of us believe the baby caught a fever, and Frida—ever mindful of her previous children—panicked and tried to christen Agnes to ensure her passage into Heaven. Others maintain that Frida had meant to kill Agnes, convinced the baby was possessed by evil spirits.

Whatever Frida's intentions, her sister-in-law Elena intervened to rescue the baby. Elena had been staying at the farm to support Frida through her pregnancy and hurried to the brook upon hearing Frida's hysterical screams. Joseph promptly removed Frida to the Mayfield Sanitarium in central Pennsylvania, where she stayed until Agnes was six years old. Elena would raise Agnes during her mother's absence.

Agnes displayed a vivid imagination in her childhood, often staging one-girl plays for an audience of livestock. She attended Butler Elementary, where teacher Alice Churchill reported, "Agnes is highly intelligent and artistic. She likes to write and draw, and her reasoning skills are quite advanced for [an eight-year-old]. Socially she does struggle. Very solitary, she tends to shy away from her peers and group activities."

The world might have caught its first glimpse of Mercy Carnahan in the Butler Elementary Christmas Pageant of 1934. Cast as a sugarplum in *The Night Before Christmas,* Agnes literally stopped the show with an unscripted jazz-dance performance. No one—not her parents, teachers, classmates, nor anyone else in the audience—anticipated this outburst from the introverted child. She dazzled the crowd with several minutes of furious action and collapsed, exhausted, to a rapturous ovation.

Word of Agnes's talent spread fast beyond Harmony, and Butler Elementary recognized an opportunity to generate revenue. The school featured Agnes in numerous recitals, which conveniently doubled as fund-raisers, billing her as "the little dancing dynamo." When Agnes reached her final year in 1939, the school notified Joyce Jacoby, founder and headmistress of the Academy of Arts in Pittsburgh. Jacoby attended a recital, *The Water Nymph,* in which Agnes played the title role. The headmistress was impressed enough to offer the thirteen-year-old a full scholarship to the Academy that very night.

Frida objected to Agnes's leaving the farm, and a conflict ensued between mother and daughter in the summer of 1940. Tensions escalated and finally erupted when Frida thrashed Agnes with a razor belt. Joseph resolved the situation by smuggling Agnes to the Academy with a truckload of chickens, enduring Frida's wrath upon his return.

Shortly after Agnes's arrival, Jacoby renamed her new protégé "Mercy Carnahan": "Mercy" because Jacoby wanted Agnes to project an angelic image, and "Carnahan" to attract Irish-Americans, who were rapidly becoming a marketable demographic at the time.

A REAL MENSCH

Mercy engaged in a rigorous course of study at the Academy, balancing drama with voice and dance lessons. She proved to be an excellent student, consistently ranking near the top of her class. Her strong supporting turns as Ariel in *The Tempest* and as Masha in *The Seagull* earned her classmates' respect in a highly competitive environment. In her senior year, Mercy won the lead in *Hedda Gabler,* and, by all accounts, astounded audiences with her portrayal of Ibsen's controversial heroine.

Her personal life during these high school years, 1940 to 1944, is more difficult to gauge. Mercy gained a reputation as a loner, joining no clubs and participating in few social functions. None of her peers have ever claimed a close friendship with her, amorous or otherwise.

We do know that Frida's condition worsened while her daughter was away. In 1942 Joseph again committed his wife to Mayfield, where she would stay for three years. Mercy was certainly aware of this situation, but the extent of its impact on her remains unclear.

Stanley Frisch, a New York–based pinup photographer, contacted Mercy late in her senior year. Frisch was a bit of a huckster, known to lure Academy coeds to his studio with false promises of Broadway roles. Jacoby despised Frisch and advised her students to avoid him, but she failed to deter the seventeen-year-old Mercy. Departing for New York soon after graduation, Mercy worked as a waitress in Brooklyn between photo shoots and ill-fated auditions. Her sessions with Frisch produced the notorious "firebomb" shot, an instant sensation among American GIs, fighter pilots, and teenage boys.

Pantheon Studios noticed Mercy's popularity and signed her to a contract in early 1945. She would appear in four films that year: Bronx Cheer, There's Always Persia, Money for Murder, and Love Served Cold. Although her parts were small, she caught the eye of noir master Dack Clancy, who cast her as the femme fatale Kataline McCade in his 1946 classic It Takes a Devil.

Mercy and Clancy did not enjoy a smooth working relationship. For all his gifts, the director was a hard-living womanizer prone to fits of drunken rage. Much of his bitterness can be tied to World War I, in which he lost an eye; Clancy was known to intimidate "soft" actors by removing his eye patch and ranting about his combat experience. Mercy tolerated Clancy until the day he repeatedly groped her on the set. She warned him to stop and even shoved him at one point. When Clancy persisted, Mercy tore off his eye patch and butted her cigarette in his eye socket.

The director passed out and spent the night in a hospital. Widely expected to fire Mercy, Clancy instead returned in a rather subdued state, bearing no grudge toward his leading lady.

Despite its turbulent shoot, It Takes a Devil was a box-office smash that boosted Mercy's stardom far beyond her pinup fame. The Los Angeles press affectionately dubbed her "La Devila," a nickname that caught on with the contemporary media and lingers to this day. She topped *Moviegoer Magazine*'s "Most Desirable Screen Siren" annual poll while beauty parlors across the country were packed with women requesting "Mercy bangs." In the wake of Devil's success, even Clancy praised Mercy as "brassy," "one hell of a doll," and "a real mensch."

Pantheon quickly capitalized on their asset, producing ten Mercy vehicles between 1947 and 1952. She reteamed with Clancy for more hard-boiled thrillers, The Savage Whim and Lady of the Dark Pleasure, and showed her versatility in lighter fare like Curb Your Man and Who's That Cat? The latter includes the dinner party scene, a rousing musical number featuring blues guitarist Bo Shepp.

All of these films turned a profit, establishing Mercy as a remarkably bankable actress. At the same time, she routinely declined interviews, red-carpet premieres, and advances from male costars. In gossip-crazed Hollywood, Mercy was often seen as odd and aloof but not unfriendly.

Curb Your Man costar Deborah Greenlea expressed the common sentiment in a *Cinefan* interview: "Carnahan was actually a sweet girl but painfully awkward. Off in her own world, awfully quiet. You'd never guess she was so big by the way she carried herself. She'd just show up and do her takes, turn on 'The Mercy,' then turn it off like a pro. We all heard about her and Clancy, but I never saw that kind of hostility from her. Though she did tell Billy Gordon a thing or two when he kept trying to get his mitts on her. Got that idea out his head right quick, and it served him right, the little rat bastard."

[Gordon was a friendly witness to the House Committee on Un-American Activities (HUAC) in the late 1940s and early 1950s, condemning several actors and screenwriters to the Committee's blacklist.]

Personal tragedy struck in 1952, while Mercy was filming Murder by Night. A Pantheon representative arrived on the set to notify Mercy that her mother was found dead earlier that morning. Frida had hung herself during a third stay at the Mayfield Sanitarium. She was forty-eight years old.

Pantheon offered to give Mercy a brief respite, but she dismissed the studio representative and immediately returned to work. When the cast and crew learned the news hours later, they were startled by Mercy's apparent stoicism. Whatever her feelings toward her mother, Mercy concealed them with "inhuman professionalism," according to an unnamed observer. As the shoot progressed, Mercy became increasingly antisocial, retreating to her trailer for long stretches between takes. We can only speculate on her mental and emotional state at that point, but we should note that eaves-dropping crew members claim they heard Mercy convers-ing with herself in the trailer, speaking in numerous voices.

Publicly her career continued to thrive, and 1953 marked its peak. She nearly caused a riot at Cannes by making a surprise appearance for the premiere of <u>The Damned Don't Love</u>. Still her most popular movie, <u>Damned</u> contains the famous "<u>testing the waters</u>" line and "<u>the evening glove slap</u>." Mercy scored an Oscar nomination for her portrayal of the seductress Eva Lane, further confirming her elite sta-tus in the business. She did not win the award, nor would she receive another nomination. After <u>Damned</u>, Mercy Car-nahan would never make another film.

EXIT LA DEVILA

Mercy's contract with Pantheon was set to expire at the end of 1955. When she informally agreed to an extension, studio president Chester Sternfeld sensed a publicity coup. On No-vember 20, he held a special press junket to cover Mercy's re-signing and celebrate her "staying home at Pantheon, where she belongs." Reporters, radio correspondents, and a newsreel film crew packed the lobby of the studio's head-quarters, angling for a view of the star.

Sternfeld stepped up to the dais first, seating himself at a table with Mercy's contract and a gold pen. White-gloved servants lurked in the wings with buckets of iced champagne.

The junket's scheduled start time, 12:00 noon, passed with no sign of Mercy. Fifteen minutes later, she still had not arrived. Nervous studio personnel scurried around Sternfeld, all whispering variations of the same troubling news: no one knew where Mercy was, nor could anyone guarantee that she was en route.

A ten-year-old schoolgirl then entered the room. Later identified as Gertrude Eukis, she was costumed as a tattered, soot-stained child laborer. The crowd hushed as she approached the dais, announcing that she had come on Mercy's behalf. Sternfeld looked on, baffled, as the girl pulled a handwritten letter from her pocket.

The message read: "Dear Johns, it's been grand, boys, but I'm cashing out. Ten years are enough, the money's enough, knowing my face and figure will move your juices now and forever. Enough. It's time for Pantheon to break some fresh fillies, to ride 'em hard and put 'em away wet. I suspect the brass will savor the task. As for me, good luck finding another; good luck with the hole in your guts. La Devila."

Insiders interpreted the letter as a veiled swipe at Sternfeld, whose sexual escapades with pubescent girls and boys were an open secret in Hollywood. Sternfeld was humiliated and enraged, but also convinced that Mercy wanted to sign with another studio. He responded by launching an all-out smear campaign. Between 1955 and 1956, Pantheon spent approximately $1.5 million—about the cost of four Mercy movies—to bury the actress with bad press.

Negative articles ran in national papers like *The New York Times* and *The Washington Post*. The former charged that Mercy "brought nothing special to the screen" and would be "forgotten by the end of the Eisenhower administration." The latter referred to her as "an instant has-been" who "betrayed the business that made her."

The Hollywood tabloids were not so kind, circulating rumors that ranged from the salacious (affairs with married costars, homosexual flings, orgies) to the tawdry (cover-up abortions, alcoholism) and the frivolous (Mercy joining a coven of witches, conducting satanic rituals). Hurtful stories about Mercy's mental health surfaced as well. *Hollywire* reported that Mercy checked herself into the Wellspring Sanitarium several times during her years with Pantheon. According to *Starwatch*, Pantheon strained to pay Mercy's exorbitant psychiatry fees and was relieved to be rid of her. *Glitz Magazine* stooped to the lowest depth, juxtaposing photos of Mercy and Frida under the headline, "La Devila Gripped by Ghost of Twisted Ma?"

[See the Temple of Mercy Urban Legends section for an extensive list of Mercy rumors. We've also included factual verifications or dismissals whenever possible.]

If any of this hackwork personally affected Mercy, she did not let it show. She never mounted a public response, and, as far as we know, never confided to anyone about it. Warner Brothers, MGM, and Paramount pursued her throughout 1957, each offering to "save," "salvage," or "rescue" her career. Mercy ignored them and chose to leave Hollywood, returning to New York in early 1958.

She spent most of the year creating her own production company, Clara Luna, hoping to finance off-Broadway plays for fledgling actors and writers. To raise money for this venture, Mercy agreed to star in *The Crimson Kiss*, a bleak drama by the acclaimed playwright Taylor Everson.

The play was scheduled to premiere in the Colonial Theatre on December 8, 1958, Mercy's thirty-second birthday.

Despite her five-year absence from the screen and reams of unflattering press, tickets sold out in record time. When Mercy made her entrance on opening night, the audience greeted her with a raucous ovation. She stood speechless for minutes, visibly moved by the reception.

When the applause dwindled, Mercy still did not speak. She stood frozen in the spotlight, gazing into the audience. Rounds of flashbulbs went off. The silence grew tense with passing seconds.

She stepped to the edge of the stage and said, "I'm not who you think. I'm not strong, brave, or beautiful. I'm a coward frightened by life. A no-talent nobody. A lie, a fraud, a fake. And I can't pretend I'm anything else anymore."

Mercy then walked directly to stage left and out of sight. Most of the audience thought that she had been acting. A long pause followed. The other actors onstage waited, as confused as the audience. As everyone began to realize what had happened, the curtain dropped.

Gilbert Pollard, executive director of Clara Luna, assumed the unpleasant duty of announcing the show's demise. Fortunately for him, the audience was more astonished than outraged. There were no boos or catcalls, only a strange hush, as Pollard advised everyone to return their tickets to the box office for a refund.

As an unnamed female witness told *The New York Times*, "I guess I should be mad that she walked off like that, but I'm not. I got my money's worth. I got to see Mercy Carnahan write her own obit. You never see stuff like that in Skowhegan."

ENCORE?

Solid facts on Mercy's post-*Kiss* life remain scant to this day. She abandoned her Manhattan apartment within hours, leaving Pollard a signed authorization to close down Clara Luna. After that, we can only guess where she went or how she has fared. Fans, journalists, and film historians have sought her with no success while tabloids continue to claim dubious Mercy sightings.

As far as we know, she neither married nor had children. We have never located the appropriate records, and no one has come forward claiming to be her spouse or child, biological or adopted. Over the years, no fewer than seventeen men and five women have courted the press, alleging themselves to be her former lovers, but each of these individuals has been discredited.

The closest thing we have to a confirmed appearance occurred on December 2, 1985. Eight staff members of Butler Valley Hospital maintain that Mercy arrived after midnight, by a special secret arrangement, to stand by her father's deathbed. Joseph Zagbroski did indeed pass away early that morning, but the hospital staff has never been able to prove Mercy's visit. In any event, she did not attend Joseph's funeral, disappointing a crowd of fans and press who overran the ceremony hoping to see her.

In my opinion, all this mystery leads to one simple conclusion: Mercy meant to vanish and stay vanished. Her disappearance might even be the most impressive feat of her career. Assuming she's still alive, she has eluded a curious public and aggressive media for over four decades. She was always an intensely private person, even at the height of her Hollywood fame, and so all of us might do well to respect her wishes and leave her alone.

Ironically enough, Mercy Carnahan never really went away. The number of visitors to this site alone indicates that her popularity is unwavering, her appeal timeless. For many of us, she will forever be the brightest star of all, and we will happily gaze upon her for ages to come.

—Her humble Temple-keeper,
Wade Endicott
wade@templeofmercy.com

6

D.T. has been working at Marchicomo's for twentysome years, which gives him seniority and makes him the unofficial foreman. I don't know how old he is—hard to tell since he dyes his hair black—but I'd guess about sixty. Don't know his real name, either, just that everybody calls him D.T. because he shakes and sweats a lot. He also smokes cigarettes by the fistful and gulps down coffee by the pot, which doesn't help to calm him. D.T.'s not an angry guy, but he'll get pissed when he has to repeat an order.

Even so, he calls for somebody to take out the garbage, and my colleagues find ways to ignore him.

Jerillo scratches the scar on his bicep where his wife stabbed him, nods his head to some Steve Miller song on the radio. I like Jerillo; he's easygoing, clownish, generous. But he also knows how to play the oblivious stoner to avoid work, and so he keeps bobbing and grooving to the music as he picks over a box of Granny Smiths.

Dockerty sidesteps into the cooler, walking like he just wet his pants. He always walks like that: feet spread wide, hardly bending his knees, pivoting his entire five-foot-two body. I think it's the result of a back injury. He also whistles when he moves. Not whistling tunes, but whistling like a toy train. I once called him "The Little Engine That Couldn't" in the heat of a verbal scrap, and he's never forgiven me.

Ross stares at the wall and breathes through his mouth. To take out the garbage, you need to haul a bin around the block with a power jack. In his one year at Marchicomo's, Ross has scraped parked cars, smashed a display rack, and dented the cooler wall with a power jack. So it's probably best for everyone if he just keeps staring at the wall.

That leaves me, and I'm fine with the break from onion duty. I pull on my gloves, hit the switch on the jack's handle. The prongs rise with an electric buzz, lifting the garbage bin off the floor. Walking backwards, I tow the load through the double doors and out to the sidewalk of Penn Avenue. Morning stragglers clear the way as I head for the corner and turn down Twenty-first.

Our trash compactor, the Mauler, sits at the back of the building where Twenty-first meets the alley Mulberry Way. The metal door groans open with my pull. One by one, then, I hoist boxes and crates out of the bin, up over my head, and chuck them into the Mauler's yawning mouth.

Yellowish tomato juice drips from sopping cardboard, burning my forearms. Bell peppers ooze through the slats of wooden crates, glopping onto the sidewalk. Leafy greens rotted beyond rust, melting to an oily sludge. Flats of strawberries growing tufts of snowy mold, watermelons fizzing white foam and ready to burst. In they go, all of them, piling up till there's no more room in the compactor.

Then I close the door and hit the crush button. The Mauler clanks and rattles while its big hydraulic press comes down. Wooden crates snap. Cardboard pops. Sickly liquids leak out along the bottom, trickling down the sidewalk's access ramp, pooling around the alleyway curb.

The Mauler then resets itself so I can reopen the door and throw more in its mouth. It will take about five of these cycles for me to empty the bin. Open, hoist, toss, close, crush, repeat. Spurts of physical work, stretches of downtime as the machine does its thing.

Sometime during these tasks, I think about that Mercy site I read last night. I've already decided that I'll never find this person. If so many others have tried for so long and failed, then how am I supposed to? I'm not, and I have to find a way to tell Lou as much.

But man, that was a lot of money in that drawer.

I'll admit that I considered it. I sent that Endicott guy an e-mail asking for contacts, just for the hell of it, pretending I was a film studies major. I even called the dog track, just to see how full of shit Lou is, and that was weird. The guy who answered said he knew Lou. In fact, he called him a "no-good son of a bitch" and said I'd have to come to the track in person if I wanted to know anything else. Then he hung up. Don't know what his problem was, and I'm not trekking to Wheeling to find out.

Still, that was a lot of money.

Another weird thing's happened since I read that site. You know how sometimes you get a song stuck in your head, find yourself singing it all day? I've had the same thing, only with images. Over and over, I keep seeing that 1934 Christmas pageant in Butler Elementary.

There's a dim room hazed with cigarette smoke, packed full of chairs and bodies. The crowd faces a stage set with a cardboard fireplace. Threadbare socks hang over construction-paper flames. A tree twinkles with white snowflake ornaments. An old lady hunches over a piano in the corner, arthritic hands ready on the keys.

Somewhere offstage, the narrator says the lines about children snuggled in their beds, visions of sugarplums dancing in their heads. Cue the old lady. She pounds out a jaunty ditty, and cue four girls dressed as sugarplums. Purple dresses, glittery wings and slippers. They dance out from behind the tree, and the audience awws.

Everything's cutesy till the fourth sugarplum starts to act out. She dances faster and harder than the other three, and she doesn't stop when they do. Instead she throws herself into the Charleston and goes nuts. The other girls gawk at her. The old lady can't keep up, wincing with pained hands.

Faster! From the Charleston to spins and kicks, the girl's dancing out of herself, unbalanced and unhinged. Faster!

The audience only sees her brilliance. Traces of purple motion, the blur of her white limbs. Her black hair flying and the blue diamonds of her eyes. They're rising now, the audience, rising to their collective feet. Clapping cheering whistling, angling for a better look at this kid, this little dancing dynamo.

Faster, faster, faster! The old lady gives up and stops, but the girl doesn't. She's breathless, dizzy, but still moving. And while the crowd's riled up in a frenzy, whooping screaming stomping, the girl's trying to say something. She's looking in their faces, their eyes, and she's desperately gasping words. But she can't sound them, not enough wind, and she can't stop her body moving till she blacks out. Drops. Hits the boards with a thud.

The Mauler finishes a cycle, ready for the last load. Just as I reach down into the bin, a familiar clickclock sounds out behind me. Gen approaches on three-inch heels, wearing black slacks and a silky white blouse. Marchicomo's opened two hours ago, and she's just reporting to work now. It must be nice to run on Managerial Standard Time.

66

She stops alongside the bin, even with those clothes, and says, "I've been thinking about the other day. I thought you were going to harass me, like your cretin coworkers do, and I overreacted. For that I apologize."

I glance at her and say thanks. But my glance turns into a stare, and she stares back, waiting. Of course I have nothing. No words, no way to engage her in a real conversation.

Gen seems to sense my trouble, and it seems to amuse her. She takes out a packet of cigarettes, taps it on the top edge of the bin. Lights up, watches me through her smoke. Daylight shows dark circles around her eyes, makes her look older. A used beauty slowly going haggard.

"You ever think about failure?" she says. "Maybe I'm strange, but I think about it all the time. Spectacular or slight, monumental or personal. If it's a failure, I'm interested. Could be anything from the Edsel to the Maginot Line, the *Challenger* to a comedian bombing on open mic night.

"When it comes to people, I've even outlined several failure types. Like the Cogs, for example. Cogs don't want much from life. They're content to wake up, go to work, come home, park their carcasses behind a TV or computer. And they lose themselves in those screens, boy, sucking hard on those binkies, filling their heads full of empty info-noise. Tax revenue and passive consumption are what they're good for. Whether it's sports or soaps, fast food or fancy cars, cozy homes or prescription meds. Sure, there's a dull, throbbing pain at the base of their skulls. A vague awareness that their lives are pointless wastes. But give them enough comfort and shiny, flashy distractions, and the pain passes, leaving them free to turn, turn, turn and grease the machine with the blood of their souls.

"The If Onlys want a bit more. Doesn't matter what they do

for money. They could be drug dealers, artists, janitors. Dayjobbers or jobless, they think they're special. No, scratch that. They *know* they're special. They know they're smart, able, and talented. Unfortunately, they're not smart, able, and talented enough, or they're inept at using their gifts to some meaningful end. So you get a forty-year-old with a drawerful of rejected screenplays telling himself, 'If I just keep at it, I know they'll buy the next one!' The thirty-year-old in his parents' basement, shredding away on his guitar, telling himself, 'If I could just hook up with the right band, I know I'll make it!' The twenty-year-old with her finger in her throat, telling herself, 'If I just lose ten more pounds and get a nose job, I know I'll make a good stripper.' The teenager busting his nuts in the weight room, telling himself, 'If I just gain ten more pounds, I know I can hit homers without the juice!' Sure, they may have their lapses into self-doubt, the occasional glimpse of truth. But give them their delusions, and they go on striving for imaginary opportunities and choking on false hope. And then they die.

"I have twenty-nine other types, too. I won't bore you with them, but I will say this: I'm damn good at matching people to their types. It's like my hobby. And yet I can't figure out which one you belong to. Usually I can tell within seconds, but so far you've stumped me. I mean that as a compliment."

"Thanks, Gen. That's depressing as hell. But thanks."

"Don't take it so bad. I'm just making nice. Almost everyone's a failure. There's no shame in it."

"So which type do you belong to?"

"None. I'm not a failure. I'm a success dealing with a temporary setback."

I smile, then realize she isn't kidding.

"Don't believe me? Watch me. I'll get out of here soon enough.

Let's face it. This town's dead. People escape Pittsburgh or retreat back to it. Nobody aspires to be here. You don't plan on staying here forever, do you? You don't think about going somewhere else, doing anything else?"

"No way," I say, and pat the Mauler. "No, you're looking at the fulfillment of my potential, Gen. The grand culmination of all my dreams and desires. Maybe that's why you can't pin me in your glass case, because I'm a success, too. Albeit a closeted one."

"I never cared much for sarcasm. It always struck me as defensive, and defensive ain't sexy."

"Getting off on other people's failures ain't so hot, either."

"I think you misunderstood. Failure fascinates me, but it doesn't get me off. You know what I get off on? Ambition. Ambition equals sexy. You're sexy, or you're not. You have ambition, or you don't. If you got it, good. Show me. Use it. Do something with it. If you don't, well," she looks down to the bin, "there's always the trash."

Gen flicks her cigarette butt, continues on toward the warehouse. The butt lands in the puddle along the alleyway curb. A burnt remnant smudged with lipstick.

Let me explain something. I'm not going to the Wheeling dog track because I'm intrigued about Lou's winnings or feuds with the manager. No, I'm going because it's Saturday night, and my original plans—sneaking some of Judd's mom's pills, hitting the cot, rising sometime Sunday afternoon for a burning, dehydrated piss, returning to the cot till Monday morning—seemed kind of lame after that last run-in with Gen. Lame if not shameful, even.

Much better to be on a bus, crushed against the back corner by a sweaty, red-faced salesman named Ted Brubaker. He smells like rum and aging desperation, his girth flabbing about in a button-down shirt. Upon settling in and loosening his tie,

Brubaker introduces himself and says, "Let me tell ya, I like the horses better. Got nothing against the dogs. They're good for a lark, but gimme the horses any day. It's like the difference between fucking a skinny broad and fucking a fat broad. The horses, they got a lot more thunder."

He bounces back and forth with a pelvic thrust, grunting what sounds like "hoogaah!" Then looks at me and says, "You got a girlfriend? I mean, hey, don't mean to infringe or anything, I'm just asking. Cause when I was your age, Saturday night, you wouldn't catch me on no bus to Wheeling."

Something tells me there's no right answer to Brubaker's question. Being about twice my age, he's determined to impart fatherly wisdom. You tell a guy like Brubaker that you don't have a girlfriend, he'll say you need one. Otherwise you're jerking off, and that's just one lonely step above being queer. Tell him you have a girlfriend, he'll tell you to dump her because she's oppressing you, limiting you to fucking only her when you should be out there enjoying your youth, fucking every half-decent piece of ass you can grab. And why not? She's probably cheating on you right now while you're sitting on this bus instead of fucking her, you fuckin' queer.

So I say, "Yeah, I had a woman. But I left her for Jesus."

That shuts him up, briefly at least, but the silence is not kind. It makes me think about things I'd rather not, like the Erin thing. There's not much left besides the books under the cot. A jumble of days at that library table, pretending to read, hoping she wouldn't catch me watching her but secretly hoping she would till finally she did. She left her post at the front desk, came to the table.

We talked there ("What is that? Emerson? [snickers] Dude was a careerist."), in cafes ("Please explain Pittsburgh's obsession with classic rock to me. People actually *like* Steve Miller here?"), in diners ("I didn't *mean* to break his wrist. Or take out three of his molars. It just kind of happened."), in her dorm ("What do you mean your dad 'sells gags for a living'?"). Talked and talked till a February night, when downpouring snow buried the roads.

We stood by her window, watching the flakes swarm the streetlights, me holding her from behind. She unbuttoned, pulled down her shirt. A yellow face ringed with flames, inked into her left shoulder blade. His cheeks red, grin devilish, eyes bright and wide. On the right was his pale blue counterpart, plump-faced and sleepy. Benign and cratered, haloed with a cosmic glow.

She touched them to my hands, the sun the moon. Let me feel them, then turned around with eyes darker than black. No smile, just a look. The kind that stays years after she's gone, that recurs in dreams and wakes you with an ache, a gut shot full of regret.

"A man of faith, huh? I can respect that. Didn't mean to offend you or nothin'. But me and the Lord, we ain't so close these days. Not after that 'Music City Miracle' bullshit," Brubaker says, shaking his head. "Buffalo. Always fuckin' Buffalo."

Soon after taking an Exit 0, the bus pulls into a lot and approaches two adjoining buildings. The taller one is a hotel, the squat one is the casino. Both are boxy and sand colored, their edges painted turquoise. Lit-up red letters spell WHEELING RIDGE across a face of each.

I follow the busload into the casino lobby. Escalators rise or decline on either side of a fake-rock formation. An angry tiki statue sits atop the rocks, its mouth gaping and drooling a weak stream. The trickle struggles down the mock-up, collects in a basin overhung with drooping palm trees.

"I don't know what you're gonna do, but I don't waste time with the slots. There's no skill in it. No, I go straight to the track.

You coming?" Brubaker says as the escalator carries us past the tiki, brings us to the main floor.

"I think I'll waste time with the slots."

"If you wanna find me, just look for the guy with the big bulge in his pocket."

We stare at each other.

"I meant my wallet! What'd you *think* I meant?!" Brubaker says, and plods off rolling up his sleeves.

I give him time, then wander my way through the slots parlor. Past a maze of machines blinking flashing clinking, making a cacophonous mess of the neon-drenched space. People, mostly elderly, perch close to the glass and smack plastic buttons, hypnotized by the spin. Their wizened faces obscured like faces masked in panty hose like faces blurred and laughing, cheering. Hitting *look at me when I bitch-slap you* kicking *admit you're a faggot* binding *I'll cut it off* cutting *hands behind your back.* Spinning lights *places everybody* ceiling, video camera, spinning, and I'm not on my knees, not in that garage again, not chained. I'm moving and refusing to lose my focus, remembering Job 1.

So I reach a stairway, go down to a hall lined with framed photos of the track's all-time winningest dogs, and arrive at the betting area. A snack bar, regular bar, and ticket counter each own a wall. Tables and chairs clutter up the floor space. Video monitors hang overhead, simulcasting the action outside. A Pac-Man machine mopes in the corner, uninvited to the party upstairs.

The crowd's younger than I expected, with a few couples in their twenties and a pack of high school kids with nowhere better to hang out. Hardly a majority of old guys in chest-high polyester pants, but there are still a few, God bless 'em, hunched over their tables and studying the program like it's the Talmud. I also count

72

one mad scientist: a guy with a color-coded system, circling dogs with a spectrum of Magic Markers, punching numbers in his cell phone calculator. And one bona fide casualty: a guy passed out, facedown on his table and a pile of losing tickets. A ticket actually sticks to his cheek, held in place with a glaze of Pabst sweat.

I step out for a look at the track, where eight handlers lead eight dogs toward the starting box. The procession stops, lets the spectators see what they're betting on. What I see is a collection of spooked canines, all frayed nerves and twiggy limbs. Eight breakable, degraded dogs born and bred for this performance. Numbered, muzzled with mouthfuls of steel wool and duct tape across their yaps. Collared and chained to a spinning disc, cheered on by featureless faces.

Lady Kraken, #6, meets my stare with glassy eyes that say, "Don't let them do this to me. Take me home. Get me out of here." And while I wish I could, her handler pulls her away. All eight dogs file into their slots of the box, locked in and left to howl.

"*Spunky in motion!*" says the PA. An electrified motor zips along the base of the track, carrying a pole hung with two dummy rabbits. "*And they're off!*"

Out shoot the dogs, thumping past in a grayish mass. My Lady's stuck in the pack while #5, Groovy Lucius, pulls ahead by a length.

The couple dozen spectators scream things like "Go! Go! Go!" "Pick it up!" "Move your weak ass!" Brubaker vocal among them, pacing the handrail, amped up like he'll charge the track and kick the fuck out of his dog if it loses.

Around the bend they come, hitting the home stretch. Lady Kraken trying but fading, Groovy Lucius surging, Brubaker yelling, "Yes! *Yes!* Make my money, bitch!" Working himself up to a seismic victory roar, and I've seen this scene before. No need to repeat.

Back inside, I find a door labeled MANAGER by the ticket counter. It's partway open, revealing an old man on his desk phone. Pushing seventy, maybe, he's still well built and sporting a gray buzz cut. Hubble-thick lenses magnify his eyes and make him look like a coked-up owl. His Hawaiian shirt may or may not have some connection to the tiki in the lobby.

"I don't know what kind of sledge it's gonna take to bash this into your skull," he says to whoever's on the line, "but for Christ's sake, clean it up! I don't care what you do with Gus. Fuck Gus. Wheel his sorry incontinent ass outside, shove him in the river for all I care. But at least throw some sawdust on that shit."

He slams down the phone, looks at me. "You want something?"

"I called about Lou Kashon."

"What about him?"

"I'm a friend of his, and—"

"That son of a bitch ain't got no friends."

"Okay, well, you said to come here if I wanted to know about him. So here I am."

"Yeah, but I didn't think you'd do it. You really got nothing better to do?"

"No. I'm kind of a cipher that way."

He looks me up and down, then nods to a chair facing his desk. Introduces himself as Dom Conte, but really saying, "Sit the hell down so we can get this over with." Conte's a busy man, see, under pressure and pressed for time.

"You want to know about Kashon? I'll tell you about Kashon. It was back in forty-five, when my pop Bruno Conte was running the place. From here to Atlantic City, everybody knew Pop was the top dog man in the East. Not one lousy mutt hit that track without his personal approval. He'd walk the stalls and check the

74

dogs' paws, their legs, their teeth. Squeeze their balls to see if they yelped like Conte-worthy stock. Pop had a hard rep, drove the breeders and trainers nuts. But they respected him cause they recognized his integrity. They knew he believed in giving the public a good race.

"And nobody got one up on him in this business, never, till May 26. Me, I was ten years old at the time, out there sweeping the floors when I first saw him, that greasy A-rab bastard. He showed up here half-looped and still in uniform like a war hero, a real Audie Murphy.

"He nailed some quinielas and perfectas on long odds. Soon he got the whole floor buzzing about the tipsy GI who's throwing down big and scoring bigger. I myself watched him drop a wad on a superfecta and win with the lead dog at 12-1.

"That's when I came running to this office, where Pop was sitting in this very chair, and I said, 'You gotta see this. There's a guy riding a streak you wouldn't believe.' Pop came out, watched Kashon play another race and rack up another couple grand, and then another. By then Kashon had a wad of hundreds, bills spilling out of his pockets. Every move he made, a wall of eyeballs followed him. It was getting to be a security risk, seeing as how we run a pari-mutuel business here."

"Which means what?" I ask.

"You're not really betting against the house, you're betting against everybody else. All the house does is give the losers' money to the winners while taking its own fixed percentage. So when somebody like Kashon walks around with a wad this thick," Conte grips an imaginary triple-decker cheeseburger, "people don't see a guy who's kicking the house's ass. They see a guy who's kicking *their* ass.

"Pop went up to him, then, tried to make small talk. Suggested

75

that Kashon lower his profile, maybe catch a cab home. Kashon looked right at him, all bleary-eyed, and said, 'Don't matter. It's just easy money. Found money. I could win this whole damn dump if I wanted, and it still don't matter.'

"Pop took exception to that, as you might imagine, and proposed a side bet on the next race: each man picks a trifecta, staking Kashon's entire winnings since they were so easy to come by. Kashon didn't even look at the program, just said, 'You're on.' His three dogs were 14-1, 8-1, 5-1 in that order. Pop's were 3-1, 4-1, 7-2.

"Bam! Bam! Bam! They all cross the line, unfuckinbelievable. Right there, Kashon scored big on his ticket, *again,* and doubled his money on Pop. Never saw nothing like it. The veins in Pop's forehead looked like ropes of licorice. I thought he was gonna murder Kashon right then.

"But he couldn't do nothing because too many people were watching, and a lot of 'em were *cheering!* All the regulars smelled Pop's comeuppance. They started congregating, getting boisterous because somebody finally got the better of Bruno Conte. But Pop wasn't going down so easy. Next race, he offered the same bet, double or nothing. And Kashon laughed as he took him up on it, the cocksure fuck."

"And Lou won again, I guess."

"This time on a superfecta, all four dogs in exact order. It was turning into Mardi Gras out there, people whooping it up, egging them on. And Pop, there was no stopping him. Nobody dared go up to him and say, 'Let it go, Bruno,' least of all me, not with the rage boiling in Pop's face.

"The next race was the last one. And one more time Pop said double or nothing, and Kashon shrugged. Fuckin' *shrugged* and said, 'Don't matter to me. We all choose our own Hell, my friend.' Like that was supposed to mean something.

"So Kashon went and picked a scrawny little runt called Will-O-Wisp to win. Scrawny by Pop's standards, at least; that mutt was 20-1, barely qualified, and Kashon put everything on it. Pop couldn't believe Kashon was serious. The crowd was begging Kashon to stop, to go home, quit while he was ahead. Pop meanwhile was all smiles. All he needed was for that little piece of shit to lose. He even went and bet on all the other dogs just to make it official.

"Of course the little shit won, of course! But that ain't even the point; it's the *way* it won that kills me. You got Spunky in motion. Up go the gates, and they're off. Kashon's dog was buried dead last, the others packed close at the first turn. It's all going swimmingly for Pop along the stretch and around the next turn. The crowd was so quiet, you'd think they were watching a funeral.

"Coming up on the stretch call, and just like *that,* the lead dog stumbled, and the pack smashed into him. One mutt hit the rail with a squeal. Another rolled clear out into the crowd, bowled over some lady in her Carmen Miranda hat. Sent her bananas and grapes flying all over while two more mutts gimped off the track. The lead dog got tangled with two behind him, their legs gnarling up in a pretzel of dogflesh. Which left Kashon's runt to trot across the line untouched.

"The crowd exploded like a riot, and Pop had no choice but to pay out. It was a bullshit fluke, but they would've lynched him if he'd called a forfeit. No, double or nothing, and Kashon doubled up for the third straight time. Pop emptied the safe, shipped the bastard and his money back to Pittsburgh in a Brinks truck.

"Pop's rep took a major hit that night, one he never got over. He was never Bruno Conte the top dog man again. He became Bruno Conte who got suckered by a drunken A-rab and lost his ass on a 20-1 runt called Will-O-Wisp. You think I'm spouting a bunch of nonsense?"

Conte opens a desk drawer, takes out a decayed newspaper. "Rumpus at the Ridge!" reads the headline on yellowed pulp. The front-page photo shows a crowd of trackgoers standing around a blob. Looking closer at that shapeless heap, I can make out a muzzled snout and bulging eye. A front paw bent backwards, a broken hind leg with bone poking through the skin. And that's just one dog; the other lies on its side, back to the camera. A man pulls hard on a crowbar lodged between the dog bodies, trying to pry them apart. Another guy stands by with a pickax.

"That's before it really got ugly. The boys cut one of the dogs when they jabbed their tools in there, struck an artery. Blood gushed like water from a busted main, and the *sound* those dogs made. I been around dogs my whole life, and I seen a lot of them suffer. But this was different. This was the work of some sick fuckin' forces.

"And your buddy Kashon had a hand in it. I know that sounds crazy, but these things don't just happen. I watched him real close that night, and even then I didn't trust him. He puts on a good front, all happy-drunk and carefree, throwing money around. But underneath that, there's something else going on, something sinister. And if you think he's your friend, you're on a crooked path to nowhere good."

7

Mercy sits on the edge of a desk in a dingy office. She wears a black dress and evening gloves that match her black hair. On the desktop lies a gun, smoking, its pollution clouding the bare bulb overhead. At her feet lies a corpse, facedown, bald head glaring at the camera. Mercy doesn't seem to notice the body or care that it's dead. She's more interested in picking lint off her glove. This world is black and white and heavily shadowed, and she's a creature that couldn't exist anywhere else. Call it her habitat.

A door opens in the background. Enter a guy wearing a fedora and a rumpled suit. The sight of the corpse stops him, then he sees Mercy. He gets all frazzled; she looks ready to yawn.

"You killed Drake! He's my partner!"

"*Was* your partner, Trent. Now he's a load of dead scum oozing back to the sewer. But I didn't kill him. Much as he deserved it, I never had the chance. And are you gonna close the door or broadcast this mess to the entire Bowery?"

Trent slams the door and approaches her. She ignores him, smoothing an unseen wrinkle in her dress. His gaze follows her hand, lingers on her legs.

"You're one pretty liar, but you can't talk your way out of this

79

jam. Drake was no saint, I'll give you that. He was a real lout sometimes, a two-bit excuse for a dick. But that's no reason to kill a man. I already got O'Grady and the cops on my back. I can't afford to let this slide."

"Then report it." She takes the phone on his desktop and holds it out to him. "But know this: I didn't put the slug in his guts. He was dead when I arrived, and that was five minutes ago. The rod's still hot. If you run, you might catch your killer."

"I think I'm looking at her."

"My prints aren't on that gun, but yours are. Everybody at the club saw me tonight, but who knows where you've been? So what do you have? No clues, no answers, no alibi. Nothing but your own motive and your own smoking gun. So go on, call the cops."

Cut to Trent, all stubble and grim-set jaw. His face registers rage and disgust, and yet some lust.

Cut to Mercy still holding the phone, eyebrow cocked. Maybe she's depraved, devious, and amoral. But she's smarter than him, and stronger.

Trent retreats to the chair behind the desk. He sits, takes a bottle and shot glass from a drawer. "I'm a detective, Miss Lane. It's my job to test the waters."

Mercy sets the phone aside. "There's a better way to test the waters, Trent. You stick your finger in and give it a wiggle."

A smile creeps upon her lips. Trent's at a loss, hand frozen on the bottle.

Cut to Mercy pulling down one of her gloves, bunching it around her wrist. She bites the tip of her middle finger, stretching off the black satin till the entire glove dangles from her teeth. Then she lets it drop with a little nudge from her tongue.

Trent's just a man, damn it. He can't resist ogling her, leaning in closer, eyes alight and seeking more skin.

Mercy belts him with a slap. A loud crack across the face, bare hand to his cheek. She comes back with a backhand. Another crack across the other cheek.

Trent's fedora falls off, his pomaded hair shakes out of place. Mercy picks up her glove and slips it back on by the time he recovers.

"Pull yourself together, man. I need you to be sober for once. It's almost midnight, Drake stinks worse dead than alive, and the Syndicate's got two hired guns on the way. We need to think of something fast."

She steps away from the desk, hands on her hips. "Now, are you gonna fix me a drink or sit there like a heap of whipped cream?"

The video stops.

I hit a few keys on the keyboard, backing up the video to "give it a wiggle." Then a key that plays the video frame by frame. The moving image ticks ahead at a glacial place, edging toward the cut.

There it is: that moment when the editor shifts our perspective, when we switch from seeing Mercy and Trent sharing the screen to just Mercy looking at Trent, and by extension us. And in the following slivers of a second—an instant stretched and made searchable by the computer—Mercy looks right into the camera.

Her façade is gone. She's not leering like she was before the cut, not staring Trent down with supreme confidence. Instead she seems scared, like she's been caught in a crime or sees something awful coming her way.

Frame. By. Frame.

Don't ask me what time it is. I've been at the Wall since eleven, and it was past two last I checked. Judd's long gone to bed, the cat's purring away on the cot, and I'm frying my eyeballs on a computer screen.

But look at her, changing with every tick. She blinks, and her eyes leave the camera. She focuses on her costar, reassumes the leer from the prior shot. No fear anymore, no hint of weakness as she begins to lift her gloved finger to her mouth. As her hand rises, her façade is restored.

I stop the video with a keystroke, back it up with a few more, and replay it at regular speed.

. . . Trent retreats to the chair behind the desk. He sits, takes a bottle and shot glass from a drawer. "I'm a detective, Miss Lane. It's my job to test the waters."

Mercy sets the phone aside. "There's a better way to test the waters, Trent. You stick your finger in and give it a wiggle."

A smile creeps upon her lips. Trent's at a loss, hand frozen on the bottle.

Cut to Mercy pulling down one of her gloves, bunching it around her wrist. She bites the tip of her middle finger, stretching off the black satin till the entire glove dangles from her teeth. Then she lets it drop with a little nudge from her tongue. . . .

Watch it that way with an untrained eye, and you never see the slip. Mercy never looks away from her prey, never seems less than divine. And though you'd never know it, somewhere in your subconscious you glimpsed her as a person.

A few hours later, I'm sitting in Judd's car, parked across from Kashon's. Chasing mouthfuls of Biggie Breakfast with coffee, I've decided to reject Lou's offer. I've already spent too much time staring at Mercy Carnahan, reading about her, thinking about her. And that episode last night—losing sleep, studying video—takes me back to an unhappy place I don't care to revisit.

Lou needs to come up with something else I can do for that cash. And if he can't, that's okay, because I wrote up a list. Hauling out all the junk in his house, painting the place, fixing the porch, stuff like that. Real, solid jobs, and all better than ghostbusting.

There's just one problem: Lou hasn't shown up for work today. His brother Eugene did, though. I watched him park his Caddy and unlock the warehouse. Watched as a truck backed up to the dock and Eugene supervised (meaning he stood around holding a clipboard) while guys in weightlifter belts unloaded bins of watermelons. But still no Lou, and I'm due at Marchicomo's.

Just as I step outside, the maroon Buick pulls up to Kashon's. Its driver, the old black guy who delivered Lou before, hurries to the warehouse door and knocks like he's worried. The door opens, and Eugene comes out.

Now keep in mind I'm observing this from across the street, so there's only so much I can hear. What I get are harried apologies from the old black guy ("I tried, man! I knocked and hollered. Was gonna bust down the door, but the neighbors was watching!"), rising anger from the old white guy ("So you just left? Christ, what if he fell and broke something?!"), which creates hurt anger in the old black guy ("Well, shit, Gene! I'm late for work as it is. You know they wanna fire me, and now you're yelling at me. I can't win!")

As entertaining as it is to watch two old men bicker, and possibly come to blows, I make a point to mosey on over, coffee cup in hand. If something's gone wrong with Lou, I'd like to know. If nothing else, I got a drawerful of reasons to care.

"Gentlemen, how we doing this morning?"

They both give me a look that says, "Who the fuck are you?"

To which I respond, "Dexter Bolzjak. I work over at Sal's."

"You're Marv's kid?" Eugene says.

"Yep, and I'm looking for Lou. Is he around?"

"No, he ain't. Apparently he's home, and God knows if he's okay. His good friend Haley here didn't bother to find out."

"Man, you want me to go back there? You just say it. I'll go. I'll lose my job, but I'll go just to shut you up!" Haley fires back.

"Well, what am *I* gonna do? I got a truck coming from Texas in an hour. You think I can just leave?"

"Okay, so he's home and you're both worried," I say. "You know what? I'll go check on him. I gave him a ride home the other day. I know the way."

"Yeah, I saw you," Eugene says. "And I gotta wonder why you've been hanging around him lately. Like you want something from him."

"Just looking for tips on the dogs. I heard Lou's good at it, figured I'd learn the game from a winner. You want me to see if he's okay or what?"

The old men size me up like I'm weighing in for a prizefight.

"I think he's a good kid," Haley says. "I trust him."

Eugene doesn't seem so convinced, but he takes a key off his key ring anyway. "I always got along with Marv. That's the only reason I'm allowing this. Call me as soon as you get there. I want to hear Lou say he's okay and coming back with you."

"And what if he's not okay?"

"He'll be okay. Just call."

I start back toward Marchicomo's, brimming with social competence. Now I just have to deal with Sal. Or Gen, better yet, who I see up ahead on Twenty-first by the Mauler. So I jog to catch up to her.

"Hey, I gotta ask you something. You care if I call off today? I got what you might call a family emergency."

"But who will bag the onions?" she says. "How will the high-precision Marchicomo machine function without you? Good God, we're all gonna die."

"I'm digging the sarcasm, boss. It's kind of sexy when you do it."

Gen stops to face me. She has a bruise on her cheek, a purplish blotch poorly masked with makeup. I try to focus on her eyes, but she's wearing sunglasses. And it's not a sunny morning. In fact, it's gray and drizzly.

"Dexter, I'm not in a cute mood today," she says, and click-clocks away.

Another knock on Lou's door, another minute spent waiting on the porch. The planks creak underfoot, eager to break like they broke under that cedar glider. I unlock and enter 809 Wellsbrook before that can happen, stepping right into the rot. At least this time I'm ready for it, and I maneuver through the stacks of newspapers, breathing the mustiness a little easier than before.

I call Lou's name a couple times, and still nothing. Up the steps I go, then, squeezing past faded magazines and paperbacks. Past the *Sports Illustrated* with the '85 Bears dancing over a crippled Patriot, past Conan the Barbarian standing atop a hill of skulls. Around the landing and its stained-glass window, up to the hallway.

The bedroom door is open. Lou's lying on his mattress, eyes closed, wearing the same clothes he wore last time I was here. For all I know, he hasn't moved since then. He's pale as hell, but it looks like he's breathing, so I knock on the door and call him again.

He rolls over, pants stained with piss, and says, "Kid. I'm having a real time here. I think . . ."

I move closer to him and step on a glob of vomit. It's chunky and laced with blood. Just sitting there on the floor, waiting for some schmuck's stupid foot.

"I think . . . I'm gonna miss work today."

At this point, a few things occur to me at once. I want to leave and forget I ever met him. Just turn around, walk out, go home. Get back to my detachment. I don't care how much money's in that drawer; it's not worth it, dealing with such a sick old bum. Or I could just call Eugene and let him handle everything. Lou's his brother, after all, his responsibility.

This is not my problem. I didn't ask for this. This is not convenient.

But call it conscience or a code, I know Lou's hurting. I know he needs help and needs it now. And I know I can be a real selfish dick sometimes. I know, I know. There's really only one thing to do, and it's just a matter of doing it.

"I'm taking you to the hospital. Where's your phone?" I see one on the nightstand, pick it up, and the line's dead. Of course. Who needs a working phone when you got a whole house crammed with dust-covered shit?

"We ain't going anywhere. I'll be okay. Sleep it off, that's all."

"No. Those are your fuckin' guts on the floor, and I just stepped on them. That's not okay. Now come on. Upsy-daisy. Can you stand, or you need a lift?"

I offer him a hand, and he swipes it away.

"Lou, come on. Be reasonable."

"I ain't going to no hospital! They're crooks, every one of 'em! Crooks! Go away, kid. Don't make me hit you."

"Listen to me—"

Lou forces himself upright on pure vitriol, fists cocked. And I can see by his sneer he's not kidding. So there we are, caught in a semi-standoff, staring at each other.

I'll admit that I blink and look away first. I need time to think, and some fresh air couldn't hurt, either. So I go over to the window and open it by its iron handles. The frame scrapes upward, shedding paint flakes and splinters. I linger by the opening, sucking oxygen and wondering what to do.

Outside in the neighboring yard, something squeaks and doesn't stop squeaking. The sound is rhythmic and annoying, and it draws my eyes to one particular tree branch. A rope hangs from that branch, and tied to the bottom of the rope is a tire, and swaying back and forth in the tire is Francesca. And when I listen closer, I hear her singing what sounds like a lullaby.

I walk out without a word, leaving Lou with his miserable pride.

Francesca hugs the rope, grazing the dirt with her toes. She's wearing earphones and singing to her music till she sees me. Then she jolts up and says, "You! You're back! What are you doing here?"

"I could ask you the same thing. It's a school day, isn't it?"

She wriggles out of the tire, yanks out her earphones by the wires. "I was supposed to cut with some kids who have a car. They said they'd pick me up an hour ago, but they never showed. So now I'm just hanging out, like literally."

"You got a cell phone I could borrow?"

She pulls one from the butt pocket of her overalls, tosses it to me. "Wicked glovehand!" she says when I catch it. I ignore that and dial the number Eugene gave me.

He picks up, and I say, "Eugene, it's Dexter. Bad news. Lou's gotta see a doctor right away, but he's being really stubborn about it. He won't let me take him anywhere, so I'm gonna call an ambulance."

"No you're not. If he doesn't wanna go, he doesn't go. You leave him alone."

"Look, I'm not gonna debate this. He's puking blood and pissing himself, for Christ's sake. Does he have insurance or not?"

"Don't you dare call an ambulance! You let me deal with it. I'll be there after work."

"Does he have insurance or not?"

"He has a right to refuse treatment! What are you gonna do when he tells the EMTs to go away? You just get out of there and leave him alone. I knew I never should've—"

I clap the phone shut, cutting him off in mid-rant. Then take a really deep breath. It's all I can do to not scream and chuck the phone through the nearest window.

Francesca watches me, her eyes big and brown and ringed with raccoon makeup. I think I mentioned that she's cute and chubby, bordering on hot in a jailbait way. Looking at her now, I think she also might be strong enough to carry half an angry bum.

"Thanks," I say, and return the phone. "Now I got a real favor to ask you. Mr. Kashon's so sick he can barely move. Would you help me bring him down to the car so I can get him to the hospital?"

"That sounds serious. Why don't you call an ambulance?"

"It's complicated. Let's just say his insurance might not cover it."

"I'd really like to help you, mister, but we've got a problem. Remember how you blew me off when I asked for help with my homework? Why should I help you now?"

"I'll owe you one, okay? Whatever you say. Let's just get this over with."

"Anything I say?" Francesca asks, blushing.

"You can think of something later. Go on ahead. You lead."

"Why do I gotta go first?"

"Because I don't like people behind me, moving around behind me. Okay? Let's go."

"Oh, you're so weird!" she says with a giggle, touching my arm as she passes.

We enter through the kitchen, Francesca surveying the wreckage. She scrunches her nose at the sight of the litter box, gives a stagey cough. Then, in the hallway, she rubs her pinkie along the newspapers and shows me the caked-on grime.

"Don't worry, it gets worse," I say as we climb the steps. "So here's the game plan. When we get to Mr. Kashon, you grab him around the chest. I'll take him by the legs like a wheelbarrow."

"Why do I gotta carry the heavier end?"

"Because he'll try to punch me, but I don't think he'll hit you. And watch your step. There's puke on the floor."

Francesca pauses at the bedroom door, looking all confused. I keep moving, though, which kind of pressures her over the threshold. But then she sees Lou, the room, and the puke, and she gasps.

Lou, who'd been dozing when we came in, wakes up and grunts, "What the— Frannie? What are you doing with him?"

"You're not gonna hit a little girl, are you, Lou?"

"Kid, I tell ya, I don't wanna go nowhere!"

I approach the mattress, get in position to grab him, and wait for Francesca to follow.

Instead she hesitates. "He says he doesn't wanna go."

"Look at him. What do you think's gonna happen if we just leave him here?"

"I knew you when you were a baby, Frannie. Don't listen to him! I don't wanna go!"

"Listen to me, Francesca. He needs help whether he wants it or not."

"No, don't! Frannie, please."

Francesca stands there petrified, fang showing in her stunned-open mouth. She looks to me for help, and I put on my best firm, resolute face. "I'm sorry, Mr. Kashon," she says. "I'm really sorry."

"I knew you when you were a baby!" Lou's voice breaks. He buries his face in his hands, hiding his tears. It's a gesture of surrender, a beaten old man's last bid for dignity.

Together we lift him off the bed and into the hallway. Lou's a short, frail guy, but it's still not easy to carry him. I keep asking Francesca if she's okay, and she keeps saying yeah, but I can see the strain on her face as we navigate the steps. At least Lou's not struggling. If he put up a fight, I'm sure she'd drop him.

We make it to the porch, hurrying before it buckles under us, and down to the car. Francesca holds Lou in a bear hug while I open the back doors. Then we slide him in, me crouching and pulling him along from one side while she feeds him in from the other. Doors closed, job done, and, as far as I can see, no witnesses.

I come back around to Francesca's side of the car. Neither of us knows what to say or do. Then suddenly she rushes into me for a hug. We stumble against the car, and the poor kid's shaking all over. Thanks, you were great, I say, stuff like that. Stuff not worth quoting, words that do nothing to soothe her.

Sorry for using you like that, I want to say. Sorry for Mr. Kashon's reaction, sorry you'll remember this forever. The truth is, I thought it was the right thing to do when I roped you into it, but now I'm not so sure. Now I wonder if we didn't just make an awful mistake.

But the truth seems too cruel to heap on her. Better to keep whispering sweet reassurances. To keep holding her till she calms down, to project all the fake strength and certainty I can.

I'm sitting in the corner of the ER waiting room, situated so I can see the comings and goings. It's been hours since guys in scrubs wheeled Lou away on a gurney, since the receptionist said a doctor would brief me if I stuck around. So I stick around.

A TV hovers overhead, attached to the ceiling. I don't need to watch it to know *The Price Is Right*'s on. The sound alone says the contestants are spinning the big wheel for a chance to advance to the Showcase Showdown. Awww! says the audience, meaning somebody just lost.

And somehow that awww! seems like a sadistic joke on the room.

Like for instance, the high school kid a few chairs away. Holding an ice pack to his cornrowed head, staring at nothing with the spacey eyes of the concussed. Or the guy in mechanic's coveralls who can't stop clutching his wrist and wincing. Or the two old women, one who keeps coughing up chest-rattling gobs of phlegm while the other rubs her back and says it's okay, it's okay. You'll get help soon.

The only levity comes from a bored kid and an equally bored grandpa who ended up in neighboring chairs. The kid's messing with his music player, and Grandpa asks him what he likes. The kid says Fat Joe, DMX, Big Pun. Yeah, they're all right, says Grandpa, though you can tell he has no idea what the kid's talking about. Now, Michael Jackson, he says, that was *real* music.

"Isn't he a freak who bones little boys?" the kid says.

"That's never been proven," Grandpa says. "That's a media conspiracy, son."

So that's what I'm listening to when Eugene shows up. He

checks in with the receptionist, already raising his voice, and I'm getting tense inside. And tenser yet as he scans the room, spots me, and comes charging over.

"Outside. You and me, right now," he says.

No argument here. I head for the exit with him following. As soon as we make it out to the sidewalk, he shoves me and says, "What's wrong with you, huh?"

I turn around and shove him right back. He almost topples, and I don't care. Push me from behind like that, and you're gonna get hit. I don't care how old you are, you fuckin' cunt.

Eugene looks at me like I pulled a knife on him. It's almost funny how fast he backs down. "What gives you the right?" he says, sounding hurt. "I told you I'd handle it."

"If I'd left him there, you would've found him dead. He didn't have all day to wait."

"Gimme back the key. And you stay away from us from now on. I don't know what you want from Lou, but you're done talking to him. No more contact, no more visits, no more!"

"That's up to Lou, isn't it?"

"No, it isn't! You don't understand him. He's just a kid. He doesn't operate like most people do. He's got troubles, okay, but we dealt with it, we lived with it. And the last thing we need's somebody like you coming around, screwing everything up."

"So you're saying he's slow, crazy, what? What's that mean, 'he's got troubles'?"

"It means our family problems aren't your business. Now gimme the key."

I dig the key out of my pocket, and Eugene grabs it like a beady-eyed weasel snatching a baby rabbit. And I'm trying not to smile because with Lou passed out in the car, it was pretty easy to stop at a hardware store on the way to the hospital. To duck in and get my own copy of the key made.

The automatic doors open, and out walks a pudgy middle-aged Indian guy in a lab coat.

"Are you here for Louis Kashon?" he says, then walks over and shakes our hands after we say yeah. "I am Dr. Khomali, and first thing is first. Louis has been hostile toward the nurses and their aides. If you could encourage him to act less difficult for everyone, we would all be very thankful."

"Well, he *was* dragged here against his will," Eugene says.

"Sorry about that. I know Lou's pretty upset," I say to Khomali, ignoring Eugene. "But what's the word?"

"The word is not good. Louis has an infection in his colon, which has created a severe blockage, which in turn caused the vomiting. That is the immediate problem, and we are removing that blockage now. Then follows the larger problem of the infection itself. We have found a tumor in his colon, and it appears to be malignant."

"Cancer?" Eugene says.

Khomali nods. "There is more. We also found a growth under his left arm, nearly the size of a billiard ball. We are still running tests, but we are certain there is a growth in his stomach as well. I am afraid this combination is advanced. Inoperable. Frankly, he is not going to get better."

"How long does he have?" I ask.

"I cannot say for sure, but I would guess a month at the most."

Between the three of us, then, there is a silence. The doors open and close, voices converse, cars enter and exit the lot. But for the moment, we do nothing but stand there and leave the not-good word alone. Just leave it for what it is.

Khomali looks at me, then Eugene, then the ground. "I can

93

meet you at the front desk if you need some time," he says. Getting nothing but more silence and averted eyes, he goes back inside.

Eugene turns to me, face twitching in a scowl. "I hope you're happy now," he says, and takes off after the doctor, doors closing behind him.

8

After the nastiness at the hospital, I still have Judd's car, spare time, and nowhere to go. I'm too wound up to go home and don't want to go back to Job 2. What I really want is to talk to someone about the Kashons. And that's a problem because Marvin Bolzjak is the only person I know who might know something useful about them.

So how agitated am I? Enough to drive back to the Strip and circle Smallman till I find a parking spot. Enough to walk up to Penn and head toward the Steel City Novelty Co. But not quite enough to go in.

Instead I hesitate, just kind of loitering by the biker bar across the street. From here I can see Dad on a step stool, taking down Pirates decorations from the front window. Soon he'll replace them with red, white, and blue crepe streamers. I know this because I still know the decoration rotation by heart. When I was little, I learned the names of the months by what they brought to that window. April: Pirates stuff for baseball season; May: red, white, and blue stuff for Memorial Day; June: beach balls and inflatable rafts for the summer; July: more red, white, and blue stuff for the Fourth; and so on and so forth, and man, am I dreading going in there. But I guess standing outside spying on him isn't making anything any better.

Bells hung from the door handle announce my arrival.

"Just a second," Dad says, his back to the door. He steps down, and when he sees me, the shock registers on his face. I'm surprised, too, seeing him up close again. He's aged a dozen years in the last six, gray hair gone to white, chin doubled, posture stooped and diminished. In a hiccup of Time, he's gone from Dad to Old Man.

"I'll be damned," he says. "I—I—"

"I won't be long."

I wander deeper into the shop, glancing around at everything but him. And unlike him, everything seems much the same. Wooden cubbyholes still fill the near wall, each cell containing a gag. What he would call "classics"—whoopee cushions, finger traps, sticky wallwalkers, chattering teeth—interspersed with more modern, harder-edged junk like rubber dog turds, squishy eyeballs, and beer funnels. There's still an aisle of party supplies, still an aisle of knockoff Pens, Pirates, and Steelers stuff. (Dad has always been careful to only sell the official Terrible Towel, though; Steeler fans will settle for nothing less.) And still more aisles and shelves stocked with still more nonessentials.

And then I look at him, and something hurts inside. Regret for wasted time, maybe, or the hard knowledge that my father's rotting away in his little world of worthless shit. He didn't just hide here when Mom left; he locked himself in and clung to this fading business. And now it's too late to break out and try something else.

"No, hey, you can stay. I got all kinds of good stuff since the last time you came," Dad says, and rummages through a bin of "Steel City Steals!" "Hey, remember these? You always liked these guys." He pulls out a rubber gorilla by an elastic cord attached to

96

its head. Bouncing it up and down like a yo-yo, Dad lets out a halfhearted "Rawwrrr!"

I fake a smile, but not too well, I guess. Dad catches the gorilla, holds it like he's not sure what to do with it. Then drops it back in the bin.

"Thanks, but I just came to ask a simple question. I got caught up in some shit with the Kashons. They say they know you, and I was wondering how well you know them."

"We go back a ways. Since the seventies, at least, when I took over here. Why, what's up?"

"I ended up taking Lou to St. Francis this morning, and Eugene's all pissed because I did it without his permission."

"Is Lou okay?"

"No. The doctor said it's cancer. He gave Lou a month."

"Damn." Dad searches the floor for something else to say and settles on a favorite refrain. "Like I always say, 'If you don't got your health, you got nothing.'"

"Yeah, well. Right now Lou's got nothing but an overbearing asshole of a brother."

"Gene's always been like that. Real protective. Lou drinks and gets in trouble, and Gene bails him out. He pays Lou to hang around the warehouse and calls it a job. He paid off their parents' house so Lou could stay there, and as far as I know, he still pays the bills on it. Gene basically subsidizes Lou, keeps him off the streets."

"So what's Lou's problem? Eugene says he's got 'troubles,' like that means anything."

"I don't know. I never could figure out Lou. I never thought he was as helpless as Gene made out. Usually, yeah, Lou was a mess. But if you caught him at the right time, you could talk to him.

"Like this one night a few years ago. I was here late, doing the

97

inventory, and all the sudden I hear this commotion out back. A horn honking, somebody screaming, something clanging off the Dumpster. I go see what's up, and there's Lou and some lumberjack-looking guy in a scuffle while the guy's SUV's sitting there idling. Turns out Lou was taking a piss in the alley, and the guy drove up and almost hit him, which led to the fight.

"So it's up to me to break it up. I calm the guy down, pull Lou in here for some coffee. And I swear, once he sobered up a little, he was a totally different guy. He told me all these stories about the service, the Strip back when he was your age. Funny stuff. We talked till dawn, just a couple old farts reliving old times and gossip."

"Did he mention Mercy Carnahan by any chance?"

"The actress? No, not that I remember."

"What about a girl named Agnes?"

Dad frowns like he's thinking hard. "Um, I don't think so. This was years ago, though."

"Did you tell him anything about me?"

"I might've, I don't know. What's it matter, anyway?"

"When he first came up to me, he called me 'hockey star.' I wondered how he'd know about that."

"He could've known from way back. I had that picture of you in the window for years before you tore it down."

"Yes, because it was hypocritical of you to put it there. And kind of sadistic, don't you think, considering how the hockey thing ended. You think I like to be reminded of that shit? You think I want *anyone* to know about it?"

Dad has no answer for that. And I have no desire to push it further. We stare each other down, and after taking a moment to maintain his cool, he says, "You're not doing this. You're not just gonna walk in here after how long and attack me. No 'Hi, Dad. How you doing, Dad. Hope you've been okay, Dad.' How many times have you walked past that window without looking in, without so much as a wave or a nod? Do you want me to apologize for skipping that game again? Is that what you're here for?"

"Fuck the game. I blew the game. That I can accept. It's everything after the game, and not just that night. I mean dropping out of school. You're gonna tell me you don't resent that?"

"No. I don't, and I never did. But disappointed? Yeah. Yeah, I am disappointed that you're still living in Judd's basement and working for Sal Marchicomo. You know, the longer you wait to go back—"

"The harder it gets. I know. And how am I gonna afford school? You really want me to move back in with you?"

"The offer stands."

"And you know I can't do that. I got *some* fuckin' pride. I can't be sleeping in the same room I slept in when I was five."

"Then sleep in the basement. Mine's as good as Judd's."

"See, this is why I don't visit. Because I know it's gonna turn into sniping and bickering and picking the same old scabs. And who needs it?"

I start for the door—have my hand on the handle, even—when he stops me with a "Dexter, wait." Dad waves me back in, and I reluctantly obey. He lowers his voice to a near-whisper, like we're conspirators, and says, "Before you go, I wanted to tell you something. I was up late watching TV a couple weeks ago, and guess what was on. *The Boogens.*"

The Boogens. One of the horror movies we watched when we first got cable, back when I was nine or ten. Whatever channel it was ran a double feature called *Friday Frightmare.* Sometimes you'd get classics like *The Exorcist* or *Magic,* but usually you'd get hackwork like *Spasms, Demonoid,* and *The Boogens.* Ugly, grungy flicks lucky to play on any big screen anywhere for a weekend.

"No kidding. Was it as bad as I remember?"

"Oh, it's pathetic. The Boogen was nifty when they finally showed him. But the rest of the movie? Pretty damn bad."

"I just remember Mom getting all pissed because we kept laughing at the old guy in it."

"But come on. Nothing beats the time with *The Texas Chainsaw Massacre*. What did she call it?"

"'A steaming heap of Grand Guignol crap,'" I say, and we laugh. "I like how she'd always sit there and rip on the movie, but she'd never get up and leave. She'd have to watch it all the way through to the end."

"Except for *Humanoids from the Deep*. Remember? She threw her beret at the TV and stormed out because it was all sexist or degrading to women or something."

"I forgot about the beret."

"Yep. The beret phase fell somewhere between her Nehru jacket phase and her Victorian phase. And that was in the eighties. You should've seen how she dressed in the sixties and seventies."

We laugh a little more, then both quiet down to a lull. By the very feel of it, and the way Dad can't look in my eyes, I know what's coming next. I telepathically hear the words before he says them, and sure enough, he does say them.

"So, have you talked to her lately?"

"No. Got the usual Christmas card and phone call, and that was it. What about you?"

He shakes his head no, negative. Then says, "I'm sure she's doing okay, though, down there in Charlotte or wherever she is. Weather's gotta be better, at least."

And then there's silence, the kind that prods you to the nearest exit.

"Anyway, I won't hold you up," Dad says. "But I just—I want

100

you to understand, I would've shown up if I knew she wasn't there."

"Dad, don't. Really, please. You don't gotta rehash it."

"No, I gotta say, I thought I was making a stand against her by not showing up, but she didn't show up, either. So it backfired, on you more than anyone, and I still feel bad about it."

"I know. It's all right. Ancient history. It's over."

"Like I said, I won't hold you up. I know you wanna go. But you could visit more often. Doesn't have to be once every six years." Dad tries to smile and can't fake it so well, either. Not knowing what else to do or say, he goes back to his step stool, back to work. It's like he's giving me a chance to escape, to duck outside and outrun the sound of the door bells.

From there I come home and drop onto the cot, alongside the already-sleeping Jeepers. Between the Strip and Lou's and the hospital and Dad, I try to sort out my busy day, figure out what's next. But instead of coming up with anything, I go back to what Dad said about those old movies.

He seemed to forget the laser disc player he brought home around that time, back when I was eleven. It was the first home-video device my family had owned. The cable network stopped doing *Friday Frightmare*, and I guess the laser disc player was Dad's attempt to keep the party going. I should also note this was 1986, when the rest of America was buying VCRs. Dad chose a laser disc player not for its superior video quality, but because some guy was selling one out of a van in the back alley for a can't-lose price. Granted, our player didn't come with a serial number, an owner's manual, or a box, but it worked.

Rental discs were a lot less common than cassettes, but Dad persisted till he found a video store with a decent selection. He brought home *Halloween,* and I must have watched that thing a dozen times. On the first viewing, it scared me so bad I couldn't sleep for a week. And yet everything about it—its camerawork and music, its darkness, its lurking villain, its relentless creepiness— just sucked me right in. You could say I was addicted or obsessed, and soon I was watching *The Thing* and *Escape from New York* and *Assault on Precinct 13* over and over again, too, convinced that filmmaking was my calling. All the other boys in school wanted to be Michael Jordan when they grew up; I wanted to be John Carpenter.

So when I finally talked Dad into taking me to Eide's, Pittsburgh's premiere punk-metal cult-movie comic-book shop, I blew a chunk of my paper-route money on an *Escape from New York* T-shirt and wore it to school with pride. Next thing I knew, some kid named Judd came up to me wanting to be friends.

We made a pretty funky team: me, a budding semi-hippie semi-metalhead, and him, a mouth-breathing geek with dandruff and steel-framed glasses. Movies brought us together, and we've stayed together ever since. And I guess I'm thankful for that, because as Judd himself would say, one friend is all you need.

But even back then, he was way more intense about ultraviolence than I was. He agreed that Carpenter was talented, but he also criticized *Halloween* for being "too soft." He also thought *The Texas Chainsaw Massacre* was "too soft." And for him, *Dawn of the Dead,* with its flesh-munching zombies, and skulls getting blasted open with bullets or cleaved with blades, was "good for its time, but getting soft."

Judd preferred movies like *Maniac* (where you see scalpings and a point-blank shotgun blast to a man's face), *Mother's Day* (where a guy gets whacked in the nuts with a hatchet, and his severed nut drops to the ground after the impact), and the Italian import *Zombi* (where a zombie shoves a woman's eye into a big wooden splinter). As far as slashers went, the *Friday the 13th* and *Nightmare on Elm Street* series were too mainstream and co-opted for him. Instead he championed *My Bloody Valentine* (where the killer ripped his victims' hearts from their chests) and *The Burning* (where the killer lopped off kids' fingers with hedge shears), but still complained about how those "pussies at the studios" buckled to the censors and trimmed the murder scenes.

Once I told Judd that I had a laser disc player, well, that was it. He'd come over after school a couple times a week, while my parents were at work, with a stack of discs he'd rented through a mail-order company called Sinephile. Imports and bootlegs mostly, and I'll admit some of them were amazing, like the original versions of *Suspiria* and *Deep Red*. But most of the discs he brought over were shit like the *Faces of Death* series or *Silent Night, Deadly Night* (a slasher movie where the killer dresses like Santa Claus.)

So we'd sit around watching this stuff, and sometimes it turned into a game of chicken: who could stare at the screen unaffected versus who had to look away. Who was hard versus who was a pussy. And honestly, I was usually the pussy. It was during *Gates of Hell,* when a guy gets electric-drilled in the skull, that Judd caught me wincing at the screen.

He picked up the remote and paused the movie. "Aw, come on. You're not really grossed out, are you?"

"It's kind of gross, yeah."

"It's fake. It's a good fake, but it's still fake. All you gotta do is stopwatch it."

Judd hit a button on the remote, slowing the footage down to half speed. Then he showed me how it was edited, where the cuts were. How the scene cycled from close-ups of the killer to the victim to the drill, creating the illusion that one man was actually pushing another's head toward the spinning bit. Then, when the bit was just about to touch the victim's face, Judd hit another button and slowed the movie down to a frame-by-frame crawl.

"Watch. Here's where they use a fake drill . . ."

The drill pressed the victim's face, spurting blood. Cut to the grimacing killer. Cut to a close-up of the victim's skin, the drill bit burrowing deeper into it.

". . . and here's where they use a real drill with a fake head."

Then cut to the victim's face; still the fake head, Judd said. Cut to a close-up of the real drill bit penetrating fake flesh, churning out fake blood and brains. Cut to the killer. Cut back to the real screaming victim with the fake drill touching his face. Cut to the killer. Cut to another close-up of the fake head, the drill bit poking out the opposite side from where it entered. And so on, till I saw nothing but cuts, close-ups, and cuts. A series of images detached from the carnage they conveyed at normal speed.

Judd backed up the video and played the scene again, and I saw his point. Once you slowed that footage down and took it apart, separated the fake from the flesh, stripped away the charade, it wasn't so gross anymore. It wasn't scary, either. It was unpleasant, maybe, but tamed. The drill-through-the-skull became something you could control with your remote, something you could study with an objective eye.

"It's nothing," Judd said, and tossed the remote back to me. "One of these days, there's gonna be a real snuff movie. Single, static camera with no cuts. Until then, all these directors and FX guys, they're just playing. A big bunch of posers. Some are better than others, but none of them are really hard core."

Not long after that, Dad caved to society and bought a VCR, which kicked the laser disc player to my room. Judd would still bring discs, I'd borrow them for a few days, and stopwatching

104

joined comic books as my top hobby. I'd close my door, blast some Iron Maiden, and lay on my bed with the remote, manipulating Time. Speeding up the footage, slowing it down, stopping on the exact fraction of a second where one shot cut to the next. It was like a video game, a test of reflexes: Could my eyes detect the edit, could my fingers hit the pause button within a frame of the cut? And then I'd go back and review the footage at regular speed, wise to the way it flowed.

Maybe I was really interested in filmmaking. More likely I was hooked on splatter, for I spent most of those hours stopwatching death scenes. To pinpoint the moment where a screaming actor became a dummy, where hidden tubes or packets spurted fake blood, felt like power. Like something that makes you stronger, smarter, and tougher than some pussy who'd close his eyes when a machete thwacks somebody's neck.

So there I was one night, age thirteen, consolidating my power as it were. I was stopwatching *The Texas Chainsaw Massacre 2,* the part where one guy bashes open another guy's skull with a hammer. *Number of the Beast* was probably blaring in my tape deck, but don't quote me on that. It might've been Sabbath or AC/DC, too. Whatever it was, it was too loud for me to hear Mom knocking on my door.

She decided to venture in, it being her house and all, and found me stopwatching the bludgeoning. Thanks to the music's loudness, and the door's position behind the bed, I didn't even notice her till she came barging in between me and the screen.

"What is this?" she said once I muted the music. "What are you doing?"

"Watching a movie."

"It's disgusting! And you're not just watching it, you're *playing* with it."

Dad appeared in the doorway, chuckling. "You get busted jacking off, huh, D.? Happens to the best of us. Call it a rite of passage."

"I wish that's what he was doing," Mom said. "Look at this, Marv. Look at what your son's watching."

Dad looked in and saw the victim on-screen, twitching in a puddle of brains and blood, slowed to the glacial frame-by-frame pace. "He knows it's fake," Dad said, more preoccupied with the Fiori's Pizzeria menu in his hand. "So, what are we getting here? Half mushrooms half pepperoni? Or anchovies this time?"

"Thanks for backing me up. You know, everything's not a joke! Everything's not a toy!" Mom said, and slammed the door before he could respond. The hallway's creaking floorboards marked his retreat.

Alone again, we resumed our standoff, though technically Mom was the only one standing. She surveyed my room, all business in her charcoal blouse and matching Cleopatra makeup. Like Dad said, she usually dressed weird and quirky, which might have fit with her being a grade school art teacher. But by the time of this particular incident, she was also working part-time at a perfume booth in the mall. And on those nights when she did herself up to sell whale oil, I daresay she looked classy and attractive.

In fact, even then I had an inkling that random non-Dad guys might look twice at Samantha Bolzjak and stop by the booth to flirt. And even then it occurred to me that she felt neglected by Dad, taken for granted. Not that I ever imagined her ending up in Charlotte, but still. Things weren't going well in that house; even the dimmest thirteen-year-old could sense the strain.

Mom found what she seemed to be looking for, the disc's sleeve plus the others I'd left on the floor. "Lovely," she said, skimming the sleeve for *Texas Chainsaw 2*. "It says this one's unrated." Then she read the others, for *Mother's Day* ("Rated X. Oh, and it's about girls getting raped.") and *Maniac* ("Ah. Another rated X, and this one's about a pervert who scalps women and nails their scalps to a bunch of mannequins?") and looked at me like I'd better start to explain myself.

"What's the big deal? They're just movies."

Mom came over and sat down on the bed, forcing me to sit up and beside her. I braced for an explosion, a grounding, something heavy. But instead she looked at me, her green eyes sad and searching for a trace of her baby.

"You're too young for this garbage. And in my house, we don't entertain ourselves by watching movies where people get raped, tortured, and slaughtered. I don't care how real or fake it looks. I know we've watched a lot of horror movies, but this is different. This is porn, and not the healthy kind."

"What about the Looney Tunes? Daffy Duck gets shot in the face, Wile E. Coyote gets smacked with a Mack truck, and we're supposed to laugh. Is that porn, too?"

"Don't be a smart-ass. You know there's a difference. Look at this," she said, meaning the skull-bashing still on the TV screen. "These movies, they're not scary. They're not even trying to be scary. They're trying to see how much gore people can take before getting upset. And when people get upset, they spread the word about how shocking the movie is, and the movie makes money. The more, the better, and what's the point? What do you get out of watching this, anyway?"

"I don't know. The effects are cool."

"Dexter, I'll tell you something that probably won't make sense to you now. And maybe it never will, I don't know. But I think one of the hardest things you can do in life is to see people as people. Not as objects, not as monsters or cattle. It's easy enough to dislike or distrust people on sight. To judge people by how they look or talk or what they do for a living. God knows our society encourages us to do just that.

"But I think it's important to be better than that, or at least to try. To fight that little disease we have inside that makes us want to put each other down, hurt each other, degrade each other. Like I said, it's a hard fight, and it doesn't get any easier as you get older. And wallowing in these kinds of movies, filling your head with these kinds of images, sure as hell doesn't help."

Mom looked at her watch and sprung off the bed like she was running late. But she still caught herself at the doorway and said, "Have all these discs on the table tonight when I get back. Don't worry. I won't ask where you got them. I won't make you rat out Judd."

"So am I in trouble or what?"

"I can't keep you under constant surveillance. I trust you to consider what I said and do what you know is right," Mom said, and left.

I lay back down, thinking, Cool, not in trouble. Then, when I considered what she said, I smiled and thought, Whatever, dude. Save the Sesame Street shit for your second-graders. The only lesson I learned that night was to never, ever stopwatch with the stereo so loud I couldn't hear the footsteps outside. And with that, I picked up the remote and replayed the skull-bashing from the beginning.

9

I'm sitting in a dingy office, and everything around me is black, white, and shades of gray. Broken glass and an ashtray clutter the nearby desk. Smoke rises from the tray, clouds a bare bulb overhead. Mercy leans against the edge of the desk, her back to me, black hair matching her gloves and dress.

I try to move but can't. When I look down, I see myself wearing nothing but a bloodstained Falcons jersey. My bare ankles are bound to the chair legs with duct tape, my wrists to wooden armrests. I try harder, though, jerking and making the chair squeak.

Mercy turns her head, her face still in shadow. Then slinks off the desk and into the light, standing before me with her hands on her hips. She stares right into my eyes, and for better or worse, that's all it takes to make me hard.

"Well. Pleased to meet you, too," she says, eyebrow cocked. "Dexter, correct?"

"Agnes."

"No, sweetie, it's Mercy. We have business to discuss, and I'm not one to pussyfoot around a point. I hear you're looking for Agnes. Hate to break it to you, but you can't have her. She's mine."

"You are Agnes. Or a character she made up. You don't exist apart from her."

"Oh? That's a mean thing to say. Maybe you should ask your buddy Louie how make-believe I am."

"If you're real, then where are you? Where can I find you?"

"In case you haven't noticed, you're in no position to probe me. You'll know what I want when I want you to know it."

"I'm just testing the waters, Ms. Carnahan."

Mercy smirks and starts to respond, but a knock at the door interrupts her. She holds up a finger as if to say "Just a moment" and goes to the door. "Someone's here to see you. Don't get up. I'll show her in."

She steps out into the corridor and returns leading a female mannequin by the hand. The mannequin's feet are nailed to a wheeled platform, the wheels rattling on the hardwood floor. Mercy rolls it in close, positions it so it's facing away from me. The mannequin's pants are pulled down around its ankles, panties down to its knees. Dirt and dead leaves stick to its back.

"Recognize her?" Mercy asks, and I say nothing. She reaches up and yanks off the mannequin's black mop of curls. "How about now?"

I still don't answer.

"Come now. Don't be rude. She's traveled eight years just to see you, and you won't even say hello? Okay. Maybe you'll like this one better." Mercy takes the mannequin by the shoulders and spins it around. It stops in her hands, facing me, and now it has Erin's face and short dark hair.

"Hmm. Cute tattoos," Mercy says, examining its back. "I wonder where she went. New York, was it? But you never did find out, did you, because after you had one of your dizzy spells in front of her, you dropped out of school. Too ashamed to face her again. But here she is, six years later. Care to say anything to her?"

"I can wake up, you know. Any second, I can wake up."

Mercy spins the mannequin around again. When she stops it this time, it has Mom's face and hair.

"Ooh. Who's this elegant lady?"

"You know damn well who that is."

"I'll call her Charlotte. And why did she leave? Did she want to, or did you push her out the door? You still don't know, do you?"

Mercy gives me a minute, but I never take the bait. Instead I just sit there glaring at the floor. She spins the mannequin once more. It stops with its back to me again, bald and mottled with bits of the woods again.

She comes over, stands so close she's touching me. Then cups my chin in her gloved hand and lifts it till I look her in the eye. "Don't be mad, sweetie. You know I'm fond of you. And . . ." she glances down as I get hard again, "I think you're fond of me, too. But I'm a bad girl, and you can't even hold on to a good one."

I start to say something, but she puts her finger on my lips and whispers, "Shhh."

She rolls down her glove, bunching it around her wrist. Brings her finger to her mouth and bites the satin, stretching it off till the entire glove dangles in her teeth. With a nudge of her tongue, the glove drops onto my lap.

"You can look for me all you want; you'll never find me. And if you even come close to Agnes, you'll wish you hadn't. Because they'll catch you first. You know who I mean."

She balls up the glove in her fist, then presses it to my mouth. The material bristles, turning from satin to steel wool. Little metal fibers burrow between my lips, squirm into my gums and tongue.

I try to scream, but she jams her hand down tight as soapy foam collects in my throat.

"Quiet! They'll hear you!" she whispers, her eyes flashing blue. "Don't struggle. Just give in. Let me take you, let me suck all that poison and fear and pain right out of you. Let me love you, and I swear you'll die smiling."

I stumble off the cot and to the laundry tubs, hawking up whatever's in my throat. Turns out it's nothing but your standard morning phlegm. No soap scum or tiny wires, no scraps of satin. And I'm still wearing the same clothes I crashed in, jeans and all. Even so, I need a round of mouth-rinsing and face-splashing before I'm sure the dream was a dream.

When I come back to the cot, the cat's still asleep, and Judd's at the Wall, immersed in his latest project: a diner waitress pouring hot coffee on a patron. He pauses the video just as the coffee streams off the spout, then enlarges the image and tinkers with the liquid's coloring.

"Hey. You left something in the printer," he says.

"I don't think so," I say, and take the page from the tray.

It's a printout of an e-mail delivered to my account in the middle of the night. "From: wade@templeofmercy.com," it says, followed by lines of earnest making-nice ("So you're interested in Mercy? Any fan of hers is a friend of mine!"), and a few names, addresses, and numbers. Gilbert Pollard and others in New York, Wade Endicott himself in Jersey. The only local contact is the Academy of Arts, annotated with "You might want to start here. It's close!" in red text.

"I swear to God I didn't print this."

"I know I didn't. I just logged you off this morning and logged myself on. So if you didn't, and I didn't, then who did?" Judd turns around, holds out his palms. "You did it in your sleep. The cat did it. There's a ghost in the machine. I don't know. But I got deadlines, man."

I stand there staring through the page, slow-burning with a feeling that I'm being provoked. Or challenged, or just plain fucked with. By who or what, I'm not sure, but it's a creepy feeling, and I don't like it.

"Since you're bound to the computer, and it's my off-day, you care if I borrow the car again?"

"Excuse me, what did you do to it yesterday? It's got this smell in it now, like puke or cigar smoke. I can't tell which."

"Don't worry, I'll air it out. Anyway, who's that you're working on?"

Judd backs up the video to reveal the young, lean Jack Nicholson flirting with the waitress. Working his famous arched eyebrows, talking in his laid-back voice that oozes smarts and obscene desires, Jack seduces the camera easily enough. But the waitress, standing over him with a pot of steaming coffee, is not so charmed.

"Nicholson? Damn. I thought everybody liked Jack."

"Well, somebody hates him, or I wouldn't be getting paid to scald his cock."

I think I said before that Pittsburgh is both defined and divided by its rivers. The Allegheny comes down from the north, the Mon up from the south, and they merge to form the Ohio, which flows out west. Between the Allegheny and the Mon lies a triangular land-wedge that is the heart of the city, and near the middle of this wedge is a big neighborhood called Oakland. Home to both Pitt (or "the University of Pittsburgh" if you want to be formal) and CMU (Carnegie Mellon University), Oakland is the higher-ed hub of town. According to Endicott and the Internet, it's also where you can find Mercy's alma mater, the Academy of Arts.

During the school season, college kids pack Oakland's streets with their mix of beer, hipness, high-mindedness, and disposable cash. Which in turn brings drunken fights, muggings, and lots of overheated political rhetoric. And if I sound cynical, I guess it's because I miss the place a little. Now that I'm caught in traffic on its main drag, Forbes Avenue, watching random kids walk by— ball-capped fratboys, girls in their navy Pitt sweats, a neon-haired punk with a pincushion face—it's hard not to feel jealous. But hey, good for them. It's their time. God bless 'em.

What's harder is to pass the old haunts. Coming up on the intersection of Forbes and South Bouquet, there's the castle-looking building that used to be the Beehive cafe, where me and Erin used to get overcaffeinated and prattle on for hours, thinking we were so profound. Before it was the Beehive, it was the King's Court movie theater, with a suit of armor in the lobby and midnight screenings of *The Rocky Horror Picture Show*. And before that, the building was a police station. Now it's a cell phone store.

There's the O (Original Hot Dog Shop) on the corner, where we gorged on a massive heap of greasy fries, her telling me how she grew up in Upstate New York. How a black bear once barged in on her dad while he was in the family outhouse. Behind the O looms her old dorm-tower *the sun the moon,* across the street from the O stands Hillman Library *Emerson? Dude was a careerist,* and behind that lurks the oppressively modern Posvar Hall.

Posvar occupies the site where the Pirates' old ballpark, Forbes Field, used to be. If you walk into Posvar, you'll find home plate commemorated and preserved on the ground floor. Outside near the Schenley Drive entrance, they've kept the bottom of the outfield wall, too, as a double row of bricks in the concrete. A plaque marks where Bill Mazeroski's home run sailed over that wall, in the bottom of the ninth of Game 7, winning the 1960 World Series for the Pirates over the Yankees.

And on opening day, 1994, Erin walked those bricks, wearing her Yankees hat, hands outstretched like she was walking a balance beam. "Nineteen sixty?!" she laughed when she came to the plaque. "You better kneel down and kiss that thing because that's the last Series the Pirates will ever see."

"They won it again in seventy-one and seventy-nine."

"Whatever. Twenty-two rings, babe," she said, pointing to her hat. "Twenty-two! How many do the Pirates have?"

"Come on, the Pens just won back-to-back Stanley Cups. When's the last time the Rangers won one?"

"Hockey? Blah. Nobody cares about hockey," she said, and hopped off the bricks. Then moved in close to me, taking my hands in hers.

"You'd be surprised how passionate people get about it," I said. "And I mean violently."

"And are you *violently* passionate about it?"

"You could say I had a thing for it. A brief thing."

"And how did this torrid love affair come to an end?" she said, brown eyes and a smile.

Forget it, I tell myself as I turn left from Forbes to Craig Street. Forget her and the entire era she occupied. I got enough work ahead that I can't keep looking back. If I must remember anything, it should be Job 1: focus, jackass, focus.

Besides, the Academy isn't a place you want to walk into all hazy-eyed. It hogs a block of Craig, fenced off from the sidewalk with black iron bars, set farther back by a moat of grass. A walkway cuts through the lawn, leads to a porch where two bronze lions guard the door. Corroded and colored green by acid rain, these lions communicate a simple message: this is an old place, built and running on old money. Slackers and the classless need not enter.

I go in anyway, to an atrium with a marble floor and wood-paneled walls. A portrait of a bulldoggish woman hangs on the near wall, her dead gray eyes glowering down at all who deign to pass. This would be headmistress and founder Joyce Jacoby, I assume. And if Jacoby was half as tough as she looks in her portrait, I can see why Mercy might flee into the arms of a sleazy shutterbug.

The atrium intersects with a hall, and there stands a tall slender lady in a suit, talking to a group of girls. I think she's who I'm supposed to meet, but if not, there's no harm in checking her out, a pretty hot sight with her golden braids and ebony skin. When she sees me, she sends off the girls, who go tittering away in their tight T-shirts and low-riding jeans.

"Dexter?" she says, approaching and offering her hand. "Valerie Hobson, the principal. We spoke on the phone. You're doing a research project on Mercy?"

"Yes. Yes, I am."

We walk the long hall, passing closed doors on either side. Intricate wood carvings adorn the top of each doorjamb, each depicting a scene out of Shakespeare. Lady Macbeth sleepwalks over Room 102, Lear staggers through a thunderstorm over 104. Across the hall, Shylock counts his coins, and poor Ophelia gazes into a pond.

"As you can see, this is our Drama Wing. Somewhere in these rooms, Agnes Zagbroski became Mercy Carnahan. Of course we don't advertise ourselves as the school that produced her. Ms. Jacoby always felt that Mercy betrayed her talents—and the Academy, to some extent—when she chose to pose for Stanley Frisch. Nor was

Ms. Jacoby a fan of Mercy's film career. To her death, she maintained that Mercy had failed to fulfill her potential."

"That must have been some grudge if the Academy's still holding it."

"There are other reasons why we downplay Mercy's time here. Factors which extend beyond Ms. Jacoby. The Academy has an interest in maintaining positive relations with its graduates. Sometimes that involves matters of discretion. If, say, a certain alumna requests that we share only specific information with the public, we would have to respect that."

"Fair enough. I take it Mercy still has some contact with the Academy?"

"I can't discuss that."

"Which implies she's still alive. I mean, all this discretion wouldn't be necessary if she were dead, right?"

Valerie stops near a door with PRIVATE painted on its glass pane. "Can't discuss that, Dexter."

"So I guess there's no chance of the Academy helping a poor, starving grad student land the interview of a lifetime with a certain alumna."

"No. No chance," she says with a hint of amusement. "All I can do is show you selected material from the archives. Would you like to see it?"

I follow her into a small room with no windows. Just four beige-painted walls and a table topped with papers. A light glows overhead, its glass dome speckled with dead bugs.

"Here we have report cards, compositions, faculty evaluations. And this, too," she says, indicating a battered spiral notebook. "It seems our Mercy was quite the little doodler."

I flip open the cover to a page of history notes, something about the Middle Ages and feudalism written in a neat, precise cursive. Flip, flip, flip through the pages till I find one of her drawings. And once I see it, my hands freeze.

It's a picture of a little girl clinging to a barbed-wire fence. She's holding on because a creature is grabbing her from behind. It looks like a big maggot with muscular arms, blobbing up out of a mud puddle by a tree. It has a grip on her ankles and pulls her up off the ground, stretching her. Its head hovers over her back, drooling a viscous slime onto her hair. She screams as blood runs between her fingers, drips down to the dirt.

The image itself is one thing, the quality another. This isn't daydreamy sketching from a bored schoolgirl. It's a nightmare carved into the page, every line so fevered and vivid, you'd think the ink was still wet. I even trace the barbed wire with my thumb just to make sure.

"What have other people said about this?"

"You're rather lucky on that count, Dexter. We were authorized to show this notebook only last month. I don't believe anyone else has seen it yet." Valerie glances around and says, "I knew I forgot something; I don't see a chair here. I'll go get one for you." So she walks out, leaving me alone to page through more notes till I find the next picture.

A seated audience, their bodies obscured in shadow, their faces a gallery of the grotesque. A grinning devil face beside a cleft-headed creature with bulging eyes and crooked teeth. A corpse with hollowed eye sockets alongside a thing with a sideways-twisted head, its long tongue lapping the air. Next row down, a body topped with a skull. A half pig, half human mutation with little tusks poking up from its lips. By the aisle, a hairless, mouthless lump of flesh with a gaping nostril for a left eye and a sightless orb for the right. In the front row sits a leering ape-werewolf hybrid with huge eyes and sharp fangs. A cyclops with an oversized eye that takes up its entire face, the eye-slit vertical like a vagina. Next, a bug-eyed lizardlike guy with beady teeth and a tongue hanging down to his chest. An old man who looks like he just crawled out of a bog, his skin caked with mud and twigs, his face sprouting ivy tendrils.

Below that, it's back to Mercy's history notes. Something about the Enlightenment written in her hand, all elegant loops and serifs. A few pages later comes the next picture.

It's another array of faces. But while her last drawing showed them as an audience, this one shows them as detached masks. I count twelve, each hung upon its own stand-up rack; two rows, six masks per row. And while the faces in the last picture were monstrous, these are merely expressions. There's Angry beside Shocked beside Depressed beside Scheming beside Calm beside Intense. Happy, Sleeping, Seductive, Confused, Teasing, Grieving.

Standing among these masks—almost hidden between the rows—is a nude girl with long black hair. She has no face, no features. In her hand she holds a mask that looks like Mercy Carnahan.

I flip ahead to the next one, not even skimming the notes.

Three drawings on the same page, and they seem to form a sequence. First, there's a pigtailed, freckled girl sticking out her tongue and crossing her eyes. Fingers hooked into the corners of her mouth, she stretches and distorts her face, makes herself a caricature of crazy. More distant, vague faces float behind her, pointing and laughing at whoever she's mocking.

Next, a girl-marionette with long black hair, wires tied to its head and wrists. Its limbs are spread wide, and a bundle of tentacles slithers out from between its legs. The tentacles branch off on either side of the puppet, the tip of each blooming with a different creature's head. One looks like a cow, another like a goat. A Valentine's heart with eyes, a horse, two goblins.

119

And last, the pigtailed, freckled girl from the top drawing. But she's not making cooky faces anymore, and her backup has vanished. Her eyes melt out of their sockets, dripping down her cheeks. Her hair falls out of her scalp in clumps, and her bloody tongue dangles by a string of tissue.

I resume flipping, nearing the end of the notebook, till I reach its last two pictures. They share the page, the first above the second.

The first shows a girl thrashing around in freezing water, surrounded by broken sheets of ice. You can't see much of her face because she's blindfolded with barbed wire. If she's trying to scream, no one can hear her because a chain gags her mouth. It coils around her throat, goes down the depths to an unseen anchor. She clutches the chain with one hand. With the other, she claws the nearby ice, trailing blood and bits of skin on the surface.

Below that, a picture of an auditorium stage, viewed from behind the curtain. In the foreground sits a platform, and upon the platform lies a sopping wet corpse. Most of its skin has rotted off, baring bones and organs. Its fluids drip onto the stage, spreading along the planks. Beyond the corpse, the curtain parts to reveal an audience. A crowd of gray featureless faces.

"Sorry about that," Valerie says, backing in through the doorway with a chair. "I had to go to three different rooms— Dexter? What's wrong? You don't look well."

"I'm fine, thanks. And thanks for getting that, but . . ." I put the notebook back on the table, nudge it away from me. "I think I've seen enough."

10

I head straight for St. Francis, taking Craig Street to the Bloomfield Bridge, trying not to think about those pictures. Refusing to let them affect me. Telling myself they're nothing but scribbles with no meaning to anyone but the girl who made them. And yet I can't un-see them, and to see them is to wonder what she was like. What was going on in her head, what made her view the world that way at that age. Wanting to understand her, I have only one strategy at this point: to remember how I felt when I was in her place.

If you say "high school," the first thing I see is Ed Durdovitch in gym class. Blue-eyed and crew-cut, a smile that said "Take it, or I'll fuck you up" as he handed me a goalie stick. His buddies Kelly and Conlan flanking him, cold, hard, and content to be his sidekicks. They were three muscled-up jocks, each capable of stomping the crap out of me, a scrawny nonathlete in a Rush T-shirt with hair halfway down to my ass. I was always among the last picks in gym; only the grossly obese Pat McAfee and some albino kid whose name I can't remember ranked lower.

"Come on, don't be a pussy," Durdovitch said. "All you gotta do's stand in the goal and stop the ball. And don't get hit in the eyes or nuts."

"We're on the hockey team, all three of us," Kelly said. "You won't even see any shots. And if you do, we'll just score more. Don't worry about it."

In no position to argue, I took the stick and went to the net. Crouched like the goalies I saw on TV, trying to look like I knew what I was doing. Mr. Block the gym teacher dropped the orange ball, and the game began. Plastic clacked on plastic. The gym filled with echoes of voices, footsteps, and squeaky soles.

My guys bulled into the other end as promised, knocking bodies around. Conlan checked some kid into the bleachers and cracked his glasses. Durdovitch plowed into McAfee, dropped him on his ass for a round of laughs. While all this was going on, I kept watching the ball. And I couldn't understand why the other goalie had trouble seeing it, why he kept shifting around and flinching with every shot.

Even when the scrum came rumbling toward me, I never lost track of the ball. Some kid took a slap shot, and it hovered like a hummingbird. I blocked it with my chest, which stung but not that bad. Then I let the ball drop but didn't know what to do next.

So I putted it toward the crowd, and another kid jumped on it and shot. Again the ball floated more than it darted, and I caught it. Dropped it, swatted it clear. To me, this was no big deal. I was just doing what I thought I was supposed to do.

But Durdovitch, Conlan, and Kelly started talking, saying things like, "Bolzjak, why didn't you say you could play?" And I had no answer for them. I just kept crouching and watching the ball, still baffled about the other goalie's struggle.

My guys put it past him once, twice, and again. He was off by a fraction, close but just missing. It was getting frustrating to watch.

Then everybody rushed back, and a kid wristed one. I paddled it away. Another kid got the rebound, shot. Dropped to my knees, took it in the shoulder. The ball rolled out, and the same kid took another whack at it. Hit my shin, rebound number three. And a third kid shot, and I grabbed it. Tossed it up like a tennis ball and smacked it across the gym.

Durdovitch, Kelly, and Conlan didn't even bother to chase it. Instead they had a quick conference, and Conlan jogged out the door. Mr. Block didn't question him. Nor did he say anything when Durdovitch and Kelly got the ball and came running toward me instead of the other goal.

I stood up and was like, "What the hell?" but Durdovitch said, "Just play! Just play!"

So I got back in my crouch and did as he said, thinking, Okay, please don't kill me. Maybe he scared my game to new heights or something, but I didn't just play; I flat-out stoned him and Kelly while they took turns teeing off.

And that's all they did for minutes on end. Durdovitch and Kelly, back and forth, quick passes and shots, and I stopped a lot more than not. The other kids and Mr. Block stood around watching, and all semblance of a game was gone. It had become nothing but a two-on-one shoot-out, two polished talents gunning all they had at me.

From Left to Right to fake, shot. Deflected off my arm, rolling back to Right. Shot. Off my chest. I swept it out, but Left caught it, backhanded it, and I kicked it back toward him. Another shot and a better save. And with the next one and the next, I didn't feel so afraid of Durdovitch and Kelly anymore. I lost that fear when I focused on the ball, and every time it hit me I felt stronger no matter the sting.

Durdovitch even tried a breakaway, came barreling toward me with his Sasquatch body and red face full of rage. I shrunk back, braced for a slam but still focused on the ball. He tried a fake. I didn't bite and took it right in the face. That shot cut my lip, and I didn't care. I spit a bloody hawker on the court and got back in my crouch. The ball rolled back to Kelly, who was too busy looking at the hawker to notice.

Mr. Block blew the whistle, and the other kids started for the locker room.

"You see that?" Durdovitch said to someone behind me. "Tell me you saw that."

I turned around, and there was Conlan and a weird old guy with a Caesar haircut and twitchy gray mustache. They'd been standing by the doors, observing us for who knows how long. The old guy never answered Durdovitch. He just walked up to me and looked me over.

"Report to my office after your next class. They'll tell you where it is," he said, and walked away, leaving me standing there all confused.

His office turned out to be a tiny room cramped between the assistant principal's and athletic coordinator's. I showed up as ordered and found the guy behind a desk, poring over papers in a manilla folder. Plaques filled the walls, Coach of the Year this and State Champion that. Pictures of high school hockey teams from the '70s and '80s, one from the '60s. A cabinet full of trophies topped with hockey players in action poses.

"You can sit down," he said, still scanning the file. "So. Dexter Bolzjak. The rap on you is this: you're a B student who could be an A student, but you're intellectually lazy and unmotivated. One of your teachers describes you as 'a cipher at a desk.' Another calls you 'a walking mediocrity.' You're a loner with no friends besides Judd Hargauer, who doesn't stack up to much himself. You have no girlfriend, and a few of your female classmates have described you as 'creepy,' 'weird,' and 'a slob.' Your male classmates have called you 'a burnout,' 'a smart-ass who's not half as smart as he thinks he is,' and 'a total fucking fag.' You don't participate in any extracurricular activities whatsoever, and your college prospects can be summarized as 'middling at best.'"

He set aside the file and leaned back in his chair. "Would you call that an accurate assessment?"

"Who called me a fag? Whoever said that's a lying sack of shit, and I'll tell you someth—"

"You're a junior, almost a senior. What do you care about? What's your direction in life?"

"I like movies. Filmmaking. But me and my parents can't afford NYU or USC, so I'm going to Pitt. Is that okay with you?"

"Did you get accepted to NYU or USC?"

"Why apply when you can't afford to go?"

"Why apply? It's easier to make excuses and not even try, isn't it?"

"Okay, look. I don't know you, and I don't see any point in talking to you," I said, getting up from the chair.

"The name's Chuck Hidio, but you're gonna call me Coach. Now sit your ass back down," he said, and stood as I kind of sank back into the chair. "I'll tell you what the point is. I don't like to be fooled is the point. I don't like raw talent going untapped in this building without my knowing it. You've been here for three years, and I never heard of you. I can't find a word about you playing anywhere. Why is that?"

"Because I never played before."

"Bullshit. You can do better than that."

"Swear to God. I don't play street hockey, and I can barely skate."

"I just watched you stop slap shots, wrist shots, backhanders, and breakaways from my best players. And you didn't just stop them, you made it look easy. How do you explain that?"

"I was trying not to get my ass kicked by your boys. They told me to play goal, so I did my best. Can I go now?"

"Not until I offer you the starter's spot."

I wanted to laugh, but I knew he wasn't kidding. Even then I saw a glint in his eyes and uneasiness in his limbs. Hints of a desperate man, a titan past his prime and terrified of retirement. He left the desk and stood beside me, arms crossed. Like we were already at the rink, me on the bench and him surveying the ice.

"How old are you? Sixteen? Right now you are standing on the summit of your biology. You will never be quicker or braver than you are today. You'll never have that *juice* you got gushing in your veins ever again. And what are you doing with it, huh? Watching movies?

"I can make you the starter. We got all spring and summer. We'll hit the rink every day, get you skating and playing in pads. I won't lie; it won't be easy. You'll want to cry, you'll want to quit. But if you got the guts and the balls, you'll know it's worth it. You'll know you got a gift, and it would be a damn shame to waste it.

"The team's almost there. The forwards, the defenders, all solid. But we need better goaltending. If you can bring it, there's no telling how far we'll go," Coach said, and went back to his desk. "It's up to you, though. I can't force you into anything. I can only offer you an opportunity. What you do with it depends on you. Are you the kid they say you are, or are you somebody else? I guess we don't know yet, do we?"

"Wow! You're really gonna do it?" Dad said, excited enough to get up from the recliner. "My man! Gimme five! You hear that, Sam? D.'s gonna be on the hockey team!"

Mom was in the dining room, laying out her kids' watercolor pictures on the table. "Since when do you like hockey?"

"Since I found out I'm good at it. Besides, it might be fun. Why shouldn't I try it?"

"But hockey's so violent. Can't you play a sport where you don't get your teeth knocked out?"

"Ah, here we go," Dad said. "You just gotta put a damper on it, don't you? He's finally interested in something, and you're gonna talk him out of it."

"I can't help but notice that he never cared about sports before, and now he does. That doesn't strike you as strange?"

"Both of you, stop. Please. Don't fight, just stop," I said. "The coach wants me to be the goalie, so I'll be wearing a mask and a ton of pads. There's no way I'm gonna get hurt. If I gotta buy the equipment myself, I will."

"Okay. If you really want to do this, then okay. Of course we'll be there for you, both of us. Of course," Mom said. "I just think it's fair to question your sudden interest."

Dad groaned and went back to the recliner, turned up the TV volume a few decibels.

"Question it all you want, but I've made up my mind. I know I'm your baby boy, but outside this house, I don't command a whole lot of respect. Girls think I'm scum, guys think I'm weak, and everybody else thinks I'm some kind of loser. I'm sick of being a loser, Mom, and I'm sick of what I see when I look in the mirror.

"But starting today, that's over. I'm invited to the party for once, and I'm not just gonna show up; I'm gonna kick ass and look cool doing it. I'm gonna prove I'm worth something. And I do need to prove that, whether you think so or not. I need to know what I'm made of."

I went to my room with a sixteen-year-old's swagger, whipped the door shut behind me. Then sprawled on the bed, tense with aimless nerves. Not knowing what else to do, I put one of the *Hellraiser* movies in the laser disc player and stopwatched it. Remote in hand, I skipped ahead to the part where a guy gets torn apart by hooks and chains.

Speeding up the footage, slowing it down, stopping it on the exact fraction of a second where flesh turned into latex. Where hidden tubes spurted fake blood, where the actor became a dummy blown apart in a shower of gore.

Bored but too sluggish to change the disc, I kept shuttling through the rest of the movie. Soon it occurred to me that my hand-eye coordination might extend beyond the death scenes. Just to experiment, I backed the movie all the way to the beginning, to the dry parts that were all talk. The content itself didn't matter; this was a test of reflexes.

Two people talking. Cut to a close-up—pause. Within a frame of the cut.

Cut back to the two—pause. Within a frame of the cut.

Cut to—pause. On the exact frame of the cut.

I lay there going through scene after scene, shot by shot. And I stopped every one as it changed to the next. Stopped every single shot.

"Holy shit," I whispered, and went to the dresser mirror across the room. I pried back my eyelids as far as they'd go, exposing the pink sockets and white orbs with their squiggly little blood vessels. My eyes still looked normal, but I knew better. All those hours of stopwatching all that death, as fake as it was, had forever changed them. And for whatever soul I'd lost, my eyes had gained the power to splinter the seconds. They had become dissectors of Time.

The elevator dings and shows me out to a floor of St. Francis. I approach Lou's room with a growing dread, knowing this won't be a pleasant visit. And however much I tell myself to be ready, to be strong, it still doesn't soften the shock of seeing him.

For one thing, they've cleaned him up and put him in a gown instead of his rags. Nobody could call him a bum anymore, not me or anyone else. But he's still sick and getting sicker, his skin drawn, his eyes glazed and fixed on the TV. Tubes run from his nose to a machine by the bed, channeling fluids from him as he lays wasting.

Lou does spark up a little when I walk in. Not that he's happy to see me. In fact, he gives me a sour look as I sit down, and says, "What do you want?"

"To see how you're doing."

"How do you *think* I'm doing?"

Well. At least he's coherent, I figure, and hold off on saying anything else just yet. And the noon news plays on the TV—the Mon Wharf's flooded again, a city council member's accused of being crooked again, the Pirates lost again—and then commercials.

"I've been doing some fact-finding on your girl. Turns out she was pretty handy with a pen. She ever draw any pictures for you?"

"I don't know what you're talking about."

"You said she'd remember you. How did you know her?"

"Sounds like she got in your head. Guess I should've warned you, kid. That's something she'll do. Get right in your head."

"I'm not worried about it. I'm just curious. A lot of people say they knew her, and a lot of people say they banged her. And they've all been proven liars. So I want to know what makes you any different."

"I got proof enough, but it won't help you find her."

"Damn it, Lou, why does everything have to be a riddle? Just tell me how you knew her."

"I'd say you're more than curious. Heh heh heh. I'd even say you're putting forth an honest effort."

"I got a thing against effort, and I'm not putting forth any till you tell me why you roped me into this. You got money, you got brains. You could've found somebody better for the job."

"I know you better than you think. Your old man told me all about you. And what he didn't tell me, I read in the papers. I don't know every detail, but I know those four guys messed you up after you blew your last game.

"But listen to me, kid. You can't let that define you. Trust me on this; I know something about it. You let one ass-kicking define your life, next thing you know, you got nothing else left. Now I'm giving you a chance to get some cash in your pocket, make something of yourself. Anyways, I got nobody else to give that money to. But you gotta earn it. You gotta show some hustle."

"Your brother and your friend Haley could use the money."

"Ah, they don't know nothing. Haley's happy slinging hash over at Jo Jo's, and Gene ain't hurting for cash. They couldn't do what I asked you anyhow. They're old, they got nothing to prove."

I sit there quiet for a while, and I can barely even look at him. It's not the tubes with the fluids or his drawn skin. It's his eyes, sunken in their pits but still alive. Still smart, and sober for once, staring right through me like they can see every hairline crack of my will.

"I'm not the Make-A-Wish Foundation, Lou, and I'm not big on promises. But I'll do what I can. Can I get anything else for you?"

"I could use some books. If you could grab some off my steps, that would be great."

"How am I supposed to get in?"

"Use the key you made on the way here, when you thought I was passed out."

We lock stares. I don't know what my face is doing, but I'm

thinking this guy's something else. Here he is, dying by the minute but still playing chess. Move, countermove, always thinking three moves ahead, studying me as I try to maintain an aura of calm.

"Okay. Fair enough. But I'm not the only one who's holding out, am I?"

"We were supposed to get married. We were together for our last year of school. I was leaving for the service, but we got engaged first. She would wait for me to get back; that was the plan. But then she went and turned into somebody else before I left. Turned into this other person, like the one you see in the movies, and broke it off.

"And I gotta know why. I gotta know if there's something else I could've done. And if you think I'm bullshitting, your proof's in the house. It's easy enough to find. I'm not saying where. God damn it, I can't tell you everything."

Lou grabs the remote and starts flicking through the TV channels, not stopping on any of them long enough to see what they are. He bombards himself with images and noise, anything to distract him from what he said. This continues for a minute, and I take it as my cue to leave.

So I start for the door, but he stops me when he calls my name. Not kid, but Dexter. I turn to look back at him, and he's still looking at the TV.

"Didn't mean to be sore at you earlier," he says, reflections flashing in his eyes. "I'm glad you came back. I knew you wouldn't just leave me here."

11

Rolled-up newspapers have accumulated on Lou's porch. Two evenings and two mornings, and I make a point to gather them, keeping up appearances and all that. While I'm at it, I check the mailbox, too, but it's empty aside from rust.

The key clicks open the lock, and I walk into the house. For a minute I feel around for a light switch, my creaky bumbling signaling every rat and roach to scurry back to their nooks. When I do find the switch, it hardly helps. By day this place is a maze of dusty junk, crammed with decayed paper and heaps of broken gadgets. Now at night it's a crypt, far too dark for the weak bulb overhead. Too many shadows, too many corners, crevices, and recesses that could hide a hostile spy.

I start up the steps, wedging my way through the magazines and paperbacks. Aiming for variety, I pick some mystery (*The Maltese Falcon*), sci-fi (*The Martian Chronicles*), Western (*The Virginian*), a classic epic (all three *Lord of the Rings*), even some Stephen King (*'Salem's Lot*) and Vonnegut (*Slaughterhouse-Five*), and I'm almost good to go. Almost but not quite, as Lou's words in the hospital still bother me.

It's here in this house, he said. Proof that he knew Mercy, and it's easy enough to find. I'm taking that as bait, a dare to snoop around till I find something noteworthy.

Lou's room looks pretty much like it did last time, except the vomit's gone. A dark spot on the floor marks where it was. My guess is that Eugene came by at some point and cleaned it up. And if that's the case, good for him.

I crouch down and pull out the bottom dresser drawer. The money's still there. Still dirty, ragged, and glorious. I grab a handful and count it just for the hell of it: $1,750, and that's just a sliver of the whole. Again I'm tempted to steal it. I could pocket it right now, and nobody would ever know. I could take four, five handfuls and still not get caught. Hell, I could dump the whole drawer in a duffel bag and just go.

Don't ask what I'd do with it. Sure, there's school, starting a business, investment, retirement, and charity. There's also Vegas and Amsterdam. Better yet, there's a whole world beyond this ex-steel town, and I know I'm missing it. Countless peoples, histories, and vistas. More than I can imagine, more than I'll ever know if I watch the Discovery Channel all day and page through every *National Geographic* rotting on Lou's steps.

And as I'm sitting there picturing giant octopi in the Barrier Reef, skulls in the Catacombs of Paris, lions in the African savannah, bazaars in Morocco, it occurs to me that I'm already plotting how to spend Lou's money while he lies dying in the hospital. I shut the drawer then, disgusted with my own mind. And yet, I'll admit, it gets harder to close that drawer every time I open it.

Anyway, proof. Lou said it's here, but all I'm seeing is that same old mess. The same dog track programs, the same Kashon's receipts with their cornucopia logo. The other dresser drawers hold nothing but clothes, likewise for the closet.

I return to the hallway and try the other two doors, always

closed. The first opens to the bathroom, and let's forget I mentioned it. The next opens to another bedroom. That much I can tell in the darkness. But once I turn on the light, the sight drops my jaw.

The room's not just clean, it's immaculate. There's no dust on the parquet floor or cherrywood bed, both gleaming with reflected light. Pristine veils hang from bedpost to bedpost, draping off the mattress in its own virgin zone. In the center of the floor lies a carpet, wine red patterned with a golden border, edges fringed with tassels. A green dragon contorts within the border, teeth and eyes white, tongue plump and pink. Down to its fibers the carpet sparkles, untouched by the very air that chokes the rest of the house.

I venture in farther, approaching a dresser banked against the near wall. Two objects decorate its otherwise bare surface. The first is a brass cross with three crossbeams, resembling a tree more than your standard Christian symbol. I pick it up—it's about the size of my hand—and read the carving on its wooden pedestal.

Louis Elias Kashon, confirmed Maronite
By the grace of Saint Sharbel
Saint Ann Church, April 20, 1941

The other object is a framed picture, a family portrait from the '20s or '30s. To the left stands the dad upright with pride, mustached and with slicked-down hair, resting a hand on a boy's shoulder. The kid giggles, a sharp break from his grave-faced mom who sits in the middle, cradling a baby. She stares ahead with wary eyes, distrusting the camera. A second, older boy stands alone to the right, looking more like Mom than Dad, an overly serious kid who doesn't tolerate a lot of nonsense.

I assume the younger, sunnier kid is Lou, and I'm guessing he's about five. Eugene would be the other, maybe ten. I have no idea who the baby is, boy or girl.

I try the bottom drawer and find a bunch of colored and ripped ticket stubs. The Warner is red, the Paramount yellow, the Nixon blue, and the Stanley green. I recognize the names; they're movie theaters that used to exist downtown. And I mean actual theaters with stages, curtains parting or closing over the screen, velvet ropes and gilded balconies, murals on their vaulted ceilings. They were dying by the time I was born, driven to extinction by the multiplex. But I still remember visiting them when I was little, gawking and wowed by stuff like *Star Trek* and *The Fox and the Hound*.

And Lou must've been pretty wowed, too, to buy so many tickets. Or maybe "obsessed" is a better word, for the next drawer is full of newspaper clippings, and they're all about Mercy. The collection goes backward through time, starting with "Carnahan Walks Off *Kiss*" to "Carnahan Leaves Pantheon" back to the days of "Mercy Stuns Cannes" (photo of her on the red carpet, lavished with flashbulb light, waving a gloved hand, masked with sunglasses) and "*Savage Whim* Another Hit for La Devila" all the way back to "Harmony Native Lands Bit Part" and "Local Actress Signs to Pantheon." The clippings feel brittle, prone to crumble, and so I slide them back to their cell.

The top drawer holds about a dozen envelopes and a small felt-covered box. I flip it open, uncovering a diamond ring. The rock twinkles, a little prism playing with the light. Capturing it, fracturing it to wisps of color while the gold band shines fierce and ageless. I don't dare touch it, not with the dust and onion oils in my fingertips, but clap the box shut and put it back.

All of the envelopes are addressed to Louis Kashon at this house, 809 Wellsbrook, and the sender is Agnes Zagbroski at the

Academy of Arts. The postmarks date them from November of '43 to June of '44. I read the oldest letter first, and sure enough, it has the same handwriting as the history notes I saw at the Academy.

> *Dear Louis,*
>
> *I can't thank you enough for last Saturday. As you know, I put myself in quite the bind. Hours before the Halloween Masquerade, and there I was, looking for decorations in a mad panic. Blame nothing but my own foolishness—always studying, ever neglectful of a world beyond my head. Only by luck did the cabbie bring me to you. Anyone less generous would have told me to get lost, but you took the time to help and spared me the embarrassment of ruining the dance.*
>
> *Of course the girls weren't pleased when I returned with all those pumpkins, and they griped throughout the carving. (Imagine their queenly hands scooping out gobs of slime and seeds . . .) By the evening, however, when the banquet hall darkened to a forest of glowing jack-o-lanterns, even my grumpiest classmate offered a grudging compliment.*
>
> *Days have passed, and I still smile when I remember us loading your truck. If you could have seen your face when I caught that first pumpkin! (I told you I knew something about farmwork. Now do you believe me?) As for the question you asked before leaving, I think you saw the answer in my eyes, but I didn't have the nerve to say it aloud.*
>
> *Yes, Louis, I do want to see you again, and I want to see you soon. I want to walk with you under the last red and gold leaves, to feel your warm kindness once more before the fall. Most of all, I want another reason to smile.*
> *Your friend,*
> *Agnes*

The next few letters continue in the same tone, mentioning trips to the movies, ice skating, and sled-riding. I skip ahead to the last one, looking for a sign of the mind who drew those pictures in that notebook, some trace of the Mercy persona. Instead a black-and-white photo falls out when I unfold the paper.

It looks like a party in a park with picnic tables and balloons in the background. Blurred kids run around back there, too, laughing. In the foreground, a young couple holds hands and stares into the lens.

The guy is a swarthy handsome charmer, well-built and broad-shouldered. His full head of dark hair shines like his smile and polished shoes. And though I don't know '40s fashion, I'd guess his suit's pretty snazzy, too. This guy seems like he's got it together, like he knows how to take care of himself, and it feels cruel to compare him to the Lou I know.

And the girl? You might not know her as Mercy Carnahan, at least not at first. Her cheeks are chubbier, eyebrows bushier, hair pulled back and tied with a white ribbon matching her dress. She has a depressive's sleepless eyes and gives just a fragile smile. For all the cold strength and confidence she'd later project, here she appears timid.

> *Dear Louis,*
> *Sunday was the best day I can remember, and I don't exaggerate. You know I love you, and you know I've been waiting for you to ask what you did. As for me, there's precious little in this life I know, but I know I want this. Forever I want you with me forever, want nothing so much as your heart, every beat shared with mine, our very souls united and undying in sweet madness.*
> *Your going away will be difficult for me, but I know you*

have your duty. Remember that I'll be thinking of you always, awaiting your return. I say this, and you haven't even left yet!

Is it too soon to think about the wedding? Perhaps, but I should mention the loveliest little church in Harmony, Saint Olaf's. They have a beautiful garden with white cherry trees, and since I was a child I've daydreamed about a ceremony among those blossoms. My father knows the pastor there, and I really do think

I hear something downstairs, a faint creak like someone opening the front door. Frozen, I listen and wait. An empty moment passes. There's no sound but my own heart and throbbing blood. Listen and wait. Standing there paralyzed, cornered with nowhere to go.

A thump breaks the silence, then another. The sounds draw closer, footsteps upon the stairs. Shoes on the hardwood, the rustle of bodies navigating the clutter. I couldn't speak if I tried; I can only listen and wait and let them find me ready.

Closer yet, they reach the landing, and they're just outside the door.

A hand curls around the doorjamb. Slowly, then, a plastic whiteness appears. A goalie mask with two eyes shining in the holes.

"Gotcha!" the mask hisses in a raspy voice. "I'll show you what happens when you sneak around!"

The mask dissolves, blurs into a white smudge across space. The bedposts move like spokes in a wheel, melting into the walls, which spin round and around again. I grab the dresser to steady myself, but that doesn't stop anything, the spinning's too fast, and my face starts to itch.

Can't close my eyes because that's when they'll come. Can't but the itch becomes a burn, and the room still spins, walls doorway window mask trailing colors, churning up a sickness in my guts. Can't but I do, clutching my face, nails scratching as I drop to my knees.

They stand over me, one wearing my own mask, the other three masked with panty hose. One holds a video camera, aims it in my eyes. Another comes in with clippers, raking them over my scalp. Cheering laughing yee-hawing, screaming faggot, pussy, cocksucker, bitch. One dangles strands in my face, awwwing, while I try not to cry, try not to choke on the steel wool's blue slime oozing down my throat. Stomps and kicks to my ribs. Grabbed by the dog collar around my neck, told to stay still and take it, faggot. They rip off the tape, laugh when I cough up the pad. And open up, one shoves a plastic pipe in my mouth. Just jams it right in there, grinds it against my molars, scrapes it over my tongue. Not down my throat, but far enough to lock open my jaw.

"Dexter! Oh, God, are you okay?! What's wrong?!" says a girl's voice. The spinning stops with her touch, her hold on my shoulder. "What's wrong?!"

I open my eyes to Francesca, the hockey mask hiked up onto her crown. She looks horrified and ready to cry, which turns my own fear to shame. I know the room didn't spin, I know they're still in jail, I know it happened eight years ago. I know, I know, I know, and all that knowledge never keeps them away for good, never stops me from going down sweating and panting and shaking like a whipped dog.

"I'm okay," I say. "It's nothing. It's just—what's with the damn mask!?"

"I saw your car out front, saw the light on, thought I'd come

139

over and surprise you with my awesome news: I'm going out for the hockey team! I got my dad to buy all the pads and stuff, and I'm gonna practice all summer and be the Sabertooths' first-ever girl goalie. And *you* are gonna help me," she says, poking a finger in my arm. "You sure you're okay? You want some water or something?"

I hold my face in my hands, pretending not to hear her.

"Wow, look at this room," Francesca says like she hadn't noticed it till now, then gets up and treats herself to a little walk-about. "This is like swank. Why's the rest of the house such a dump?"

I climb back to my feet, wobbly but well enough to put the letter back in the drawer. "I don't know, but it's time to go."

"What are you doing here anyway? How's Mr. Kashon?"

I start for the door, but she hurries over to block me.

"Hey, wait! What about what I said, about you helping me play goal?"

"No way. Absolutely not."

"That's not fair! You owe me a favor, remember? First you don't help me with my homework, but I help you with Mr. Kashon. And now you're blowing me off again?"

"Look, it's not that I don't think you can play. And it's not that I don't want to help you, but I can't. Think of something else I can do for you."

"Anything else?" she says. Her brown eyes ringed with raccoon makeup lock onto mine, a blush rises in her cheeks. Her lips part just enough to reveal that fanglike tooth, that little glitch that makes her mouth so kissable, while her breath feels warm on my face.

"Nothing that'll get me arrested," I say, which makes her blink and back off a step. "Come on, we both know you don't really like

140

hockey. You're trying to impress people, and that's not a good reason to play."

"Nuh-uh! I *do* like hockey. I've loved it ever since I saw you play."

"You never saw me play. You're too young."

"*Hello,* your game's online. It's not that hard to find. You really do live in a cave, don't you?"

"Yeah. Gladly. And I'm getting sick of you sneaking into it, reminding me of crap I'd rather forget."

"Don't get mad at me. I didn't post that video. I just happened to find it. You're not still bummed about those goals you gave up, are you? Aside from those, you were amazing. I'd love to play like you did, and you could teach me."

I try to move past her, but Francesca grabs my wrist and pulls with all her weight, whining, "Pleeeeease!"

I jerk free, and she staggers. Before she can react, I cup her face in my hand and squeeze her cheeks so hard she puckers. And I crouch down so we're eye to eye, our brows almost butting.

"You don't get it. They'll hate you, they'll degrade you. They'll rip you to shreds. They'll rape you and piss on you while you lay there crying. Is that what you want?

"You know what they told the cops? They wanted to 'purify sports.' Get rid of the fags, the pussies, anything feminine. So they started with me because I looked like a fag to them. What do you think they'll do to you, huh?

"You think they're in jail? They're everywhere whether you see them or not. They're around every corner, in every shadow, every time I close my eyes, and they're just waiting for me to let my guard drop so they can fuck me again. And you? You keep bringing them back. So no, I'm not gonna help you. No way, never," I say, and let her go.

The mask falls off her head, hits the floor. Francesca grabs it up and backs toward the doorway. Red-faced with a shaking voice, she says, "I don't know what they did to you, but I didn't do it! You're making excuses. You don't think I can play because I'm a girl. Maybe you're afraid I'll do better than you. Or you just don't like me because I'm not pretty enough for you. Well, I'll show you, Dexter Bolzjak! I'll show you real good!"

She runs downstairs crying. Slams the front door. Sands of eroding cement tinkle in the walls, then all falls quiet again.

I wheel up to the Wall, open a search engine, and type in "Truman Falcons 1993 Championship." The computer pulls up a list of links, topped with one called Ultimate Sports Chokes! I click on it, and the screen flashes.

A cartoon picture of a baseball catcher appears, the guy crouching behind home plate. Halves of his shattered mask lie scattered about his cleats. He clutches his throat with both hands, gagging on a ball lodged in his mouth while blood and teeth drip down his chin. His eyes bulge out of their sockets, sweat rolls down his brow.

Welcome to Ultimate Sports Chokes!
reads the text above the image, and below:

Here it is! The quintessential collection of the world's greatest gack-attacks, from the "Wide Right" Bills to the fat baldy at your local bowling alley gutterballing the last frame of a would-be 300 game. From Buckner to a therapy-bound tyke giving up a walk-off homer in his Little League championship. And yes, we got your Greg Norman, your 1992 Houston Oilers, even your 1942 Red Wings.

Built on contributions by You the People, we proudly present this ever-expanding gallery of Nervous Nellies in desperate need of a Heimlich. Indulge on this Feast of Fail, this Panoply of Monumental Collapse, and remember—it's only the Agony of Defeat for the loser. For the rest of us, it's just damn funny.

A blank Search field awaits at the bottom of the screen, so I type in the keywords again. And just like that, the link appears. <u>1993 PA State Championship Blizzards v. Falcons</u>. Nothing but pixels, and yet I hesitate, my hand jittery on the mouse.

Remember Job 1, I tell myself. You already lapsed once today. Let's not spin again, shall we?

The button clicks with my touch, activating RealTime, Judd's favorite video player-editor. RealTime downloads the file and fills the screen with a paused image: Cooper Rink viewed from an elevated perch, as it appeared on TV eight years ago. Players mottle the surface of the ice, the crowd is a frozen crush of noise.

Then everything moves. The players skate. The camera shakes with the quaking rink. The crowd flickers, their roar muffled under one grating voice.

"Hell-ooooooo, ladies and gentlemen, this is WPIT's Kip Larky broadcasting from historic Cooper Rink! Smile, because tonight you're live on public access!

"We got ourselves a real blockrocker here, a clash of the titans. Rob 'Da Bomb' Bomley in goal for the Ropersdale Blizzards versus Dexter 'The X-Factor' Bolzjak of the Truman Falcons. Both have been near-perfect throughout these playoffs, but tonight only one can be a champion. The other a mere footnote. Forever remembered as a loser, if remembered at all."

I turn off the Wall's speakers. Once was enough, thanks. Don't need to hear it again. And of course I've seen it all before, too, but not from this perspective. Not so detached. Not filtered through a camera and confined to a screen, every moment prone to research and review.

Maybe it's no surprise, then, that I don't feel much while watching it. Like I said before about people getting thwacked in movies, there's a basic difference between watching something and having lived through something. An unbridgeable gap. In this case, inevitability widens that gap, too. A couple of third-line Falcons take a few shots on Bomley, and I don't perk up because I know they'll give him no trouble. Durdovitch slams into a Blizzard, drops him to the ice, and I don't think "ouch" or "nice hit" because I know Durdy will end up getting ejected on a bone-headed game misconduct.

And the Falcon goalie? That kid bouncing around like a half-assed acrobat, deflecting shot upon shot after shot while cameras flash and the crowd pounds the glass? I can't even stand to look at him. If I knew how, I'd delete him right out of the footage, erase him from the collective memory. Doesn't matter whether he was good, great, or awful. What matters is that people like Lou, Dad, and Francesca think he still exists, and they keep confusing me with him.

So it's a pointless, empty exercise, this revisiting Cooper Rink, and I don't even know why I'm doing it. But I don't stop. I sit there staring at Kelly dumping the puck, the other Falcons chasing. Cut to the second camera, the one closer to the ice, as Durdovitch scrambles for the puck among the Blizzards. They knock it away from him and start back the other way. Cut to the higher, more distant camera to keep up with the Blizzards, the crowd blurred in the background.

There it is—I hit a button, pause the video—there's your reason

144

why. Somewhere in that pulsating mass is a face I need to find, and I don't mean the sadistic redhead. No, one of the four fuckers was there in the stands, the old one with the gray beard. The ringleader, father to the one who hid in the woods with the knife. Even now, even in this form, I can't have Graybeard lurking unseen among the crowd. I have to expose him, root him out before he infects any more of my head.

After years of watching Judd use RealTime, I think I know enough of its tricks. Like for instance, the zoom-and-render combination that lets you magnify an image and focus it. With the cursor I draw a box around the crowd, highlighting it, then hit the keyboard command to blow it up. The crowd expands to a colorless splotch that fills the screen. I type another command, and a red line moves back and forth across the screen like a windshield wiper. The line clears up the splotch a little with each pass till a clear image appears: a middle-aged woman, multichinned and henna-haired, screaming in a Blizzards jersey. Lights glare off her glasses, turning her eyes to white voids. The two fans on either side of her are visible, too, plus a few before and behind her.

By using the arrow keys, I move through the crowd, scrolling past the woman and her neighbors, scanning from left to right and covering three rows at a time. Past the girls with falcons painted on their cheeks, the tubby watery-eyed guys in Pens jerseys Jagr and Lemieux, a mom in mid-scold as she grabs a kid who's grabbing another kid's pink cotton candy off its paper cone.

He's in here, I know it. Blending in with everyone else, a sixty-three-year-old gray-bearded bastard with glasses. And no, I won't say his name because he doesn't deserve one; when he dies, he can die nameless. He'd watched me in this crowd like he'd watched all my games. My practices, even, studied me, tracked my route home, knew where my parents were, hoping for a night

145

when he might corner me alone. As it turned out, he got his chance.

Face after face, tapping the arrows, trusting my eyes and reflexes like I did in the old days. Past faces old and young, male and female. Past concerned moms and proud dads and drunken uncles flushed with beer and rage, Ropersdale natives cheering for their Blizzards. Hated them so much at the time, but now they're benign, harmless compared to the one I'm trying to find. Past a redhead—different redhead—past junior high kids happy to act up and scream with no one telling them they can't.

Graybeard watched from the bleachers, and once he saw no Mom and Dad, he went ahead with the plan. Called his son who rigged the trap on Old Watermill, the pulled-over Taurus, the mannequin. Called the one at the garage who prepped everything there, the spinning wooden disc and video camera. Maybe left his seat at some point to confer with the fourth one. The fat rink-worker with curly hair, always hanging around the snack bar in his yellow STAFF shirt.

Faces, faces, and faces. My fingers rap the keys too fast for the computer. It lags but still moves the picture along, past so much distorted flesh. Mouths frozen open, laughing, chewing, gusting fury or chanting "Goalchick." Eyes sucked of color, dark little twinkles demanding blood. No wonder I saw monsters in the stands that night; no wonder Mercy saw them, too, when she performed and scribbled them into her notebook. You see so many faces and try to think the best, but in every crowd you find one who means you harm. You search long enough, hunched over a keyboard, monitor frying your eyes and brain, computer sucking your energy as it tightens your muscles, and there he is.

Right there.

Just sitting on a bleacher, all casual in his jeans and dark green sweater. Bald like I remembered, gray beard and glasses. He slouches, paunch sagging over his belt, head tilted toward my end of the ice. A completely ordinary-looking old creature. You'd think nothing of sitting next to him or letting your kid sit next to him. You'd never take him for a kidnapper or molester, and if somebody told you he was, you might not even believe them, he seems so normal.

I hit the keys that play the video frame by frame, then wheel back from the Wall. Too wound up to stay in the chair, I stand there and watch him move. His eyes leave the ice, his head turns toward the camera. He might even see it, might be looking right into it.

My body's shaking, my nails digging raw divots in my palms. I can feel my face twitch, my throat burning to scream. To say, yeah, I see you, you cockstroking old fuck, and I hope you're dying in jail. Slowly, painfully, and knowing you're going to hell. I want to wake the whole sleeping world and say, see, this is what a monster really looks like. This is why we make them so fantastic, because in reality they look so boring, so human. And this one, this fucker's still after me eight years later. Him and his son and their friends, they got my heart and they keep coming after my head, my soul. But I'm not afraid of them, I swear to God I'm not afraid.

The video cuts to the second camera, closer to the ice, turning the screen white. So he vanishes, and when the video cuts back again, he'll be hidden again. Back to the cover of the crowd again, waiting to be found again, forever stalking his prey.

12

Almost a week later, and I'm getting nowhere. I worked my way down that list of contacts Wade Endicott sent, calling each number and leaving unreturned voice mails. The only live one I caught was Gilbert Pollard, Mercy's ex-associate. The guy has to be pushing ninety these days, but he was still sharp enough. So sharp he refused to discuss Mercy over the phone, insisting on a face-to-face meeting where he promised to present an "exclusive artifact." "You won't be sorry for making the trip, I assure you," he said, his silky voice exuding an air of the upper crust.

Endicott also put himself on that list. After exchanging a few e-mails, we agreed that if I do go to New York, I could stop to see him, too.

And so these are the leads. A doddering husk in Manhattan who's luring me up there to show me God knows what, and an obsessive alpha-creep on all things Carnahan. But they're willing to talk, and I'm in no position to pass.

Stewing on this lack of progress, I roll into the Strip early and head toward Jo Jo's, the diner where Lou's friend Haley works. It sits on Smallman and Twenty-fourth, a couple blocks from Kashon's, nestled in the not-yet-gentrified section where big empty buildings still linger. Massive brick monsters stranded by Time, abandoned by the fickle buck. The most noticeable, and maybe the saddest, is the Armstrong Cork Factory. The old hulk broods on the river, its boxy towers linked by a rusted, elevated walkway. Every few years, the news says some developer plans to turn Armstrong Cork into condos, and maybe one day someone will. But these days it rots, its countless windows smashed, dead machinery cluttering the gap between the towers, walls graffitied (APES! scream glaring letters across the façade) and charred from the occasional fire.

Jo Jo's, by contrast, huddles low to the ground, its cement-block walls painted off-white and decorated with smiley chefs. It's a blunt and functional building, a gas station in a past life now thriving as a greasy spoon beloved by truckers, barhoppers, and every hungry body in between. The signature dish is a triple-egg omelet bursting with veggies, sausage, and potatoes. God bless you and your guts if you can finish one.

No maroon Buick in the lot yet, so I guess I made it before Haley. With the downtime I riffle through a mess of printouts from the Wall, meaning maps but mostly quotes for buses and hotels. No way around it, a weekend in New York spells a hit to the wallet, and my brain aches with dollar signs and decimals by the time Haley coasts in from Smallman.

I step out and wait for him to approach. He stops when he sees me but plays it cool, even gives a nod. A gesture of recognition, respect. I think I can work with him.

"Got a minute? I want to ask you something."

"About Lou? I know you got his brother going. You are one persona non grata over at Kashon's, I can tell you that much."

"Yeah, well. That's Eugene's problem. Mine's that I promised Lou I'd look into something, try to find somebody."

"Let me guess. Somebody famous and mysteriously vanished. A certain blue-eyed, black-haired porcelain beauty."

"So what do you know?"

"I know your search ain't going so good if you're fishing from me."

"Then where else do I fish?"

"If I knew that, I'd be fishing there myself, get me a big-ass payday from the press. Way I see it, if *anybody* knew where Miss Movie Star was, she'd've been found long ago."

"You ever see the two of them together back then?"

"I didn't meet Lou till after the war, so no, I never saw her. I only heard things. Whispers on the street." Haley looks at the diner, at Twenty-fourth, back toward Smallman like the street might be eavesdropping even now. "They say she dumped him at the Haddonfield. A glitzy restaurant used to be Downtown before you was born."

"Who's they?"

"They's my boys that worked there bussing tables, washing dishes. They say Lou showed up, got himself a table for two and sat waiting. And kept waiting, alone, getting antsy while the minutes ticked by. Waiters was buzzing about him in the back, everybody's sneaking looks at the poor guy getting stood up.

"But then an ominous hush fell over the place. Palpable, man, even the boys in the back felt it and peeked out to see what's up. And what they saw was folks clustered by the front windows, gawking at a Rolls-Royce pulled up to the curb. The girl stepped out of the car, came right into the restaurant.

"Every single person was checking her out, and she basked in it, letting everybody get their look. Like she knew this town never saw nothing like her before and never would again. Stood there awhile all sexy with her sleek hairdo and shiny black dress and gloves, then walked toward Lou, her high-heeled shoesteps making the only sound.

"They say Lou stood up to meet her, nobody else even moved. He called her Agnes, told her how incredible she looked, pulled out her chair. But she didn't sit. She reached down into her cleavage, plucked something out, and tossed it on the table. Was a diamond ring, and it spun there on the table like a coin before it fell over.

"'The name's Mercy Carnahan. Remember that,' she said, and looked around, stared down the whole restaurant, face by face, eye by eye. 'All of you, remember that. Next time you see me, I will glow down upon you. A shaft of magic beamed off silver screens and straight to your dreams. For I am the Fallen Goddess, and as long as I am bound to this sphere, no soul is safe.'

"And she walked out, leaving them all silent behind her. Got back in the Rolls and rolled out of town. Next thing you know, she's big just like she predicted. And Lou? Shit, man, they say when she left, you could see the life draining out of his face. And that was *before* he went off to the service. Who knows what happened to him in the war?"

"Damn. I knew he got dumped, but damn."

"And that's all I know about that. Like I said, I didn't meet Lou till later, till after Gene had him working over there. I known 'em both going on fifty years, and I can tell you, too, don't take it personally with Gene. You saw him yelling at me. He gets like that over Lou. I guess you can't blame him when you figure he lost his other brother, too."

"What other brother?"

"I thought you knew. Between your old man and Lou, I thought you knew. Lou's the youngest, Gene's the middle one, and the oldest was Tommy. He died when they were kids, right back there in the railyard. Killed himself, allegedly. The cops found him with a bullet in his head, the gun in his hand. I think he was twenty years old."

"Jesus," I whisper, thinking of that family portrait on the dresser, revising who was who. "Lou must've been about ten."

Haley lifts his floppy cap, scratches the sparse gray fuzz atop his head. "I could tell you some stories about Tommy, but that's another talk for another time. And right now I gotta work. So good luck, Sherlock," he says, and heads to the door with a laugh. "You let me know how your fishing goes."

I stand there alone for a moment, in no hurry to walk over to Marchicomo's, and end up gazing skyward to the nearest big empty. OTTO MILK CO. reads the fading sign painted on its brick skin. Just below the sign, on the corner of the side wall and façade, a mason-made bird perches with spread wings. The old-timers will tell you it's a phoenix, a remnant of when the building housed the Phoenix Brewery back in the 1800s. Before it became Otto Milk in the days when the stuff was delivered to doorsteps in bottles, before the company went broke and the plant shut down. History upon history in these back streets, there's no escaping it.

A muffler backfires then, jolting the morning calm. The culprit, a putty-spackled orange Datsun, appears on Smallman. It U-turns onto a gravel patch at the bottom of the Otto building and sputters to rest. The door grinds open, and who should emerge but Genevieve in a short black skirt and shiny purple shirt.

She approaches, heels clickclocking as usual, and stops when she sees me. "It's not mine," she blurts. "Just borrowed till I get my Firebird from the shop."

"So what if it's yours? That CMU tuition can't be cheap."

"You have no idea," she says as we head toward Marchicomo's together.

Three blocks stretched longer by silence. "Awkward" isn't the word for it so much as "guarded." We've never been friendly, but we've settled into roles and a routine: I start nice, she belittles me, we skirmish, and she softens it with enough contrition that I'll come back for more. And she knows I'll always come back because I've wanted her since we locked stares among the wicker. What do I get out of this? Not much, but I guess when you're broke you take the attention of attractive women wherever you get it, even if it feels like a paper cut to your pride.

So now we're walking, she's waiting, and I begin with a compliment. "You look less bruised today," I say. And it's true. The mark on her cheek has turned yellowish, no longer caked with makeup.

"Is that supposed to be a joke?"

"No. Try genuine concern. I don't like seeing you with a black eye. And I would've told you so last week given the chance."

"You have no reason to care, and whatever bumps and scrapes I get, there's nothing you could do about it anyway."

"You don't know that. Tell me what happened, and I'll tell you what I can and can't do."

"I'm trying to help you, believe it or not. I'm flattered that you like my unblemished looks. Thanks. You're not so bad-looking yourself. But that's it. That's as far as we go."

"So if somebody walked up to you right now and punched you in the face, I shouldn't care?"

"What, you thinking of trying it?"

"Oh, and *I'm* the defensive one? I ask if you're okay, and you ask if I want to hit you. Think about that for a second."

Back to silence as we draw closer to work, coming up on the

corner of Twenty-first with St. Stanislaus and its cross-topped turrets. I sneak a look over at Gen, who seems rattled off her confidence. A slouch has crept into her posture, her eyes are downcast. As she grips her purse strap, I notice something wrong with her hand, too. A discoloration between her thumb and index finger.

I stop, and before she can react, I grab that hand and slide back her cuff, enough to expose a flesh-colored bandage wrapped from wrist to forearm. She lets me hold it up, this brazen proof of pain, then jerks free and points into my chest.

"Quit it, okay? Just quit. You can't know me, Dexter. I know that sounds silly, but you can't. Do you think I like acting like this? I'm not such a bitch, you know, and I get sick of having to be one. But I have to protect myself."

"From what?"

"Letting you in. Hurting you. I don't need another wounded boy on my conscience."

"You're talking in riddles, Gen. And besides, you shouldn't worry about hurting me. Not when you've been looking so roughed-up lately."

"I'll say this one last time: there's nothing for you to worry about, and nothing you could do. Know your place. Back in the cage with the apes, sorting onions."

"For somebody who doesn't like being a bitch, it sure comes easy to you."

"Look, asshole, you just saw me in my shitty-ass car. What more do you want?" she says with venom, enough to hold me there while she walks the last block alone.

The day goes like they all go. No end to the fifty-pound sacks of onions—red, white, yellow, Vidalia—piled up on pallets in the back of the warehouse, smelly in different stages of rot. Carry to the table, slit the mesh. Dump, sort, bag, weigh. Poke airholes in the plastic, stock, and restock. Wipe hands with crusty rag every so often, knowing it'll take a long soak in lemon juice to get rid of the stink. Nothing else, not even grit soap, seems able to fight those onion oils.

D.T. works a crate of brussels sprouts, peeling off the yellow leaves, dropping the manicured buds into a Styrofoam carton at a hopped-up pace. The old bone-thin soldier just doesn't quit; he's like the conscience of the place in a way. Quiet and always working, a model machine if you can overlook his constant coffee and smokes.

I like D.T. for not abusing his authority. It's understood that he's the foreman, and he rarely resorts to screaming. As far as I know, he's never ratted anyone out to Sal, and he's cool enough to let everybody screw around within limits. Like how he happens to not notice Jerillo picking up a sprout and chucking it at Dockerty, who flinches as the missile grazes his head.

Then all four of us flinch when Sal comes charging in through the plastic flaps that curtain off the doorway to the store. "Where is that fuckin' imbecile?" he says, and we all relax a little, knowing he's looking for Ross. Sal doesn't wait for an answer and barges into the cooler, throwing open more plastic flaps. Poor blindsided Ross can't even say hi before the tirade starts.

So Sal reams Ross for his latest fuckup. Dockerty carries another box to the garbage bin, due for another trip to the Mauler. "Gimme Shelter" plays on the radio. The Stones after Zeppelin after Floyd after The Who. Great bands trapped in the grind of the classic-rock format, their most famous songs worn down by an endless repetition fitting for a place like Marchicomo's.

Between New York and Gen, I have enough distractions to

pass the hours anyway. More than once I review the morning's run-in, and I keep wondering what I might find if I followed Gen home. Of course it's a bad idea. But it's also tempting because as harsh as she gets, there's always gamesmanship in her put-downs, a dare in "you can't know me," a tease in "there's nothing you could do." And her flash of anger? That was the first naked feeling she's shown. If it was supposed to push me away, it did the opposite. Now I only want more of her, to expose another piece of her real self, and the least I'll settle for is seeing her exist away from this place.

I bail a few minutes before closing time, then, absorbing unhappy glances from D.T. and the rest. Oh, well; I'll deal with it tomorrow. What's important now is getting to Judd's car before Gen gets to hers, and it looks like I've made it. The Datsun remains where it was this morning, and I have time enough to sit and wait in the Corolla, watching Gen as she walks past.

She pulls onto Smallman, and I roll out after her. Keeping up won't be the challenge, but keeping a safe distance will be. The trick is giving her enough space so she won't suspect she's being followed, but not enough to lose her. And it's harder than it sounds, I realize, as the cross streets tick down from the twenties to the teens. She hooks a left onto Eleventh, skirting the construction zone where they're building a new convention center, passing the dreaded Greyhound station, then turns right onto Liberty.

Now we're Downtown, heading toward the tip of the triangular land wedge, that point where the Allegheny (to our right) and the Mon (to our left) converge to form the Ohio. Liberty cuts a diagonal path across the wedge, a borderline between two street grids that meet on a slant. If you look at a map, you'll see a slender grid along the Allegheny, the grid of the Strip with its east-west avenues and numbered north-south cross streets. The other grid, larger and less constricted, fills the majority of the wedge, from Liberty to the Mon; its east-west avenues are numbered, the north-south streets aren't.

It's like two different guys designed two different grids for Downtown, neither aware of the other till their construction crews ran into each other. Then, with no room to adjust his plans, each guy shrugged, rolled up his blueprint, and walked away whistling. These mismatched grids are just the kind of quirk that drive out-of-towners nuts. Even if you're a local, navigating Pittsburgh can be pretty arcane. But Gen continues right on ahead like she knows where she's going, unfazed by all the streets crossing Liberty from both sides at odd angles.

We clear the packed Downtown blocks, nearing the Point (Point State Park, officially), the green space at the tip of the tri-angle. The Point has the big fountain you see whenever Pittsburgh ends up on TV. This mini-geyser marks where the three rivers meet, a confluence considered the gateway to the West since the French and Indian War. (Lewis and Clark also launched their ex-pedition right near the Point, for what it's worth.) Liberty veers south short of the Point and ramps up onto the Fort Pitt Bridge. Another nightmare for visitors, Fort Pitt offers a brief span of cut-throat merging before its lanes split. The left enter a tunnel, the right branch off to run alongside the rivers.

Gen takes the tunnel, and we come out on the parkway. She tries to speed up to match the rush-hour traffic, punishing the Datsun's wheezy engine. Everybody passes her anyway, forcing me to hang back and ignore the cars and SUVs tailgating me while I maintain the gap.

We hold this pattern for about ten miles till she exits onto a four-lane road called Washington Pike, still bearing southwest. The city lies far behind us now, gone for shopping centers with names like Great Southern or Chartiers Valley. Land-hogs blobbing into each other, wallowing in a sprawl of asphalt, their overbloated units branded with light-up signage. Kmart, Sears, Home Depot, Office Max, JCPenney for boredom; Wendy's, Taco Bell, Pizza Hut, Krispy Kreme for gorging, the choice is yours.

I follow Gen into the Chartiers Valley lot, parking far enough away to stay unnoticed. At first she seems to be going to the Giant Eagle, most likely for groceries, but instead walks into the neighboring Petey's Cove. Which is odd, since Petey's Cove is a "family fun" restaurant, one of those kids' joints with an arcade, robotic puppet shows, and pizza that tastes like cardboard.

I give her time, trying to guess what she'd want from such a place, and only now does it occur to me that I'm stalking her. The funny thing is, I don't really care. After how she's talked to me, *What are you good for? Nothing you could do. There's always the trash. Know your place,* and led me all the way out here to the fiefdom of freakin' Bridgeville, I want a payoff. Something I could use for the next run-in, like a glimpse of whoever's been roughing her up.

But so far nothing. More time passes, enough that I finally throw open the door and head for Petey's Cove, fresh out of patience.

The place has an arcade and dining area on opposite sides of a central hallway. Thinking that Gen might have come here for a kid's birthday, I try the dining area first. Sure enough, there's a party going on. A bunch of kindergarten-age kids scream and carry on over gnawed, rejected pizza crusts while the birthday girl rips open another gift to join her stack of Bratz stuff. A woman who's most likely the mom paces around the table, talking to someone on her cell phone, and a waitress comes by to take away some plates. The only open stage is dark and crowded with robotic puppets. Lulu the pelican, Blip-Blip the barnacle, Ollie Oyster, and Petey Parrot, finished with their canned jokes and songs for now, silent and staring at nothing with golfball-sized eyes.

I cross the hall and try the arcade. Ski-ball lanes, banks of crane games and Whac-A-Mole tables, a ball pit called the Treasure Trove. Loud kids jump into the pit, burying themselves, tackling each other, gunning the yellow balls at each other's heads. ("Remember, kiddies," Petey says in a sign posted on the Trove, "DON'T throw the bullion!" He even points a wing at you, trying to look all tough in his eye patch and tricornered hat.) Video games take up the rest of the space, junior high and high school boys slouching over the screens and causing explosions, car crashes, gunshots, and every other kind of computerized mayhem. All this and still no Gen.

Baffled and resigned to having blown it, I drop a few quarters on the Marvel Heroes Vs. Heroes game. It's a shame DC never made one of these; I'd spend good money being Batman and kicking Superman's smug, self-righteous ass. But as it is, there's still fun to be had being Spider-Man, taking on Captain America. Beating the crap out of Cap, showing him up for the lame clown Axl Rose always said he was.

The kids in the Trove erupt with more noise, then come hurrying out and brushing past me while I play. I glance over to see them rush a live, in-person version of Petey's sidekick Scurvy. Even by cartoon-character standards, Scurvy is a misconceived mess. For starters, he's purple, fuzzy, and named after a disease. Clothes-wise he always wears a derby and baggy pants like a cut-rate Charlie Chaplin. And his face, with its bugged-out eyes and gaping toothless grin, is a picture of dementia.

The kids swarm him anyway, grabbing for his hands, hugging his legs. They even laugh when he does a series of stagey gestures: snapping his suspenders, flicking the brim of his hat, rocking back and forth on his heels. And so Scurvy performs while I,

Spider-Man, advance to a scrap with the Hulk. Ducking his fists, dodging his earthshaking stomps, getting boxed in by the big green lug.

My focus slips away from the game. Something seems wrong in the room; I'm feeling a hostile vibe. When I look away from the screen, I catch Scurvy staring at me. The little kids have moved on to other amusements, leaving him to stand there alone. I return his stare and can't return to the game. My hands freeze on the controls, and I abandon Spidey to a certain pummelling.

You could call this a standoff, then. Me and Scurvy locked in on each other, neither daring to move.

I'm trying to think of something to say. Something witty, something to ease the tension, but I never get a chance. A junior high boy leaves his video game and takes a run at Scurvy, spearing him right in the gut with a flying tackle. Scurvy lands with a thud. Two other boys join the fun, whooing and whooping.

The kid who threw the tackle, a stocky freckle-face, gets up and stands over Scurvy. "Suck it, you purple faggot," he says, crossing his hands over his crotch and thrusting it toward Scurvy's face. A taunt learned from pro wrestling. Then he and his buddies break for the front exit, red-faced and laughing.

Scurvy lies on the floor, clutching his gut. A few stunned kids linger around him, and at least one little girl runs off crying for mommy. As I walk over, he sits up with a grunt and rips off his own head to reveal Gen. She throws the plastic globe of a mask aside, derby and all, and looks up at me.

Her face is anger laced with pain. A hard-set jaw, eyes glaring but hurt. I hold out my hand to her, and she takes it.

We sit down at a sports bar in the shopping center, a place called Alley-Oops. It's bland and crammed with the typical trappings:

160

pool tables, electronic dartboards, three big screens each tuned to a different ESPN. A dry-erase board by the door hypes Happy Hour, ninety-nine-cent baskets of wings, the Monday-night WWF wrestling special. The two bartenders, guy and girl, wear green polo shirts embroidered with an interlocking AO logo. Neither seems happy, and the guy's been shooting me peeved looks since I ordered nothing but water.

Maybe they're hurting for tips. Aside from me and Gen, the place is almost empty. A few scattered gray middle-agers sip at their foam and pretend to watch the TVs, though I keep catching them ogling Gen with the desperate glint guys get when they know they're going home alone. Over at the tables, there's a group in their twenties, four beefy guys in black T-shirts and jean shorts and ball caps. They're louder than the Metallica on the jukebox, calling each other "bitch" and "fag," trying to impress the drunk fake blonde among them.

"You don't drink?" Gen says as her Yuengling arrives, her first words since we left Petey's Cove.

"I got nothing against it. I just need to be sober."

"For what? How can you live in Pittsburgh and not drink?"

Job 1, I want to say. You can't afford to get drunk or even tipsy. You stay sober, alert, and ready because they're always out there, the fuckers still waiting for their chance. "I don't know, but I've managed."

"Yeah, and you managed to stalk me all the way out here. Are you proud of that?"

"Not really, but I don't regret it. You baited me into it."

"So what do you want, then?"

"Respect. For you to admit you're no better than me."

"Okay, fine. I'm no better than you. But I did go to CMU. For a semester, fourteen years ago. And I never went back.

161

"What happened was I ran up some credit cards, which led to some legal problems I don't like to talk about. Then my brother's leukemia got worse, and the hospital bills got bigger. So I dropped out to work, and that's all I've been doing ever since. Working, taking care of my brother and my dad, whose health isn't so stellar anymore, either."

"You never got a degree anywhere else?"

"Dexter, you can't tell Sal. I need that job, at least for now."

"Of course I won't. But that's a tough spot you're in."

"That's life," she says, and takes a swig.

"So if you did your semester fourteen years ago, you're now, what, thirty? Thirty-one?"

"Something like that. Why?"

"You said you came up with thirty-one failure types, which struck me as odd at the time. But now I'm starting to think you make up a new one every year, like some kind of twisted birthday gift to yourself."

"You're perceptive. But you're not—you are *not*—going to get me to say I'm a failure. Okay, so I work at Marchicomo's, and yeah, I dance around in a funny costume at a pizza joint. And maybe I blew my shot at going to a good school, maybe I'm in a world of debt, and maybe I got caught shoplifting once or twice. But I'm still fighting for a worthwhile life. I still have my brains. I still have my looks, enough of them. And I still have time to find something better. Not much time, but some. So I use what I have. What else am I supposed to do?"

She finishes the bottle, sets it on the bar. The guy in the green polo swipes it and gives her another. Then he looks at me and says, "You okay, Aqua-Man?"

I give him a go-to-hell smile, enough edge on it to send him away. "See, this is why I don't go out in public," I say to Gen.

"Everybody's a wise guy. Everybody's a smart-ass. Always cracking jokes, trying to be funny when they're not. It's boring, it's depressing."

"What *is* your story anyway?" she says.

"It's boring and depressing."

"No, really. I know you don't belong at Marchicomo's any more than I do. So what are you doing there? I told you my excuse."

"Yeah, but see, mine involves these four guys kind of jumping me. Doing a number on me as it were, and so I kind of crawled into a cave to lick my wounds but ended up hibernating. For eight years, more or less, and now I feel like I just woke up."

"I thought *I* talked in riddles. And this thing, whatever it was, happened eight years ago? You know, it might be time to—"

"Get over it. I know. I'm trying to do that, Gen, I really am. I don't sit around brooding. I keep busy. In fact, I'm working on a major project as we speak. Right now I'm trying to figure out how to get to New York for a weekend."

"Oh, yeah? What're you up to?"

"I'm looking for Mercy Carnahan."

Gen blinks, waits for a punch line that never comes. Then says, "You're not kidding."

"You know the Kashon warehouse over on Smallman? One of the Kashon brothers was engaged to her before she was famous, and she dumped him for no reason. Now he's sick with cancer, and he wants to talk to her again before he dies. And he asked me to find her."

"Why you?"

"Lou knows my dad, and my dad told him I'm struggling to get a foothold. I guess Lou thinks he's doing me a favor by offering me this job. And he believes in me. He thinks I can do it."

"This sick old man is paying you for this? You don't feel like you're scamming him?"

"Hell no. First of all, he hasn't paid me yet. Second, I'm making an honest effort. And you know what else? I'm gonna find her, Gen. I'm gonna do what nobody else has done. What people have been trying to do for fifty years. I am going to find Mercy Carnahan. How's that for ambition?"

Gen smiles. For the first time today; maybe her first real smile since I've met her. And we let ourselves look at each other. No words, just a shared silence. Then each to their drink, and I'm scrambling, wondering if I just missed a chance at something.

"And you think you'll find her in New York?"

"I don't know yet. But I gotta go up there to see some guy who claims he has an 'exclusive artifact' I can't find anywhere else. It might help, it might not."

"Well, you'll have to tell me all about it when you come back."

Another silence. Now I know the chance I missed, and this time I take it. "Why don't you come with me?"

"Sounds fun, but I can't afford it."

"Neither can I, so we'll split the costs."

"And that's why you asked me?"

"Not the only reason. I asked because I want you to go. Look, I'll go alone if I have to, but I don't want to. And if I could pick someone to go with me, I'd pick someone who's smart, strong, and hot. That means you."

She searches my eyes and says, "I have to get back. The kids need their punching bag." As she moves to leave, I feel her bandaged touch on my arm. Down it slides, down to my wrist, and she whispers, "I'll sleep on it."

A squeeze, and off she goes.

The bartender takes her bills and empty bottle. The group at the table gets louder and drunker as the blonde screeches along to Limp Bizkit or Korn or Linkin Park blaring from the jukebox. And with Gen gone, the gray middle-agers have nothing to look at but the TVs, a nonstop barrage of sweaty athletes in their prime.

13

Alley-Oops happened on a Monday night, and by Friday morning I'm waiting in the Greyhound station. The New York bus won't leave for another hour, but a line has already formed to the door. Ahead of me, an exhausted mom tries to separate her two brat-boys, who keep fighting over a handheld video game. Behind me, a college-age couple with backpacks prattle on about their wonderful hiking trips in South America and Europe. Off to the side, a ragged old woman paces the line, seeking eye contact while she rants about a mansion where the floors were gold, the doorknobs were diamonds, and the pillows were stuffed with shredded cash.

Back and forth she goes, dragging a plastic bag full of clothes, limping in shoes held together with duct tape, her silver wig slipped off-center but held on with a ribbon tied around her head. And the longer she has to wait, the louder she gets, her voice boiling up to a shout. The rest of us sneak looks as she passes and look away before she catches us, and I suspect we're all thinking the same ugly thoughts: Please don't let me be the one she approaches. Keep walking, crazy lady. Go away, way far away.

Even so, I can't fault her for wanting to leave. The station's a relic of the '60s, a throwback to a gee-whiz Space Age that petered out by the '70s. Walls clad in dull green tile, embedded with the occasional stainless-steel text. SNACKS over the vending machines. RESTROOMS over the restrooms. INFORMATION over the information desk. Whooshing sliding doors with arrival/departure marquees missing numbers and letters, communicating nothing but neglect. Banks of coin-operated TVs defunct for decades, now serving as a stopover for a homeless guy shaking a cupful of change. And any hotshot architect who thinks a slick, modern space improves our lives should see the people stuck working here, like the rough-voiced redhead at the info desk or the elderly guy hobbling around with a broom and dustpan, laboring with looks of beaten-down defeat.

On top of all that, I have my own personal reason for hating this place: it's where I last saw Erin. Our sophomore year had just ended, and so did we, though neither of us would admit it yet. She was going to New York to spend the summer with some friends. I was supposed to go, too, but had another spinaround the week before.

It was the second one Erin witnessed. Both happened in her dorm room, both during sex. The first hit that winter. At the time I didn't realize how tough it must've been for her to see me freaking out, and I was too embarrassed to be anything but defensive. Afterward she tried to get me to talk about it, and I stonewalled her. Stopped all her shots, and years later, what's left but a collection of echoing phrases:

What happened to you? This isn't okay. This isn't normal. Why can't you tell me what's wrong? You can't go through life like this, always so close to a breakdown. You need help. If you can't tell me, then you'd better tell someone. You know they have counseling on campus.

That last one caused some trouble when I said, "No way. I'm not going to therapy. I won't sit in a room with someone who couldn't care less, whining and bitching about my problems. That's for women, all that constant talking about feelings. Men don't do that shit."

"What?! Since when have you become so macho? Tell me, what's the manly solution to debilitating trauma?"

"Jesus, you make it sound like I'm crippled. It's no big deal. Something bad happened, and I don't like to discuss it. I don't think I owe you or anyone else a detailed account of my lowest moment. And to answer your question, you suck it up. You be a man. You stop talking and thinking, and you *do* something to keep yourself busy."

"And resort to clichés," she said.

The second one hit around finals time. Though she tried to hide it, she was more bothered than shocked, more spent than sympathetic. For months she'd hyped our summer in New York, saying I needed a change of scene. To get out of stifling Pittsburgh for a while, meet some new people, experience a new place. But after I ended up on the floor again, dizzy and scratching my face, Erin didn't argue so much when I said she'd have more fun without me.

So here we were, waiting in line at this very same door for all I know. We'd hardly spoken since I'd picked her up, and with every quiet minute I felt a little more sick inside. Like everything good was dying, and I was powerless to stop it, too weak to mutter a word of protest. When the door opened and the line started to move, I reached for her hand.

She stiffened and said, "Are you okay?"

"No," I said, and damn it if I wasn't choking up right there in public. "I love you."

168

"I love you, too. But I can't help you if you don't help yourself. You have to decide what's more important: me or your secrets. I hope you pick me." She tried to smile, though her voice and brown eyes wanted to cry. Before I was ready for it, she kissed me. And before I could give her one of my own, she'd stepped away to keep up with the crowd. Then she was gone, and that was all.

Someone brushes against my arm, and I look over to see Gen standing there in her sunglasses. She surveys the station with in-difference, turns to me, and says nothing. Which I guess is her way of saying hi.

"What did you tell Sal?" I ask.

"Don't worry about Sal. He's old, he's soft. Doesn't matter what I told him." She hands me some papers. "The hotel. Taken care of."

"You get shit done, Gen. I admire that."

"You should," she says, and pokes a straw through the lid of an iced mocha.

The crazy lady stops in mid-rant and mid-limp, stares right at Gen, who's sucking on the straw. Gen meets her stare and lowers the drink. For a moment they're frozen. Then Gen takes off her glasses and says, "What?"

The crazy lady blinks. Her mouth twitches to a smile, though her voice drops to a hurt murmur. "Don't be hating, sister. Just thought you was someone else. That's all." She resumes her march and recovers her volume, back to the mansion with the golden floors.

"I hate this place," Gen says. "It reminds me of the first time I ran away from home. I was fourteen. My boyfriend was thirty. The cops caught us waiting for a bus to Florida. Denny had pot and coke on him, and it was not pretty when that K-9 sniffed him out."

She puts her glasses back on, still watching the woman retreat. "The worst part is, she's probably right. She's been here every time I've been, probably saw that exact bust. You live anywhere long enough, you get saddled with ghosts, that's for sure."

After five hours of mountains, farmland, and forests, I think I've seen enough of Pennsylvania to get the idea. It's lush and green and a natural beauty, yes, and might spark some kind of spiritual awakening if you explored it on foot. But there's only so much you can see from the turnpike—so many horses and silos, so many rest stops and billboards—before boredom takes over and the bus becomes oppressive.

Gen has no trouble sleeping, but I'm all tensed-up nerves confined to a seat, waiting for something violent to happen. Much of this comes from a bearded guy who's blocking the aisle, resting his ass on an armrest a few rows ahead. He once had a seat but gave it up to an Asian teenage girl who boarded the bus after it was already full. The driver was about to kick the girl off, but the bearded guy got all chivalrous and insisted she take his seat, claiming he could sit on the armrest for the entire seven-hour trip to Philly, no problem.

After an hour, the beard decided he didn't like sitting on the armrest so much, and he's been bitching about it ever since. Worse yet, he's starting to get nasty toward the girl he'd supposedly helped.

"I pay ninety fuckin' bucks for a ticket, and they make me sit on the armrest. That's Greyhound for ya. When I get to Philly, I'm going right up to the manager's office with this fuckin' armrest, and I'm gonna slam it down on his desk and say, 'There. That's what I got for going Greyhound.' Christ, this thing's killing my back. Bruising my tailbone, too. You know what the technical name for the tailbone is, China doll? The cock-sex. You like cock-sex? I got big cock-sex. You wanna massage it for me?"

"Go sit on the toilet and shut the fuck up," somebody says.

Which quiets the beard, at least for a while. But once he stops, the guy right behind me starts again. All bulked up and wearing a wife beater and orange do-rag, the guy keeps calling people on his cell phone and cursing them out. Between calls he threatens his girlfriend, who's holding a baby and trying to lull it to sleep.

"Yo, what up?" the guy says to his phone. "Where you at? I'll be in Philly in two hours. Put my cousin on. Not Lonzell. *Liozell.*

"What? He's dead? What the fuck you mean, 'He's dead'?!"

My seat jerks forward. The baby starts to cry. Mom gets up and hurries for the bathroom.

"What, I embarrass you? Do I fuckin' embarrass you?" the guy shouts at her back.

Gen wakes up and looks around with a yawn. "So I've been thinking," she says. "I can't figure out whether your old friend's a senile romantic or a douche. I don't mean to be callous, but let's face it, we all get our hearts ripped out some time or another. You get over it. You move on. I just can't understand somebody who lets it ruin his life."

"He must be one of your failure-types. You got one for cancer patients?"

"Come on, don't get like that. I'm making a reasonable observation."

"Yeah, but it's always easy to tell someone else to get over it. I mean, how can we really know what happened between Lou and Mercy? Maybe they had a kind of love neither of us will ever have. Maybe she had a power over him that most women don't have over anyone. Or maybe he was never a stable guy to begin with, and the war really jacked him up. Who knows?"

171

"You're too charitable," Gen says. "I read up on this chick, and I'm not impressed. She was a farmgirl with a wackjob mom. Just another piece of hick trash who tramped herself out, got too big too fast, and went nuts seeing what she could get away with. It's an old story, as old as showbiz."

"And what makes you better than her? By the time she was your age, she'd made a fortune, walked off her job, and did whatever she wanted with her life. Kind of beats Marchicomo's and Petey's Cove, doesn't it?"

"Hey. I told you why I'm stuck."

"You think some credit card debt and hospital bills would've stopped Mercy Carnahan? You should love her; she was nothing if she wasn't ambitious. But instead you're jealous, I think."

"Listen to you! You sure *you're* not the one who loves her? Well, I've got some bad news for you, Dexter. She's old now. If she's still alive, she's in her seventies. She ain't hot no more."

"When it comes to her, I'm detached. She's an object to me. She's a car, and I'm the repo man."

"You are such a bad liar," Gen says with a laugh. "You should see your face when you talk about her. You want her as much as the old guy does. Seriously, if she still looked like she used to, can you tell me you wouldn't do her? If she laid herself out on a bed for you, in all her glamour-puss glory, and arched one of her little eyebrows, you wouldn't jump on her?"

"No. I'd walk away just to prove I could."

Gen searches my eyes, seeking a breach. Finding none, she says, "Boy, your exes must have some tales to tell."

"I don't have exes. Just souvenirs of somebody I let down."

"Just one girlfriend, at your age? Ouch. No wonder you relate to that old guy."

"Told you my story's boring and depressing."

"Well, then. If an opportunity came along to make your story less boring and depressing, would you recognize it? Would you know how to take it?"

"I think I'm doing that, Gen."

"I'm not talking about finding Mercy Carnahan."

"Neither am I."

Point taken, Gen reclines with a crooked smile. Within minutes she's sleeping again, and when her head rolls onto my shoulder, I don't bother to move her. Instead I relax just enough to breathe and ease into her touch.

Sleepy PA falls back for the Jersey Turnpike, its lanes racing with traffic. Swerving, weaving, cutting off, tailgating, horn-blaring, hordes of faceless drivers taking angry chances. Even in the bus I feel the stress, sense the approaching City. And when its skyline first appears—Empire State, Chrysler, Twin Towers instant and blunt—it still grabs me no matter how much I've seen it on TV. Familiar and alien at once, impossible to grasp: centuries of history, millions of lives and dreams among those close-packed buildings. The limits of what we've made with our hands and machines, the leading edge of how we live. It's all just a few miles ahead and closing fast, and all I can do is gawk.

More humbling, even, to step off the bus and into the crush. Luckily Gen has been here before and leads the way. Otherwise I'd wander around Times Square all night, overwhelmed with the spectacle of big ads. She keeps me on a straight line from bus station to N train, and I spend the ride in a minor stupor. Trying not to stare but still curious, still imagining where everybody else came from, listening to Spanish overlap German and Chinese and a dozen other languages, sneaking glances at people's faces. Realizing for the first time how small my town is, how I'd always considered myself a city boy till now, when I might as well be Dorothy in Oz.

Or better yet, Mercy in the '40s.

Don't ask how she tackled this place all by herself, because I couldn't tell you. As I sit there watching some kids break dancing in the aisle, one jumping up onto the seats and swinging around the poles like a gymnast while most everyone else strains to ignore him, I wonder how she did it. To be a teenage girl from Harmony, PA, throwing herself headlong into this craziness, it must've taken some guts. And to not just survive here, but do well enough to catapult herself across the country, that must've taken even more guts. More, I'll admit, than I'll ever have. So I guess I have to say this for her: whatever her faults, Mercy was no coward and no princess.

We step off at Broadway in Queens, walk the blocks to a Comfort-8 near Fourteenth Street. The check-in guy (name tag: ROCCO) gets pissy because we've interrupted a crucial Mets at-bat on his portable TV. Strike three, and Rocco shoves the paperwork and key at us like it's our fault.

The room is about what you'd expect from a place called Comfort-8. Lots of drab, from carpet to curtain to bedspread, but neither of us care. After eight hours on a Greyhound, no decor is prettier, and nothing feels better than bellyflopping onto the lumpy mattress.

Gen does just that, sprawling on the bed, while I go to the bathroom. Standing over the sink with a bottle of lemon juice smuggled from work, I soak my hands in the acid, letting it dissolve the onion oils in my skin. Substituting a bitter stink for a sour one, listening to the sounds of Gen on the other side of the door.

174

She stretches, letting out a groan that rises and blossoms to a yawn. Her clothes rustle off and land on the floor.

So here we are. I wanted this from the moment I saw her in the wicker-filled basement, kept at her till she agreed to be here, and now it's happening. The question is, can I hold it together? I did with Erin, back in the beginning *the sun the moon February snow* but then those last times *always so close to a breakdown*. Job 1, I think. As long as you remember Job 1, you should be okay.

When I come out, Gen's lying there in nothing but a lacy black bra and thong. The look on her face isn't exactly "Come hither," more like "Well, we both knew this was coming. Let's do it already." But the longer I challenge her stare, going on a full minute, maybe, the more something else creeps into her eyes. A growing suspicion that I'll end up hurting her just like all the rest, but a sad giving-in anyway. A settling for more hurt because it beats fading alone.

I take off my clothes *take 'em off you fuckin' faggot* cheering laughing yee-hawing, and stand naked before her. She looks me over, her gaze a video camera. "Not bad," she seems to think, "maybe good for a fuck after all." Moving toward her, remembering Job 1. Focus, don't go dizzy, focus. Don't let the screaming pussy cocksucker bitch voices throw you. Don't think about the clippers raking your scalp, the dog collar on your throat, the duct tape. Don't think, period, just block it out and fuck like everybody else.

We kiss, Gen tasting like tobacco. I unhook her bra, throw it wherever, and stroke her small breasts, pinching her nipples, licking them to hard little nubs. And so far so good. Judging by her hot short breaths, she has no idea what I'm fighting. No clue that poisonous memories are infecting my mind. That they *you know who I mean* made me wrap the same balls she's holding with duct tape and tear it off, ripping out the pubic hairs. No, she'd never guess,

175

and still we kiss while she puts on the rubber, neither knowing where the other's been.

Gen slides me in with a gasp, eyes closed like it hurts. Six years since Erin break away with every push, crumbling with every moan I coax out of Gen. Harder, faster, pushing to win for the times I lost. Pushing to get back to the sun the moon the snow downpouring outside.

"Oh, God, yes!" she whispers, the headboard thunking against the wall. "Oh, *yes!* Don't stop. Don't stop! Fuck me. Fuck me hard!"

My guard slips more the longer we go, jarred loose with our rhythm. The room begins to spin, my face starts to burn. But I don't stop, not with Gen writhing, her cum wetting my skin. I close my eyes to focus but find a world gone black and white. I'm back in the dingy office, bound to the chair, and there's Mercy. Slinking off the desk, out of shadows and into the light. As I keep pushing, Mercy. Erasing every trace of Erin, Mercy. Cupping my chin, lifting my face close to her breast.

"Say my name," Gen whispers. "Say my name!"

Go on, sweetie. Mercy drags a single finger across my cheek. The burning cools, the dizziness stops. *Tell her who you want.*

Nice try. You think I'd fall for that?

You've already fallen. I'm just making it feel good. She smiles, cocks an eyebrow. *Or am I just an object to you?*

I don't answer, and she doesn't seem to expect or want one. Still smiling, she stoops to kiss me, and I can't resist. I let go, gushing without touching her, high but unsatisfied as she vanishes. As she leaves me with Gen, who claws my back and shakes with a scream. Gen, whose name I remember on the last spurt.

We collapse in a sweaty heap, breathing as one till I pull out and lie beside her. Then we snuggle and kiss. And thank each other, say it was great, say we'll do it again. I can't speak for Gen; I don't know who she's thinking about or what she really feels. I only know that if fucking her means kissing Mercy again, then I'll fuck her again.

And again and again.

14

The next morning, we wake up, take our showers, and don't say much to each other. Call it an awkward vibe, but not a hostile one. My guess is, we're reorienting ourselves, trying to figure out what we are now. Friends? Boyfriend-girlfriend? Two confused people who don't know what they're doing? Neither of us wants to ask, so we leave the Comfort-8 skirting the issue.

Once we board the N train, Gen takes my hand and gives it a squeeze. I look at her, and she's smiling. Her sleepy green eyes search mine, and I can't help but smile back. And put aside whatever was in my head last night and enjoy being with her, just her and nobody else. If that doesn't clarify what we are, maybe it doesn't matter. It seems we've struck an unspoken deal to have fun now and worry later. Which works for me, considering the pressing business at hand as we get off at West Twenty-eighth and join the midtown crowd.

From what I've read and heard, these seven years of Giuliani have pretty much defanged Manhattan. Violent crime is way down from the '70s and '80s, largely because Rudy's running a police state. He chased the hookers and porn out of Times Square and replaced them with the more wholesome whoredom of Disney:

Beauty and the Beast and *The Lion King* playing a few blocks from each other, a big Disney store right in the heart, at Broadway and Seventh. Hell, my map even labels it as "Times [Disney] Square," and I don't think the mapmaker is being ironic. Meanwhile Bill Clinton's moving into Harlem. And the Lower East Side, once so dangerous the NYPD plowed a tank through it to squash a riot, is gentrifying into a hipster mecca. The kind of place where you need a trust fund to rent a room.

Even Rudy can't scrub and bleach every nook, though, and West Twenty-seventh somehow slipped his reach. From Broadway to Fifth, the block darkens in the shadows of its buildings. More than one storefront displays stockings and wigs, fake nails and fake eyelashes, and just when you start to think the block might be home to hookers, you run into the Sentinel Hotel. With its entire façade painted turquoise, and its name flashing in purple and green neon, the place might as well say "Hey, sailor" to all passersby.

"You sure you got the right address?" Gen says, unamused by the scenery.

I have no answer for her as we enter a building across from the Sentinel. In the vestibule there's a panel of door buzzers with a list of names and numbers. Gilbert Pollard at 22, as he said, and I don't even have to hit the buzzer; the security door's already open. The jamb's metal is bent around the hinges like someone pried it with a crowbar, and the busted lock emits a quiet, wounded drone.

The building itself might have been beautiful once, back when the tile floors—white patterned with black flowers—weren't stained with piss, and the ornate molding on the walls wasn't smothered under layers of gray paint, and the steps weren't crunchy with broken glass and dead roaches. If nothing else, me and Gen get a healthy whiff of pot-smoke on our climb to the fourth floor. And

179

overhear some blasting Latin hip-hop, a flamenco hybrid that hasn't made it to Pittsburgh yet and probably never will.

I knock on the door numbered 22. A series of locks and chains slide and click, and old Pollard shows us in. Upon seeing the guy, I want to apologize for having bothered him. He's bony and so badly hunched you can count his vertebrae by the bumps of his flannel robe. His face stretches tight against his skull, the skin as thin as wax paper. His arms seem to be stuck in piano-playing position, his hands limp and quivering. But he still has his wits and a rich, Shakespearian voice offering us tea or spirits, regretting the wretched state of his flat.

Gen takes him up on the tea, sending him off to his kitchenette.

I wouldn't call Pollard's little studio "wretched," at least not compared to Lou's place, but it is dark. You'd never know the sun was shining outside, as neighboring buildings block out the natural light. There's little in the way of furniture, just a recliner draped with an afghan, the edges of its armrests fraying. No sofa or sign of a bed. A combination radio–record player collects dust in the near corner, flanked by stacks of albums with the Philharmonic, Gershwin, and Jolson on top. Bookshelves tower around the recliner, tilting and bowed with the weight of so much paper. Alone in its own little space, a film projector sits upon a nightstand. At first I figure it's a nonfunctioning antique, but there's also a screen nailed to the opposite wall. So who knows. Maybe Pollard gets all nostalgic watching newsreels from the 1930s or something.

Framed black-and-white photos fill the rest of the wall space, the same youngish guy appearing in almost every shot. This was our host, I guess, as a steamboat captain. As a migrant farmworker. As a zoot-suit-wearing gangster, as the Mad Hatter. A playbill for *The Crimson Kiss* hangs among the photos, including a picture of Pollard laughing with Mercy, their arms slung around each other like the best of pals.

"So, what was she like?" I ask when he returns with Gen's tea.

"Agnes? She was wonderful. A lovely, gracious woman alive with passion, intelligence. Yet she was humble, not at all like the demon-witch she played in all those silly movies. No, she was quite the opposite, actually. Far from the madding crowd, she was a vulnerable soul rife with insecurities and torment."

"Did she ever talk about her time in Pittsburgh, when she was going to school?"

"No, I'm afraid not. She never discussed the past. Never talked about her family or love life. She was guarded in that sense. Extremely guarded at times."

"She had a love life then?"

Gen chuckles, seating herself in the recliner. "What does that have to do with anything?"

"If she was going through a rough time with something personal, like her love life, it might help to explain why she bailed on *The Crimson Kiss*. Right, Mr. Pollard?"

"I assure you, I never knew why she abandoned the production, and I still don't. She did express concerns with the script before the debut. Some minor quibbles, perhaps, but she gave no indication that she would walk out as she did. None whatsoever."

"Do you have any idea where she went? Or whether she's alive?"

Pollard grins with his liver-colored lips. "I appreciate your forthrightness. Unfortunately, I know nothing of her whereabouts. Nor do I have the luxury of pondering them. As you can see, I am living in rather reduced circumstances, which in turn brings us to the delicate matter of the artifact. Or, namely, remuneration for your chance to see it."

"Excuse me?" Gen says. "You want to get paid? For what?"

"I understand your trepidation, my dear, but this is Manhattan. The rent is our bogeyman, and a tenacious one at that."

"Fair enough. What is it, and what are you charging?" I ask.

"A film," Pollard says, and gestures to the projector. "And I promise you'll never see it anywhere else. I possess the only existing print, for I personally confiscated it from its creator. The deviant carved a concealed hole in the wall of Agnes's dressing room, positioned a camera in the opening, and captured her shortly after the final rehearsal for *The Crimson Kiss*. The result is silent and brief, only three to four minutes, but it does give you a glimpse of her in a rare, unguarded moment. Would you like to see it?"

"What did Agnes think of this little movie?" Gen says.

"I never told her about it. Prudence dictated as much, for she was so very distraught at the time it was filmed. Upon discovering her voyeur, I immediately seized the film and ejected him from the premises. Then of course Agnes herself left soon thereafter, never to return."

"Well. It's a good thing you kept a piece of her."

"The current rate for a single viewing is one hundred dollars," Pollard says, ignoring Gen or not hearing her. "I'll accept nothing but cash. There are several automated tellers on the block if you need to step out."

Fine. If that's how he wants to play, fine. I kneel down, take off my shoe, and dump out a hundred-dollar bill. It's the one Lou gave me that day at Biggies, stashed underfoot in case of disaster. Gen watches me acting all casual as I hand it to Pollard, who brightens at the sight of his contemporary, Ben Franklin.

"You won't be disappointed," he says, and totters off to a closet between the kitchenette and bathroom, disappearing into a deeper darkness. From there comes the sound of a combination lock, its dial spinning, latch clicking. While Pollard tends to his safe, I face Gen and her stare.

"Hey, it's your money," she says, and rolls her eyes away, sipping her tea.

Pollard emerges from the closet holding a puck-sized reel. He loads the film and dims the overhead light. The projector whirs and throws its glow onto the screen.

After some blurry confusion, the camera settles and focuses on a desk mounted with an oval mirror. Brass ivy frames the glass. Hairbrushes and makeup clutter the desktop, along with a torn envelope and folded letter.

Mercy enters the shot, seats herself before the mirror. She's wearing a black dress, which matches her eyelids, lips, and hair. Her face, powdered with stage makeup, looks even paler than usual. The camera's position gives you her reflection, and you can see she's upset about something. This isn't the cool man-eater of the movies. She looks tired and worried.

It reminds me of the time I stopwatched her on the Wall. How I found that sliver of Time where she'd slipped out of character, then slipped right back in. But now there is no character. Now I'm seeing her real self, and I'm starting to feel a weird kind of guilt, like I'm violating her somehow. And yet I can't look away.

Mercy picks up the letter, reads it, turns it over. A splotch marks the top of the page, a small drawing or picture I can't make out. She slaps it down, glances at her reflection. Grabs up the paper again and rereads it, eyes racing over the text.

She takes a pen and tablet from a drawer and writes a letter of her own. Scribbling across the page, hand manic but still lagging behind her mind. Impatience creeps into her face, rises to anger, and down goes the pen. She crumples the paper and throws it aside.

183

Another try. Again she scribbles lines, but then doesn't write so much as slash at the page, and stops again. Crumples the paper and throws it aside.

She's edging beyond anger. In her short breaths, skittering eyes, and scowl that makes her nostril twitch, she teeters. Like a disturbed person one itch away from exploding.

But she tries yet again. Picks up the pen, starts to write, but can barely eke out a line. She runs her hands through her hair, covers her face. Convulses with sobs. Then lowers her hands to reveal tears and melting makeup.

Her eyes meet their reflection, and there's your itch. For she clenches her jaw, pulls back, and punches the glass. Rams her fist right in her own face.

The glass cracks. She hits it, and hits it, and hits it till shards land on the desk. Then clutches her face and rakes her flesh, scratching down to her throat, down to her chest and breasts, clawing at herself like she wants to rip open her entire being.

About half the mirror remains in its frame, enough to show her face smeared with blood from her gashed hand. Blood glistening black upon her failing mask. Now she looks upon herself—a shattered, ruined beauty—and appears content with the sight. She doesn't wipe away the coagulating blood and tears and makeup. Instead she looks relieved, maybe amused. And as the film flickers out, she even seems to smile.

I don't know what I just saw, but it gouged out a piece of me. Right out of my gut, left me feeling a noxious mix of sad and sick. Worse yet, I'm even more curious now because something in that footage tripped a wire in my brain. My eyes detected something besides her breakdown, something that wants to connect to another image I've seen. But I'll be damned if I can figure it out yet.

Pollard turns off the projector, turns on the overhead light. Gen leaves the recliner to stand by me.

"I need to see it again," I tell her.

"Then talk to him. I'll see what I can do," she whispers, and heads for the kitchenette with her empty cup. Pollard tries to object, but she eases past him with a smile and a thanks.

He looks at me with a giddy twinkle in his eyes. "Worth your while, yes? Will it help with your research project?"

"Maybe. What was she reading, do you know?"

"No, I'm afraid not. As I recall, a number of us heard the breakage and rushed to her door. I led the charge and observed the deviant fleeing the scene, so it fell to me to accost him while the others attended to Agnes. She had cleared the desk and cleaned her face before allowing anyone to enter. As far as we knew, she'd simply had an accident. She said she'd stumbled and clumsily reached for the mirror to steady herself."

"And then she left."

"The following night." Pollard totters toward me, licks his liver-colored lips, his breath smelling like sour milk. "You have been to the Colonial, haven't you? Why, you should go while you're in town. They've kept her room just as she left it."

"Why?"

"It began as a bit of gallows humor, a perverse good-luck charm for the Colonial's next production. With a run of success and time and Agnes's continuing popularity, the room became a fixture, a superstition no one wanted to disrupt. Even the theater's most base, philistine owners have upheld the tradition. Thus it stands, an enduring portal to the past, a hidden gem of Gotham."

"No kidding. Guess I should check it out."

"And on that note, it's time for us to go," Gen says, barging in between me and the old man. "Mr. Pollard, you were a superb

185

host, and I thank you for having us. I wish we could stay longer, but we have many more interviews to conduct. Take care, sir. It was our pleasure, truly it was."

She kisses him on the cheek and walks right out the door. Pollard stands there red-faced and flustered, while I'm torn between chasing her and being polite.

"So, uh, thanks, like she said. I guess, yeah, we should get going. I'm sure you're tired of talking about Mercy. I bet you'd be happy to never mention her again."

"Oh, not at all! Not at all! It's no bother. If it weren't for her, no one would call on me at all, I'm afraid. For that I resent her, I protect her, and by God I still love her. I don't know what became of her, but for her sake, I hope she's dead. I would rather she decay to dust than become another walking corpse, like so many left in her wake."

With that, we shake hands. His clammy palm squishes against mine, seeps a moist chill into my skin. While little beads of phlegm ooze in the ridges of his lips.

Gen must've really booked out of there. She's not in the hall, the stairs, or even at the front door. When I step outside, she's waiting all the way at the corner, giving me a look that says, "You coming or what?" Then she starts away so fast, I have to jog to catch up to her.

"He didn't notice, did he?" she says as we head north toward the Empire State Building.

"Notice what?"

Gen pulls the film reel from her purse and tries to hand it to me. I stop right in the middle of the sidewalk and get jostled by the surrounding crowd. She never pauses, and again I hurry to keep up.

"What the fuck, Gen?! You can't do that! He'll call the cops!"

"Oh, listen to you. He won't call the cops. Nobody's supposed to have this, especially him. It's a peep show gone wrong, and I guarantee you he filmed it himself. Think about it. If Pollard caught the guy who filmed it just as he filmed it, then who got the film developed? And when Pollard saw what was on the film, why didn't he destroy it? Because it's his; he made it by himself, for himself. And now he needs to pimp it to pay the rent. Fuck him. That repulsive old creep's been making money off your girl's misery forever. Serves him right that I took it."

"After drinking his tea and kissing him, even."

"What did you *think* I meant when I told you to stall him? Do you want to find this chick or not?"

"Yeah, but did you really have to steal the thing?"

Gen lets out a frustrated grunt, stopping our walk on a Broadway block crammed with jewelers and silver-dealers. "I didn't steal it; I appropriated it for the greater good. You said you wanted to see it again. Were you going to pay him another hundred bucks?"

"No, but—"

"Then take it to somebody who converts eight-millimeter to digital and put it online. If she's alive, you'll hear from her lawyers. Then work from there. It's further than you'll get otherwise."

"So broadcasting her humiliation online, that's better than what Pollard did."

"Wake *up*! God, I could slap you! She doesn't *want* to be found, Dexter. You think you'll pull it off because you're such a nice guy? You gotta get some balls about this. You gotta play rough, fuck some shit up. Or do you want to go home and tell your sick old friend you came up with nothing?"

I don't answer her, trying to stay calm. Trying to deny that she might be right. And while I'm standing there like a fool, she walks to a mailbox. Opens the hatch and holds the film to the chute, one flinch from dropping it.

"No, don't!" I blurt. "Okay. You made your point."

Gen tosses the reel to me, smirking as I bobble it. Then takes her cigarettes out of her purse, lights one up. "If you're going to that theater, I'm going to Macy's. There's a cafe on the third floor. I'll see you in two hours." Off she goes, glancing back with a puff of smoke, saying, "You're welcome, by the way."

15

So I walk the ten-plus blocks north till I reach the Colonial. The theater announces itself with a cast-iron banner on the façade, gold letters on black. Below the banner, a marquee juts out over the sidewalk and reads DE SCANDALE in blazing cursive. Down on the street level, posters combine the title with an image: a chic Frenchwoman in a feathered hat that looks like an ostrich's ass. The box office, a tube of glass braced with decorative brass, bulges out between the front doors.

A spectacled gray-haired woman fusses around in the tube, riffling through some papers. I break from the pedestrian crowd and stand near her window, and when she doesn't notice (or ignores) me, I rap on the glass. She looks up with wary contempt, the kind that infects anyone who's worked with the public for way too long.

"We're not selling tickets for another hour yet."

"I'm not here for the play. This might sound weird, but I heard you guys have preserved Mercy Carnahan's dressing room, and I was—"

"Oh, you're one of those," she says, and looks me over like I'm a degenerate. "It costs twenty bucks. I'll get Jorge if you're interested."

"Great. Do that." I jam a twenty through the money hole; the old bag grabs it and retreats inside.

After a few minutes, a Latino guy in green coveralls opens the front doors. He's about thirty, I guess, with a goatee and hair hanging down to his eyes. If nothing else, he already seems friendlier than his coworker.

"Yo, come on. We gotta do this quick before everybody gets here. Management only allows it a couple hours a day, and you got here right at the cutoff."

I follow him to the lobby, where two stairways curve down from a balcony overhead. A sculpted, cast-iron panel is fixed to the balcony, depicting a harbor bathed in moonlight and frosty mist. Waves splash the moored boats and wash foam upon the dock planks. Sails unfurl as figures struggle to unload cargo. A cart stacked with freight rumbles away, chassis rattled by cobblestones, the driver's lash raised and ready to crack, horses snorting jets of frozen breath.

Jorge goes under the balcony to a door with a plaque that reads AUTHORIZED PERSONNEL ONLY. He unlocks it, and we enter a dark corridor lit with bare bulbs little better than candles. The floor slopes downward, the walls papered with playbills for obscure titles like *Burnt Offerings, Rusty Folly,* and *Now You Run.*

"I gotta say, you're not the usual. Usually it's Goth girls and old drag queens. The Goth girls think this Mercy's their patron saint. I don't know what the queens are thinking, but they show up dressed like her. Maybe they wanna raid her wardrobe."

"The owners haven't changed the room at all? They don't clean it or anything?"

"They don't even let the exterminator spray it. It's a bit much if you ask me. We had this one psychic-lady come here once, said she could still 'sense Mercy's presence in the ether.' I'm thinking,

190

'Lady, that's just mold spores you're smelling.' Not that I wanna put down your beliefs if you're into all that."

"I'm just wondering why the owners go through the trouble."

"I don't know, but we still get people. Not big crowds, but a steady trickle. Too steady to turn away. And it's money, so nobody's complaining. I know I'm not. If people still want to see this lady's room, and they're willing to pay for it, let 'em."

We come to the end of the corridor, climb a few steps up to another door. Jorge finds the key from the dozens on his ring, unlocks it, and leads me out to a wider, brighter space. We're backstage now, and as much as I'd like to see more of what goes into giving the world *De Scandale*, Jorge keeps going. Into another hallway, our footclops echoing, around a corner.

Door after door, and Jorge doesn't need to point out which one leads to Mercy's room. Prior visitors have left roses on the floor around it. Candles in glass. A card telling Mercy to get well soon, another declaring that we miss her. Homemade portraits in pencil, pastel, and paint. Somebody even left a little Mercy teddy bear decked out in a black dress, evening gloves, and bangs. A star remains nailed to the door, its stenciled letters faded by age and countless touches.

Jorge unlocks and opens the door. "You'll see the boundary line. You're not allowed past it, and you're not allowed to touch anything but the star. Okay? Take your pictures, say your prayers, do what you gotta do. I'll hang back if you need some space."

Brass poles and black velvet rope section off a quarter of the room, the area around the door. Mercy's castoffs fill the rest of the space, the forbidden zone as it were. To the left, an open trunk full of clothes. Her desk in the far corner, the ivy frame still mounted upon it, half the glass still intact. A black-and-white print on the wall straight ahead, a lakefront cottage with swans on the water.

191

Another picture on the right-hand wall, facing the desk, but I can't make it out from here. Closer to where I stand is a fold-out dressing screen, its cloth panels embroidered with a lakefront scene to match the print.

I head for the desk, overstepping the velvet rope.

Jorge lays a hand on my shoulder. "Yo! Didn't you hear me?"

"I need to see something. Look, I promise I won't break or change a thing. Nobody will ever know the difference. Besides, I dropped twenty bucks for this. Come on."

Jorge thinks it over with a put-upon breath and lets me go. Maybe I'm wrong, but I'm betting he's bent the rules more than a few times before, resigned to the passion of fanatics. He follows me over the rope, though, determined to hold me to my word.

I stand behind the desk, inhaling dust and stale air, looking for where the camera must have been. A concealed hole in the wall, Pollard said. Which brings me to the wall opposite the mirror, to the picture I couldn't make out before. Closer now, I see that it's a painting of a brook flowing diagonally across the canvas, fallen leaves speckling the bank with dull reds and golds.

The water runs clear, its streambed lined with pebbles. One chalky rock breaks the surface, round and textured with squiggly cracks. It takes me a moment to recognize that rock for the half-buried skull it is. One eye socket lies just above the waterline, the other below. Cheek lodged in the mud, jawbone detached and settled toward the bottom of the picture. The space between skull and jaw suggests a mouth stretched impossibly wide, forever unleashing a drowned scream.

"You notice something funny about this picture?" I say.

"Yeah. It's weird and fucked up," Jorge says.

I lean closer into it, poring over the canvas. A faint groove outlines the underwater eye socket, like someone traced it with a

192

razor. Within the socket are two metal slivers painted black to match the picture. I poke the eye socket with my finger. The canvas gives, popping loose to reveal a pre-cut hole.

"What are you doing?!"

"It was already like that. You know why? She had a peeper."

I lift the painting off the wall, uncovering a rectangular gash in the plaster. It measures about an inch wide and a few inches high, an opening to darkness. Something drops to the floor as I set the painting aside. Jorge picks it up: a length of coat-hanger wire ending in a loop. The cut patch of canvas is fastened to the loop with staples, which explains those metal slivers. It's a clever, effective plug, and I assume there's a matching deception on the other side of the wall.

"What's next door?" I ask.

"Utility closet."

"Then that's where he hid. My guess is, he cut the hole in the picture first, then the hole in the wall."

"Holy shit," Jorge says, and rolls the wire between his thumb and forefinger, spinning the stranded eye socket. "But that's no little pinhole. How could he pull out this piece of the picture, put his eyeball in there, and not get noticed?"

"Because he didn't put his eyeball in there. He spied on her through a camera. That's why the hole in the wall is shaped like that, so he could wedge the camera in deep, get the lens right up to the canvas. And the lens was dark and blank enough to blend into the painting, to pass for an empty eye socket."

"How do you know all this?"

"I've seen the footage myself."

"Jesus, man. What are you, some kind of detective?"

"Something like that."

I walk over to the desk, its surface dusty but otherwise bare. It has three drawers, and I open the top one to find makeup—lipstick, compacts, eyeliner—and pens and a tablet. The same objects I saw in the film, thrown together and closed off. In the middle drawer, a stack of typed pages that turns out to be *The Crimson Kiss*. I scan it for something written in her hand, some mark by her pen, but no luck. Bottom drawer, nothing but a roll of black ribbon and a pair of scissors.

"Anything in here besides clothes?" I say, going to the trunk.

"Not as far as I know," Jorge says.

I rummage through it anyway, a heap of black silk robes and gowns.

"Whatever you're looking for, you better step it up. Like I said, everybody's gonna be here soon, and if they saw me letting you snoop around like this, they'd fire me no matter what you find." Jorge hangs the painting on the wall, fitting the loose piece back into place. "What are you looking for, anyway?"

"I don't know yet. But I think I'll know when I see it."

"Why don't you check her garbage while you're at it?"

Sure enough, there is a wastebasket alongside the desk. I hadn't even noticed the damn thing till Jorge mentioned it. So I ditch the trunk for the wicker container. Glass shards weigh it down, swept into it after the crash and abandoned like everything else. I shake the wastebasket around, sifting through the mess.

"Yo! I was *joking*! I didn't really mean it!"

Once I glimpse crumpled paper among the glass, I reach in to fish it out. Toss it on the desk and reach in for another. And again for another, minding the edges. Three discarded letters, three re-covered wads. I spread them flat on the desktop, then arrange them by the amount of writing, from most to least.

Jorge stares at the letters for a moment, then at me, then goes to the doorway to see if anyone's coming.

194

Dearest,

I know I hurt you. I know I don't deserve you. I know you have every right to deny me. I know all of this, and yet I ask you to search your heart—the heart I know you still have—and question whether you needed to be so cruel. Does hurting me in return truly make you feel better? I was wrong, and I've begged your forgiveness. Of course you have no obligation to accept my apology, or to forgive me, but did you need to lash out with such rage? Please understand me. I am struggling to be the person once worthy of your love, and I fear that I can't endure alone. I merely implored you to have an open mind, to possibly consider coming here

And that's where she stopped and pitched it. On to the next one.

How dare you attack me? If you insist on undying resentment, consider this. That night was a test, and you failed. You could have recognized that I wasn't myself and taken action to restrain me. At the very least, you might have tried. I never claimed to be blameless, but I never acted alone. You men and your pathetic submission to beauty, your frailty at the promise of a fuck, you deserve to grovel, every one of you. If you could have seen how weak you looked when I kicked you! How you wilted when I sucked the soul from your carcass!

From there her writing breaks down to unreadable scribble, a couple more lines before she gave up and tried the last one.

she's grinding my mind to pieces her claws scraping the walls of my skull I would pluck her out through my eyes if I could stab my fingers in deep and bleed her back to hell

195

"Anything special?" Jorge says, trying not to sound antsy.

"No. Just garbage. Thanks for indulging me, though."

"If you call that 'indulging,'" he says with a chuckle.

I crumple the letters back to wads, drop them in the basket. Then shake it around, shifting the broken glass. Burying her words as she left them, under layers of shards.

That night, me and Gen end up in a bar in the East Village. I don't know what it's called because it doesn't have a name or sign, just a door and word of mouth. It's a memorial to the New York rock of the past, if its posters of the Ramones, the Dolls, and Blondie mean anything. Behind the bar, photos of Patti Smith and the Talking Heads and even KISS flank a framed poster for *The Warriors*. The Clash's version of "I Fought the Law" plays on the jukebox while most everybody in the room looks too young to have seen a Clash concert: stick-thin boys with carefully mussed hair, black T-shirts, and canvas sneakers, stick-thin girls with dyed-black hair and black T-shirts, knee-high leather boots that used to say "hooker." Which I guess is the style these days; I'm not criticizing or objecting, just observing.

Anyway, the matter at hand: I'm sitting in a booth alone while Gen's at the bar talking to some guys. Besides a glass of water, I have Greyhound schedules and a map of Gurgon, New Jersey, on the table, trying to plan tomorrow's visit to Wade Endicott's place. Mercy's self-described "humble Temple Keeper" lives only a half mile from the stop, so that's something of a break. Beyond that, I don't know what to expect or ask him. And maybe that's because I can't concentrate on anything but Mercy's letters.

Somebody really got to her, that much is clear. Her letters make me wish I could've found the one she read in Pollard's film,

196

the one that set her off. Or at least find out who wrote it. With her references to hurting that guy on "that night," I have to wonder if that guy was Lou.

Highly unlikely, I know. She dumped him in '44 and bailed on *The Crimson Kiss* in '58. That's a fourteen-year stretch, where she worked her way up and lived large while he wasted away between Kashon's and his parents' house. I doubt she'd feel so strongly about him after all that. Unless, of course, there's more to their story, and that's a possibility I can't ignore. Not when Lou's held out on me before.

And then there's the downward turn her writing took, all just before she flipped out and left the play. Again and again, I come back to the same questions: What was going on in her head? If she was insane, did anybody try to help her? Was disappearing the only way she felt she could help herself? And if she's still alive, how mentally healthy can she be?

Somewhere between The Stooges and The Pixies, I start sketching the dressing room mirror. Call it my own personal answer to her notebook doodles. And though I'm no artist, it's a passable picture of what I've seen. The oval bordered with ivy, the cracked glass, her face reflected in the intact half. I'm starting on the eyes by the time Gen approaches the booth.

She's wearing a new shiny blouse and silk scarf from Macy's; I don't know where she got the plastic tiara perched crookedly atop her head. Holding both a wineglass and cigarette in the same hand, she slides into the opposite seat. A guy with floppy hair joins her. He looks about twelve, dressed as expensively as Gen. Together they could be a couple of high-powered professionals gleefully slumming.

"Can I get you something?" the guy says.

"That's okay, I—"

"He doesn't drink," Gen says, her breath a fog of liquored smoke. "He's a teetotaler."

"A teat-totaler?" he says, and leers at her tits.

"Oh, stop it!" she says, laughing.

"So what're you doing there? Maps? Drawings? You know, this *is* a bar, not a library."

"He's a schemer, too," Gen says. "Always scheming and plotting. He needs to chill out."

The guy leans over for a better look at my sketch. "Interesting. Though I wouldn't hold out hope for a graphic arts career."

"And what do you do?" I say.

"I'm in publishing. Maybe you've heard of Norman Mailer, Kurt Vonnegut, John Updike. I've worked with all of them. My name's Howard," he says, and holds out his hand.

I shake it and say, "Dexter. I dropped out of college and work in a warehouse full of rotten produce."

A moment of silence befalls our table. Gen and Howard exchange looks. He then sees someone he knows—someone important, no doubt—and scoots out of the booth.

"You are an ass," Gen says. "He was going to invite us to a party. Who knows who we could've met? Would it kill you to be a little social?"

"That was an honest exchange. If it embarrassed you, Gen, then go with him. You're an adult. You have free will."

"Then maybe I will go."

"Maybe you should."

"Dexter, you don't know how to live. You're in Manhattan on a Saturday night in a pretty happening place. It won't get better for you anytime soon, and you're wasting your time on a fuckin' actress. Can't you lighten up and have some fun?"

"I didn't come here to party. I came to do a job. I'll have fun when I'm done."

"You really don't care if I go with him?"

"I'm not going anywhere with that condescending shitbag. I don't care who he knows. If you want to go, then go. How do you want me to stop you? Grab your wrist and smack you around?"

"See you tomorrow," she says, sliding out of the booth.

"Remember, we have to leave early to catch the bus."

Gen flips me off with her free hand, the one without a wineglass or cigarette, and rejoins Howard and the crowd around the bar.

So. Where were we? The eyes. And the glistening mixture of tears, makeup, and blood. All of which I would lick from her cheek if I could. If a glitch of Time and Space gave me the chance, if scrapping this life was the price of tasting her suffering, I would swallow.

16

I wake up alone, stagger to the bathroom half asleep. Turn on the light, and find Gen on the floor, curled against the base of the toilet. Pieces of tiara lie scattered about, as smashed as their owner, and a layer of orangish gray scum floats atop the toilet water. I piss on it, curious to see if it changes color, but it doesn't. It just becomes orangish gray scum plus piss. The tinkling does rouse Gen, though, enough to say, "Don't even think about it."

"I wouldn't dare. Unless you were in the tub," I say, and flush the toilet.

"If you're done, turn out the light."

"Come on, let's get you to bed."

She groans but doesn't resist as I pull her up, carry her to the mattress. I lay her down and rub her back for a while, till she looks up at me with bleary green eyes and a face ten years older than it was yesterday.

"Now what do you think of me?"

I lean down and kiss her on her brow. On her cheek. On her lips. "You're a drunk train wreck. And I'm the prize you deserve."

"Is that so?" Gen says, laughing. Another kiss, and she starts to take off her blouse. "If you're so great, then do something for me. Make me forget where we're going. Make me forget who I am."

Slowly her smile gives way, leaving a trace of sadness. I do what I can for her, braced and focused on Job 1. But nothing happens this time like it did last time. The room never spins, the four fuckers never bust in with fragments of the past. I close my eyes and wait for Mercy, but she never appears. It's like they're all holding off, waiting for something, because I can't believe they're gone for good.

Gen locks her fingers with mine, pins my hands back, and rides me hard. I push and listen to her whisper, "I don't want to go back. Don't take me back." And keep pushing till she writhes and cums, freed from herself and her life for a few precious seconds.

The same Gen sits beside me in the subway, resigned and hollow-eyed. Sleeps beside me on the bus, wakes up wincing when we pull into Gurgon. Says nothing as we gather our luggage and step off at our stop.

The bus leaves us in the lot of a bankrupt shopping center. Once the home of a RadioShack, Blockbuster, and Arby's, the strip mall has lost them all, keeping only their vacant shells with soaped-out windows. The corpses of underdog operations lay gutted among the name-brand dead, their signage doubling as headstones. Kelly's NailCare, Simply Super Hair, Best Pets, King Video, gone and forgotten.

Aside from me and Gen, there's nobody in the lot. Not a single car, either, but a few overturned, banged-up carts. Cracked bubbles of asphalt sprouting with weeds. Some tires thrown together in a heap, near a garbage can that's giving off a yellowish vapor.

Gen looks at me and says, "You better know where we're going."

We head for a hill at the edge of the lot, a steep and winding climb that brings us to a housing plan. Nothing noteworthy here, just bland suburban houses with SUVs in their parking pads and the odd flag hung out for Memorial Day. Chemically green lawns stretch from doorsteps to the street, leaving no room for sidewalks, and so we trudge down the middle of Glen Elm Road. The wheels of Gen's luggage rattle off the pavement. Otherwise there's a strange hush over the place. No chirping, no barking, no engines. No voices, nobody outside even though it's a pretty, sunny morning.

We take Glen Elm all the way to its cul-de-sac end, where Endicott's house awaits. It sits back in a pocket of woods, locust trees its only neighbors. Their canopy keeps the house in constant shadow, their massive trunks leaning over the roof at perilous angles. Straight on, the house looks like a standard ranch, but as we close in, I see an addition in the rear. Normally I wouldn't notice such a thing, but in this case, there's more than a little discord between the two units. The house is rectangular with wooden siding painted white. The addition a sleek black cylinder with metallic skin, a stunted silo trying to look badass.

"Are you sure this is the place? I'm getting a weird feeling," Gen says as we reach the porch.

"Gen, some faith, please," I say, ringing the bell.

A sandy-haired man answers the door, a preppy catalogue come to life in his khakis, loafers, white button-down shirt, and plaid sweater vest. He looks to be in his forties, in full flabby meltdown with puffed-out cheeks and jiggling chins. Beads of sweat wet his brow and oil the lenses of his glasses. His hazel eyes project a feverish eagerness.

"Hi, Dexter. I'm Wade. Oh, and you've brought a friend. Come in, come in!" he says with handshakes and back slaps, ushering us to the living room.

A Mercy figurine stands atop the coffee table in the center of the room. About a foot and a half tall and modeled on her *It Takes a Devil* character, it faces two other figurines on the mantelpiece: Mercy in a nurse's uniform, as she wore in *Curb Your Man,* and Mercy in a WAC uniform, as she wore in her Korean War romance, *Hearts of Containment.*

Pillows embroidered with needlepoint portraits of Mercy decorate the sofa. A black-and-white cartoon plays on the widescreen TV, Mercy seducing a professor whose bow tie spins when she winks at him. Framed pictures of her hang all over the walls, too. Mostly stills from her films, but also a few color shots that stand out from all the noir.

"Feel free to have a seat. Or look around if you want," Endicott says, then claps his hands as if to summon a servant.

I gravitate to the color photos, which show Mercy and Endicott goofing around at Niagara Falls, hugging and laughing. Mercy in denim and flannel, hiking up a mountain trail with Endicott panting behind her. Mercy and Endicott aboard a yacht, her lounging on deck in a bikini, him wearing a captain's hat and sipping a piña colada.

"These pictures are interesting," I say.

"Ah, yes. Colleen. It's been fifteen years since she passed but still feels like yesterday. God rest her soul, and God damn God for taking her!" Endicott says with a forced laugh. Then he pulls a handkerchief from his back pocket and dabs the sweat on his brow.

I look at Gen, whose face says, "Don't look at me, jackass. This was your idea."

"You clapping for me, Daddy-O?" says a husky voice behind us.

Me and Gen turn around to see Mercy standing in the doorway, in a dark blue dress and gloves. She cocks an eyebrow and sashays into the room, past Gen as if she weren't there. Stops right in front of me, checks me out with a dirty smirk.

"Well, what have we here?" she says. "A real hunk of handsome."

"My daughter Desiree," Endicott says. "Desi, ask our guests if they want something to drink."

Before Desiree can ask anyone anything, Gen says, "No thanks. I'm just gonna go smoke on your porch, if that's okay. Oh, and Dexter, remember. We have a bus to catch." With a parting glare, she leaves me with Endicott and his daughter.

"And you?" Desiree says, standing so close we're nose to nose.

"Coffee. Thanks."

"Cream and sugar?"

"Just cream."

"You want a little cherry on top, too?"

"If you have one to spare, yeah."

"Mmm. I'll jump right on that," she says with a smile and sashays away.

As I sit down with Endicott, it occurs to me that Desiree was the name of Mercy's character in *Lady of the Dark Pleasure*. Something tells me this is no coincidence.

"If I remember correctly, you're working on some kind of research project?" Endicott says.

"Yeah. The project has evolved since I started it, but yeah. At first it was about Mercy's impact on postwar pop culture, feminism, that kind of thing. But the further I go, the more I want to talk to the woman herself. I'd love to know what she has to say. Getting some quotes from her would make all the difference."

"I bet it would," Endicott chuckles. "But you know that's not possible. She's been gone for more than forty years. Poof! Vanished."

"But you've read all the biographies. Among all the people

who've studied her, is there a leading theory about where she went or what she's up to?"

"No, not really, and they've never stopped trying. Her biographers, historians, the tabloids, and other scholars like yourself. And they've all come up flummoxed. You know why? Because you can't find Mercy Carnahan.

"She's a paradox. She's nowhere, and she's everywhere. She hasn't made a public appearance since 1958," he gestures to his collectibles with a sweep of his hand, "but she's still with us every day. My Web site gets a million hits every other month. All these videos and posters and postcards and T-shirts and dolls, they still sell. You watch a late-night comedy show, and they still crack jokes about *The Crimson Kiss*; an actress has a public meltdown, and she's pulling a 'Mercy Carnahan.' Everybody still gets the joke, everybody laughs. Why? Because she's entrenched in our psyches.

"You can't locate that kind of entity. You can't interview it and quote it. All you can do is worship it. Respect its power. And artfully evoke it."

High-heeled footsteps click along the hallway, approaching the living room. I assume it's Desiree returning with my coffee, but instead another Mercy lookalike walks in carrying a silver tea tray. This chick's wearing dark red—gloves, dress, shoes, eye shadow, lipstick—and when she sets down the tray, she bends over so I can see her cleavage. In case I missed the point, she winks at me, too.

"You gonna introduce us, Pops, or just sit there and sweat?"

"Oh, Ani, quit being a brat. This is Dexter, a film studies major. Dexter, my daughter Anastasia."

"Charmed," she says, and offers her gloved hand for me to kiss.

I hesitate, but with both of them staring at me, I end up taking her hand and kissing her satin-clad knuckles. She strokes my cheek and sashays away. Anastasia, by the way, was the name of Mercy's character in *The Savage Whim*. Just thought I'd note that.

"Insouciant, aren't they? What can I say? My girls are free spirits."

"How many kids do you have?"

"Just the girls, whom you've met. There was another once, a son. But he, too, has passed."

"I'm sorry, Wade. I, uh, didn't mean to—"

"Ah, no, no, no. It's no problem. He's still very much with us, too, like Colleen. Come to think of it, I'll be paying my respects to her shortly. So please don't take it the wrong way if I cut out soon."

"Fair enough," I say, and pour some cream in my coffee. "You mentioned your Web site. It sounds like a pretty heavy commitment. Is it like a small business or a part-time job or something?"

"I wish. No, it's just a hobby. Cosmetic surgery is my full-time gig, though I prefer to think of it as 'corrective surgery.'"

With the coffee cup halfway to my mouth, my brain connects Endicott's words to his daughters. I stop, lower the cup. Return it to the tray with a trembling hand.

"You okay, bud? You look a little peaked all the sudden."

"It's nothing. I'm fine," I say, clasping my hands together to fight the shakes. "So, uh, back to the paradox. I think I get what you're saying about Mercy, but what about Agnes? She's a flesh-and-blood person, isn't she? If she's alive, she has a body, she has an address, and she can be found, right?"

"That may be true, but I don't know where she is. And I don't want to know. If she's alive and has half a brain, she'll never come forward. It would kill Mercy, and why would she do that?"

"You think she'd lose all her fans if they saw her as an old woman?"

"I won't deny that's part of it, but it goes much deeper. It's what Mercy represents. She's one of the last bastions of stardom when stardom was something to aspire to. When it meant dignity, self-respect, a right to privacy, and a sex appeal of suggestion rather than exhibition.

"There will never be another Mercy Carnahan, not in this day and age. What is fame today? What is stardom? In Mercy's era, you had to know how to sing and dance, and you at least had to be literate. Nowadays, all you do is get drunk and take off your clothes for a guy with a video camera, and there you go. You and your titties go right online, and voilà! You're a star!"

"To be fair, didn't Mercy get her big break by posing as a pinup girl?" I ask.

"It's different, totally different. She still had to work hard for that opportunity. But now, thanks to all these digital gadgets we have, it's easy to put yourself in the world's living room. Who needs hard work and talent? All you need is the willingness to be filmed doing something embarrassing. Sometimes you don't even need that much, if someone films you without your knowing it.

"And now that everyone's a star, stars have become disposable. And now that stars have become disposable, what do they do? They submit to humiliation, desperately clinging to their ever-dwindling relevance. They subject themselves to these disgusting game shows, stuffing worms and cockroaches in their mouths. Or they mock themselves in TV commercials, or invite film crews into their homes to exploit their daily lives.

"Why would Mercy reenter the arena when this is what the arena has become? Why would an icon from the Golden Age of Hollywood participate in this Age of Degradation? She shouldn't, and she won't. And I shouldn't have to explain this to you, of all people, should I?"

"You can explain whatever you want. I'm just writing a paper."

"I'm not talking about your paper, Dexter, I'm talking about you. You know exactly what I mean by degradation, don't you? Our obsession with broadcasting each other's humiliations?"

"No. I don't know what you mean."

Endicott studies me, fresh droplets on his brow. He pulls out his handkerchief, dabs himself again. "You are Dexter Bolzjak, the former hockey goalie, aren't you? Surely you know how easy it was for me to find your star-making performance."

"Yeah, well. There's nothing I can do about that. I don't own that footage. If some snide jerk wants to put it on his stupid little sports Web site, along with everybody else who ever blew a big game, I guess I have to live with it."

"You have no idea, do you?" Endicott says, a note of pity in his voice. "You haven't even considered the possibility."

I say nothing, waiting for him to elaborate. He doesn't, though, and we sit there locked in a stare till shrill beeps pierce the silence. Endicott checks his watch, hits a button on it to kill the alarm.

"Time's up," he says, and rises. "I mustn't keep Colleen waiting. Please, feel free to finish your coffee. The girls will show you out when you're done. Best of luck with your project, bud, and may you never know what you already don't."

We shake hands on that bit of weirdness. Endicott hurries out of the room, leaving me alone with his Mercy figurines and cartoons. And while the animated Mercy walks down the street, making a random guy's tongue wag and eyeballs pop out, I try to decipher what Endicott meant. Something about me having no idea. Missing a possibility. Never knowing something I already don't.

High-heeled footsteps approach, and not one but both daughters enter the living room. They stand over me, side by side, hands on hips, eyebrows cocked. By their identical leers, I reckon this will be no simple good-bye.

"You're already leaving?" Desiree says. "We hardly got to know you."

"A shame, isn't it?" Anastasia says. "Say, Desi, maybe we should give him a memento before he goes. A little something to remember us by."

"Mmm, yes," Desiree purrs. "Come, Dexter. Let's give you a hands-on forget-me-not."

"Now, ladies," I say, standing, "as much as I'd like that, Gen's waiting outside."

"Let her wait," Anastasia says. "You know you'll have more fun with us."

"You know you want to, you know you will," Desiree sings.

They hook their arms around mine and walk me to the hallway. I'll admit I don't fight them off. After all, Gen went to a party without me last night, didn't she? We pass a few doors on either side, turn a corner, and arrive at a bedroom. The sisters slide their hands down to mine and pull me toward a bed fluffed with pink blankets and pillows.

"I don't know about this," I say. "Your dad—"

"Forget about him. There's no distracting him when he's in the Temple," Desiree says.

"And it's not often we get one like you," Anastasia says. "Young, in decent shape, enough juice for two."

"Easy, sister. I got dibs, remember. You stand guard at the door," Desiree says, and sits me down on the edge of the bed.

She undoes my fly, pulls my jeans down as she kneels. Somewhere in my mind, I know this is a bad idea that won't end well.

But once she wraps her plump lips around me and starts stroking with her tongue, there's no thinking. There's just clutching the bedsheets and trying to hold on.

Desiree bobs her head back and forth. Slowly at first, but faster as we fall into rhythm. And as we breathe harder, I hear a mix of sounds from under the floor. It's like squealing, grunting, and a chain lashing around.

"Wait. Wait. What is that?" I say.

Desiree looks up, lipstick smeared about her mouth. "Nothing."

The sounds continue, getting louder. Squealing, grunting, chain links. Then a wail that's inhuman but unlike any animal I've ever heard.

"No, that's something," I say.

"Oh, that's just our dog in the basement. He's going bonkers because he knows we have company. Ani, go calm him down."

"Why do *I* gotta go? It should be *my* turn to—"

"Just go!" Desiree snaps, and her sister obeys.

We hear Anastasia's footsteps going down to the basement, her muffled voice, and the wail quieting to a whimper.

"It's okay. You need to relax," Desiree says, and sees that I'm no longer hard. "But not *that* much. Don't tell me you're done already."

For the first time, I take a close, unsparing look at her. Faint scars run along her hairline at her temples, down past her ears, to her jaw. Her nose is unnaturally narrow, nostrils pinched. Her brow and cheeks smooth but unmoving, lips inflated. Only her eyes seem real, and the longer I look into them, the more pain I detect.

"We can't do this. It's not right," I say.

"You know how lonely it gets in this house? Come on, just pretend. I know I'm not her, but I'm as close as you'll ever get. That counts for something, doesn't it?"

Before I can answer, she goes down on me again. And man, I try to resist, I really do. But this chick is skilled and sucks me right back to where we were. Back to our rhythm, back to that thoughtless, joyous space where wrong and right don't matter so much. Back to where there's nothing but holding on till I'm just about to burst, and that's when Anastasia screams.

"No! Stop! Get back here!"

Footsteps thunder up from the basement and toward the bedroom.

Before either me or Desiree can react, this thing appears in the doorway. It's wearing a skirt, fishnets, and a black wig slipped halfway off its scarred, bald head. It has whittled cartilage for a nose and a lidless eye bulging out of its cheek. Its few teeth are cracked to bits, and a grayish green fluid leaks out around its tongue. Drips down its chin, glops onto its breasts bound in a purple bra.

I jump across the room, screaming, "Jesus! What the fuck is that?!"

It comes lumbering in, trailing a broken chain from a dog collar around its neck. Anastasia runs up behind it, grabs its arm. Desiree, too, leaps up to restrain it. But it fights them off, slamming Anastasia off the nearby dresser and shoving Desiree aside. While I'm pulling up my pants, it keeps coming, groping the air between us.

"Hegghhmeh! Hegghhmeh!" it grunts, its tongue slathered in viscous ooze.

The sisters get back to their feet and rush it again, yelling at it to stop. Once all three of them grapple, I jump onto and off the bed and bolt for the door.

"Don't go! He's harmless!" Desiree says even as it knocks her to the floor.

I stumble out to the hallway, but the space blurs around me in a dizzying swirl. With each step I hit something solid—door, wall, hanging picture, wall—though everything looks transparent. The hallway spins faster, and around and faster, and around and faster, and aroundroundaround till I close my eyes and take my chances running blind.

That's just what they want, and they're waiting. One wearing my mask, three masked in panty hose. The video camera on a tripod as they stand over me. Naked and chained to a wooden disc, a dog collar around my neck. Balls raw from ripped-off duct tape. Kneeling, bent backward to face the ceiling. Jaw locked open with a cut of plastic pipe. Crying as they say shit like *shut up, faggot. You crying now, you pussy? You like sucking cock, don't you?*

My face burning, I keep running. Not knowing where I'm going, just barreling ahead through space, hands outstretched to fend off the walls.

Their faces upside down, floating over me. *Places, everybody.* I can't see their hands but hear their zippers and the rustle of their pants dropping.

I reach a door at the end of the hall and throw it open. Then run into a light so harsh I open my eyes to see where I am. My blurred sight has cleared, my face has cooled. The spinaround subsides, tamed by this room I've entered.

It's the addition to the house, the silo-like structure I saw outside. Here, inside, its circular wall and floor are silver, blinding with a shine cast down from a halo-shaped skylight. The room is bare except for Endicott and a large glass box in its center.

That box is a coffin. Within it lies Endicott's wife, a dead ringer for Mercy. Her black hair remains lustrous, eyes open and blue, pale skin radiant. Black rose petals speckle her swan neck, lie sprinkled about her black dress and lace gloves.

212

Like I said, Endicott's in the room, too, paying his respects. Which means he's sprawled naked atop the coffin. Yes, naked, with sweat dribbling down his face as he dry-humps the glass, eyes closed and grunting like an ape. So loud with every thrust, he hasn't even noticed my standing there. His doughy buttocks shimmy, gut and breasts pressing the glass with sounds of moist suction. He may be impotent; for all his exertion, his dick is a flaccid stub buried in flab. And no matter how hard he pushes, he still hovers over and apart from her, forever powerless to break her plane.

"You're sick," I say, the words falling out in a rasp. "You're sick!"

Endicott looks up. The shock paralyzes him. Then it sends a twitch through his mouth, the lids of his gaping eyes.

"What's that thing you keep in the basement? *What is it?!*" I scream, but I don't need an answer. I know it's his son. I don't know everything he did to the kid, but I know enough.

Endicott still can't speak. He climbs down from the coffin, covering himself with his hands, mumbling ums and uhs.

I turn and walk down the hall. Not running yet, my whole body too numb with tension. All I can do is plod ahead, leaving Endicott to his temple. The siblings are still fighting in the bedroom as I pass, the sisters begging the brother to calm down as he keeps grunting, "Hegghhmeh! Hegghhmeh!" I glimpse all three of them in my periphery, even brush past them, but I never stop.

I reach the porch, where Gen is sitting in a chair and lighting another cigarette. A shirtless, barefoot Endicott blunders out after me, zipping up his pants. Gen looks at him, looks at me. Then looks away, exhaling smoke and shaking her head.

"Don't get the wrong idea, bud. We're a happy family. Nothing illegal's going on. It's just a misunder—"

"Back off, you sick fuck! Don't touch me! Do *not* touch me."

He keeps his distance, nervously looks around for witnesses. I grab my duffel and Gen's luggage and go. She follows me to the street, lets me walk off some steam before taking her bag.

"So," she says, "should I even ask—"

"No."

"I thought I heard some scream—"

"No. Didn't happen. Nothing happened."

She doesn't press any further, at least for now, and we walk back the way we came. It's not till we're on the bus, speeding through central PA, that I hear what the son was trying to say. *Help me.* The same thing his sister was trying to say, too, through her mask of an altered face. *Help me.*

17

I show up at Marchicomo's the next morning, dragging on a lack of sleep. After the events at Endicott's, plus the stress of impending failure, I couldn't get an hour's rest. But that trip won't pay for itself, however badly it went, which means I have to suck it up and get back to work.

From the moment I walk into the warehouse, though, I can tell something's wrong. Jerillo and Dockerty glance at me and act busy without saying hi. When I say, hey, what's up, they mutter some heys and nothins and nothing else. When I ask how the weekend went—one of the few I've ever missed—they mutter okays and all rights and don't elaborate. Ross, meanwhile, diligently sorts through a box of banana peppers. And that's the ultimate tip-off, for Ross doesn't just avoid diligent work, he avoids any and all work, especially so early in the day.

Whatever, I figure. Maybe they're just sore that I called off. So I head to the back of the warehouse to grab a sack of onions, but D.T.'s already there, smoking and reading the paper.

"Sal wants to see you downstairs," he says, keeping his voice low. "I don't know why. I just know he's not happy. Thought I'd tell you back here instead of out there, in front of everybody."

"Thanks, I guess."

Downstairs I go, then, down to the wicker. Gen's sitting on the same love seat I first saw her sitting on, looking pale and rattled. Sal paces the space between her, the bathroom, and the surrounding furniture. His little frame shakes with rage, his orange skin burning to the color of tomato soup.

"Oh, good! Bolzjak! Please, sit. By all means, have a seat," he says, gesturing for me to join Gen. "That's why I called you down here. So I could see the two of you side by side. See your faces sitting together."

Neither me nor Gen has a response to that, which pisses him off even more.

"I see how it is. You're gonna play dumb, the two of you. Well, it's too late for that. You know why? I had a surprise this weekend. Heinz called, wanting a couple pallets of celery. You know Heinz? One of the biggest fuckin' companies in this town? One of the most important buyers? Heinz, who I been doing business with for twenty-four years?

" 'No problem,' I said, 'you got it.' I call Bucchinelli, and three hours later, I'm standing around like a fuckin' jag-off waiting for the truck to show up. Heinz calls, asks what's going on. I call Bucchinelli again, and he tells me the truck's not coming. Why? Cause my fuckin' credit's been downgraded from an A to a D, he says. So what the fuck am I supposed to tell Heinz? *What*?!"

Gen says, "Sal, I understand you're upset—"

"Shut up! Twenty-four years and not once has my credit been questioned. Never! Can you comprehend the shame, the embarrassment? The detriment to my honor?

"Oh, but it gets better. I was so desperate to cut a deal with Bucchinelli, I went to the safe. Surely I got enough cash to pay him up front. But guess what I found when I went to the safe?"

Sal focuses on Gen, lowers his voice, "I spent all weekend going through the books, double-checking your work. It didn't take me long to wonder how you ever got through CMU. So you know what I did? I called them, made an inquiry. Expelled in your first semester for stealing computer equipment. Aren't you something?"

Gen says nothing, staring at him with her own anger simmering.

Sal turns to me. "And what do you gotta say for yourself?"

"I, uh, don't really know what to—"

"Leave him out of it, Sal. He doesn't know anything," Gen says.

"She said the two of you went to New York for the weekend. Is that true?"

"It is," I say with a gulp.

"On whose dime?! What did you do, fuck each other on a bed of my money?!"

"Okay, we got the point. We don't need the histrionics," Gen says.

"Oh, you trollop," Sal growls. "If you were a man, I'd sock you silly. Trollop. *Trollop!*"

"Are you done yet?"

"Am I done? *Am I done?* No, I'm not, but you are. And you better thank fuckin' God I'm not pressing charges. That's my good-bye kiss to you."

Gen looks at me and says, "You coming?"

"No."

She blushes, her face betraying a tremor of hurt. But ever herself, she stays hard enough to simply walk away with no pleas or whimpers. Me and Sal listen to her departing clickclocks, then share one ugly silence.

"You should've went with her," he says. "You're fired, too, you know."

"Sal, come on—"

"Don't even start. I trusted you, but I'd be stupid to trust you again, wouldn't I? No, I won't hear any excuses. You were with her when she was blowing my credit. That's all I need to know."

"I had nothing to do with it! I'm sorry she stole from you, but I didn't!"

"Just go, for Christ's sake," he says, and crumples onto a nearby chair. "You think I'm *enjoying* this, as long as I've known your old man? Just get out of here. Go before I throw something at you."

I hit the sidewalk thinking, Sal didn't just fire me. I didn't just lose the job I've had for six years, a job that pays under the table with no safety nets. I'm not broke with no prospects. No, none of that can be true, and besides, all that matters is catching Gen before she gets to her car.

She's two blocks away, rounding the corner of Twenty-first and Smallman. I go running after her, closing in as she nears her Datsun parked alongside St. Stanislaus. She notices me while opening the driver's door and waits, arms folded across her chest.

"Hey. I got fired, too," I say, still not believing it, but saying it anyway. "Thought you should know."

"That's regrettable. Mistakes were made."

"That's all you can say? What the fuck am I supposed to do now?!"

"Get another job."

"That's real clever, Gen. If you're so smart, why did you rip off Sal? Did you really think you'd get away with it?"

"I didn't care! I wasn't thinking. It was just something I did. Something I do and keep doing no matter how much bullshit counseling I get. I warned you, didn't I? I said you'd get hurt if I

218

let you in. But you kept after me, I let my guard down, and here we are. What else did you expect?"

"Look, I care about you, okay? I could put you through a wall right now, but I do care about you. And I don't want it to end like this."

"It doesn't matter what you want, it's who we are. Two fuckups too consumed by our own failures and ghosts to ever truly open up to anyone. It's nice that we made each other a little less lonely for a while, but be honest with yourself. Don't pretend we had a chance."

Gen leans in and kisses me. Right on the lips, so quick I can't react. She looks back just once, her glassy eyes on the brink of tears, and ducks in her car before anyone can see her cry. Off and away she goes, leaving me choked up and alone.

With a sudden abundance of free time, I end up doing two things I'd planned for later.

First, the film. I take a bus to Oakland and go to the Pittsburgh Filmmakers building. Filmmakers is a nonprofit in a converted warehouse. As I understand it, their mission is to help people create video art, whether it's photography or films. So they have classrooms, darkrooms, rooms full of video equipment they lend out, gallery space, and a movie theater all under the same roof. I figure it's a decent bet that somebody there could help me, or at least tell me where to take the reel.

I walk up to a check-in window. A college kid sits on the other side, watching anime in a small room crammed with tripods and klieg lights. I show him the reel and ask if he can make a disc out of it. He sighs something vaguely negative, so I show him one of the hundreds I got for burying Lou's cat and tell him I'm willing to negotiate. The kid's eyes pop open and he promises to have a disc ready in a couple hours, no questions asked.

Second, visiting Lou. From Oakland I catch another bus to St. Francis, glad to keep moving, to stay active so I don't dwell on what happened earlier. But that gladness collapses once I enter the hospital. The last two trips here weren't exactly holidays, after all, and this one doesn't promise to be any better.

The elevator shows me out to Lou's floor. I walk to his room and stop in the doorway; for a second I don't even recognize him. The cancer has eaten away at him, shriveled him down to a skeletal trace of his old self. The bum who staggered into Biggies was a picture of vigor compared to this.

He is awake, though, and musters a smile when he sees me standing there. "Kid. What've you been up to?"

"Keeping busy, man. Believe it or not, I've made some progress on the Agnes front. I'm close to a breakthrough. I can feel it."

Lou closes his eyes and keeps them closed. A sign, maybe, that he doesn't want to talk about it. Or that he's disappointed, I can't tell. In the lull that follows, I spot the paperbacks stacked on the windowsill.

"You read those already? I can bring you more."

"I didn't read any of 'em. I tried, but all they did was remind me of the last time I read 'em, so I stopped. I don't wanna remember being young anymore. I don't wanna remember being healthy anymore."

"Well, is there anything else I can do while I'm here?"

He considers it and says, "This food they got's no good. I could go for some Biggies. The chicken nuggets and fries. You know, number seven."

"I don't know, Lou. That's probably against protocol. I mean, the doctors and nurses wouldn't allow it, would they?"

"Fuck 'em! I'm the one who's dying here! Is a decent meal too much to ask?"

"No, of course not. I'm just saying, I don't want to make things worse."

"*Now* you worry about making things worse? It can't get worse, kid. We both know I'm never leaving this bed. Which I wouldn't be in if you hadn't dragged me here."

"Hey, come on. We're not gonna argue about that again, are we?"

"Nobody's arguing. You asked what you could do, and I told you. Can you do it or not?"

"Okay, fine," I say, and get the hell out of there before I say something too nasty to retract.

Once again the elevator shows me to Lou's floor, but this time I walk in with a sopping bag of Biggies. Lou grabs it from my hand and wolfs down every piece of that greasy crap so fast I wonder if they've fed him at all lately. And for a guy with such decayed teeth, it's almost impressive how he tears his way through so much food, but regardless. I give him time, let him savor his decent meal while I watch a soap on the TV.

But I can take only so many minutes of model-pretty people gazing at each other, reciting faux-romantic nonsense. Especially after this morning. So I say to Lou, "Hey, I need to ask you something, and you gotta answer me truthfully. After that night at the restaurant, did you have any contact with Agnes again? Any whatsoever?"

"Never saw her or heard from her again, and I never tried to reach her. I knew her people would screen me out, and then she disappeared. Why?"

"It's nothing. Just a theory I had."

"Kid, stop worrying about it. Take the money and forget it."

"What?"

"You heard me. I don't got a will, and it's too late to make one. So I'm telling you now. Empty that drawer and go do something with your life."

"No, Lou. That wasn't the deal. The money's not mine till I find her."

"Don't tell me what the deal was. I came to you, remember? And I'm saying it's too late. I'm trying to help you. You did what you could. Now take the money."

"No! I'll find her, Lou, I know it! I'm one break away, and I'm not giving up, you hear me? And I won't just find her, I'll bring her here. Wherever she is, whatever shape she's in. If I gotta wrap her up in duct tape and stuff her in a car trunk to bring her here, I'll fuckin' do it. No, if it's too late for anything, it's too late to turn back. You gotta try, old man. You gotta hold on. You gotta give me just a little more time, and I swear I won't let you down. Please. I'm this close to begging you. Don't give up yet. Don't give up!"

He closes his eyes, sinks into his pillows, and says, "Keep it down. I'm not deaf yet."

I sit there waiting for him to say something else, and he never does. A commercial for denture glue leads to a commercial for a laxative, which naturally leads to another soap, and that feels like my cue to go. I collect the Biggies trash and paperbacks and say, "Anything at the house you want me to take care of? Pick up your mail or anything?"

"Nah. All my mail goes to Gene. He handles the finances, taxes, bills. I don't got the mind for that shit."

"Okay, then. Guess I'll see you soon," I say, and start for the door.

"Wait," Lou says. "I gotta tell you something."

He lifts his hand from the bed, his fingers like brittle twigs. I go back to him, and not knowing what else to do, I take his hand

222

in mine. He clenches hard and raises himself from the pillows. His watery brown eyes stare into me, his emaciated face twitching toward tears.

"Listen to me," he says, his voice shaking. "I'm afraid. Afraid it was all a waste. I didn't have enough guts, and now the time's gone. It's all *gone,* Dexter."

"It's not all gone, not yet. You don't have to be afraid. I'm here, Lou. It's gonna be all right."

"No, it won't. It's—" Lou coughs, tries to speak, then coughs harder.

I ask if he needs help, but he just keeps coughing. Then he lurches forward with a sharp retch and vomits up a gutful of gray sludge. It spatters his chin, his chest. Liquid and wet bits land on our clasped hands. He retches again, blurting forth another acid splat. The grayness even leaks into the tubes in his nose, mixing with the fluids already flowing from him.

"God damn it!" he cries, and lets go of my hand. "God damn it to hell!"

I rummage through the Biggies bag, looking for napkins. A frazzled, big-shouldered nurse appears in the doorway and surveys the scene, her face creased with stress.

"Did you give him that?" she says, meaning the food.

"Yeah, I—"

"You shouldn't have. This is what happens when he doesn't eat what he's supposed to."

"I didn't know. I'm sorry, I—"

"You'll have to leave. You can come back later."

Instead I linger near the doorway, watching her tend to Lou, who's crying with his face in his hands. She gently pulls on his wrist, but he swats her away and says, "I want outta here, God damn it! I wanna go home!"

"You *can't* go home, Mr. Kashon. Now, please, let me clean you up."

"What's the fuckin' use? It's all a mistake, all of it! Every minute, a waste of fuckin' time."

"That may be so, Mr. Kashon. I'm not here to justify your existence, I'm here to clean you up. Now let me get this gown off of you. Oh, my. We *did* make a mess of ourselves, didn't we?"

18

After picking up the disc, I spend the bus ride thinking about what Gen said in New York. Her idea of putting the footage online, baiting Mercy to respond. It's desperate and not very promising, but I don't know what else to do. And judging by the shape Lou's in, I'm almost out of time.

I'm still pondering the idea when I come home to the basement. Jeepers lies all sprawled out on the cot, licking his paw. He pauses to look at me, then keeps licking. The Wall's monitor glows though Judd's chair sits empty. I wander over to see what he's working on, and even by his standards, what I find is one sick image.

There's a naked woman on a bed, handcuffed to its metal posts. She's blindfolded and gagged, her face bruised and nose broken. Blood runs from her nostrils and lips, trickles from her nipples pierced with fishhooks. Welts and more bruises blotch her body, which writhes in muted slow motion.

I hit a key to play it at regular speed. Other figures become visible. Two stand by the bed as a third mounts her. As he penetrates her and pushes while she cries and tries to scream. I pause the video but can't look away, not yet.

Of all things, it reminds me of Endicott. *You know exactly what I mean by degradation, don't you? Our obsession with broadcasting each other's humiliations?* As twisted as he was, he might've had a point. I mean, if people want to watch something like this, that's fucked up enough. But even more fucked up, maybe, is how it's just sitting out there on a server somewhere, waiting to be seen on countless screens all over the globe.

He said something else, too. Something that struck me as weird, that sounded almost like a warning. *Surely you know how easy it was for me to find your star-making performance. You have no idea, do you? You haven't even considered the possibility.*

A chill prickles me as I realize he didn't mean the game. He meant the tape. *That* tape, the tape the four fuckers made in the garage. But no, I tell myself. No. It can't be online. There are laws, safeguards. You can't just broadcast somebody getting molested. People can't watch that as entertainment. It's not possible. No way, even if I'm standing here staring at a rape on the Wall. Even if I'm holding a disc of private humiliation I'm tempted to make public. No, you still can't tell me it's possible.

The upstairs door opens, and Judd jogs down the steps in his saggy gray sweats. He stops when he sees me, and says, "Whoa, you're home early."

"It's real, isn't it?"

"Oh, that. That's a special project I'm doing for this top-dollar guy. Technically it's real, I guess, but you never really see anything from the waist down. This is the only view you get. It's mostly her face."

"I thought you didn't do rape, Judd."

"I prefer not to. But you gotta understand what I'm competing with these days. There's a tape out there now where a guy chops off his own cock with a hatchet, gouges out his balls, and puts them on a table right in front of the camera. With no cuts, no edits, nothing, I swear to God. Clear as day, right there on the screen. Now that's some hard shit. So if somebody wants something like this, I can't afford to say no if I'm gonna stay in business."

I say nothing, but stare at him, studying his skittery eyes, wondering what else he'll confess given the chance.

"Come on, it's not like I *filmed* it. I'm just touching it up, adding little details like those hooks. I know it's ugly work, and I'm not proud of it. And maybe it's not the quote-unquote 'right' thing to do, but Christ, everybody's gotta pay the bills. Anyway, if I'd known you'd be home early, I would've drawn the curtain. I know this one's pretty upsetting. Look, I'll draw it right now. You won't see or hear anything."

Judd moves toward the curtain, but I reach out to stop him.

"No, not till you tell me something. You've seen it, haven't you? You know where to find it. Don't you?"

"What are you talking about?"

"*Shots on Goal.*"

His blush is answer enough.

I wait for the room to spin, but it never does. No dizziness creeps upon me, nothing itches or burns. The four fuckers don't try to bust in with fragments of that night because they don't have to anymore. They're already here, and with a few keystrokes you, me, or anybody else can watch what they did. Not as pieces churning around in my head, but as the home movie they'd always intended.

So much for my supercharged eyes, for dissecting Time. Now all I see are the last eight years vanishing in a fraction of a second. Everything I thought I knew, every assumption I made to protect myself, every moment I spent believing that tape would stay my secret. All ripped away like stitches from a fresh gash.

I don't even need to hear Judd say it, but he does anyway. "Yeah. It's, um— I got a copy."

"You've had it all this time?"

"Not *all* this time. For a few years. I was gonna tell you when I thought the time was right, I really was."

"And where did you get it?"

"There's a black market for this shit, a whole network of guys buying, selling, and swapping it. This one here's from a guy who traded for it from another guy who bought it from another guy. I don't know where it originally came from. I don't know who filmed it, but it's circulating. I don't know how yours ended up online, either, but somebody got his hands on it and digitized it to sell. And now there's so many copies of it out there, it's just *there*. You look for it, you trip over it. I don't know what else to say. I'm sorry—"

"We're watching it. Right now. Me and you."

"No, come on. I'm not gonna—"

"You're gonna pull it up right now, and we're gonna watch it, Judd. Or I'll go to the cops and personally put your ass in jail. Then you'll get your chance to survive some sick, brutal shit. Call it inspiration for your art."

"I said I'm sorry, okay? I'm *really* sorry—"

"I don't give a fuck. Just pull it up."

Judd searches me for a sign of give and finds none. He lets out a labored breath and seats himself before the Wall. With a jittery hand, he starts up RealTime and navigates his archive till he finds a file labeled "SOG."

"We don't have to do this," he says, looking up at me. "We really don't."

I reach over him, hit the key to load the video. RealTime fills the screen with two frozen silhouettes who then begin to move.

228

They're aiming the camera on themselves and jostling for control of it. All the while they lighten, the silhouettes, and become two distinct people.

The short, fat one is twenty-three years old. He's got a head of blond curls, plump lips, and squinty blue eyes. I'll call him Yellow for the Cooper Rink Staff shirt he's wearing. Only later did I find out he worked there, that he'd hung around and watched me so much that Graybeard noticed him and roped him into the plan. Hell, I even made eye contact with Yellow when I fled the building that night; he was one of the staffers who smirked at me as I wedged through the turnstile.

The other one I'll call Handy for being such a tool-belt type. He's a tall, skinny forty-two-year-old with a goatee and a backward ball cap for the Little League team he coached. Dirt streaks his white arms and neck, darkens his jeans and work boots. Sweat soaks his armpits. He's been holed up at the rendezvous point all day, in that dank little garage in a wooded corner of a West End neighborhood called Crafton.

"Come on, gimme! We gotta call it *Face-Off*!" Yellow says.

"No, we're calling it *Shots on Goal*."

"That's stupid."

"Shut up. What do you know, fatboy?"

The camera shakes back and forth between them till Handy jolts Yellow with an elbow. For a minute the screen goes black. Then SHOTS ON GOAL appears in white letters, and you can hear Handy saying ta-da and laughing offscreen.

Somebody pounds on a door with a secret-code knock. One-two, one-two-three. The title disappears, and the garage reappears. Handy's holding the camera now as it captures Yellow approaching the sound. He opens the door just enough to peek out, then steps back as Graybeard enters.

He comes blobbing in, his lard sac of a gut sloshing, looking around all worried and sweaty. Like his plan ended up being more work than he thought. Panting with spit on his lips, the sixty-three-year-old does nothing but hunch over and suck wind for a minute. Hands on his knees, green sweater bulging with breath.

Once he gathers himself, Graybeard looks at Yellow and says, "What the hell's the matter with you, wearing that? Are you trying to get caught? Change it before he sees you, dumbass."

Handy laughs as Yellow scurries offscreen.

"They'll be here any second," Graybeard says to Handy and the camera. "Everything ready?"

The camera pans around the garage. Cinder-block walls with no windows, rusty chains dangling from the ceiling, worktable cluttered with jars of nails. Around and down to a wooden disc hovering just inches off the concrete floor. The disc measures about three feet in diameter. A pair of metal handles are bolted to its surface, each wrapped with a chain and padlock. Electric wires trail out from underneath it while four chalk Xs mark the floor around it, evenly spaced like the NEWS points of a compass.

"Check it out," Handy says, and clicks a switch offscreen. The disc spins slowly with a motorized hum, its chains clinking along the floor.

"You did it!" Graybeard says. "I knew you'd nail it. Good work. Really, I mean that."

"Aw, thanks," Handy says, humble and touched, and lingers on his work before turning it off.

Graybeard takes off his glasses, pulls a ball of nylon down over his face. "Hurry up, put these on before they get here," he says, with more panty hose in hand. He tosses one to Yellow, who's now wearing a white T-shirt. The video cuts out for a few seconds so Handy and Yellow can mask themselves.

Another coded knock on the door. One-two, one-two-three. The camera jerks toward the sound, focuses on the door as it opens partway. A plastic female face pokes in from the darkness. The mannequin from the woods, missing her black mop of curls.

"Yoo-hoo!" says a shrill voice behind her, offscreen. "Who wants a blow job? Don't say no, fatboy. We know you'd buy one from a dummy."

Handy and Graybeard laugh as the camera bounces over to Yellow, standing there taking it. Their little whipping boy, even after he helped them get this far. If they were smarter, they might've been nicer to him. After all, he's the one who ratted them out when the cops came sniffing around the rink.

The door swings all the way open, and the mannequin goes flying past the camera. He comes in after it, the one who jumped me in the woods. Camo, I'll call him, for his green-brown outfit with combat boots and bandana. He stands no taller than Graybeard (his father) or Handy (his cousin), and he's built thick but not chiseled, like he used to lift weights but quit.

"Get ready. I got him," he says, and goes back outside.

Then someone stumbles through the doorway, shoved from behind. A kid in a Falcons jersey, eyes crazed with fear, his mouth a gray duct-taped blank. Hands still bound behind his back. Camo follows him in, wearing the kid's goalie mask, and slams the door. The kid turns around, and Camo punches him in the face, dropping him to his knees.

Graybeard and Yellow rush in and start kicking him. The kid lies there, grunting with each hit. He curls up but can't protect his head with his hands tied. They stomp his ribs, step on his head. Camo hawks up his best gob of phlegm, spits at the kid's face. The other two do the same, laughing at how funny the kid looks.

Already tired, Graybeard looks at the camera and says, "You want in? Hand it over."

Yellow takes the camera from Handy and closes in on the kid's face wet with spit and blood. Handy's foot swings into the picture, hits the kid in the mouth. Then the foot comes down on the kid's temple, clicking his skull off the concrete.

"Ohhh!" "Ohhhhh!" "Ohhhh! That had to hurt!"

"Don't knock him out yet!" Graybeard says through the noise. "Keep him conscious, for Christ's sake."

Camo grabs the kid by the ponytail, yanks him so he's sitting upright on the floor. He cups the kid's chin in his hand, aims his face to the camera. "Get a close-up. Show everybody how pretty she is."

Yellow does what he's told, holding the camera as steady as he can.

"Okay, now here's what you're gonna do," Camo says offscreen. "You're gonna look in the camera and say you're a faggot. Because you *are* a faggot, right? You're my little bitch, aren't you?"

The kid closes his eyes hard, tears dripping out anyway.

Camo slaps him across the face. "What? I didn't hear you! Anybody hear him?"

"No!" "No!" "No!"

Camo slaps him again. "What? Speak up!" Then yanks the kid's hair again. "Admit you're a faggot. That's all you gotta do."

The kid sobs out a muffled sound, sobs it out again louder.

"What?" Another slap. "Look at me when I bitch-slap you!"

"All I heard was a girly squeal," Handy says, and they laugh.

"Time. Watch the time," Graybeard says.

Camo clutches the kid by the neck, pulls him up to his feet,

232

pushes him to the wall. "Okay, listen. I'm cutting the tape off your hands. And then here's what you're gonna do, you're gonna strip for us. And if you even think about looking at that door, I'll slice your throat open. Got it?"

"You getting all this?" Graybeard asks Yellow, who says yeah. "Stand over here. You'll get better lighting."

Yellow does what he's told again, moving over and back to show Camo cutting away at the tape. Once he's finished, Camo leaves the frame. The kid leans against the wall, alone, and barely able to stand.

"Come on, take 'em off!" "We don't got all night!" "Take 'em off!"

The kid pulls off his jersey, lets it fall in a heap.

"Face the camera, God damn it!" "Keep going!"

He takes off his T-shirt, revealing pale skin speckled with bruises. His whole body shakes, his breaths rapid. It seems he'll collapse at any second.

"What are you waiting for?!" "Take 'em off, you fuckin' faggot!" "Keep going, bitch!"

He fumbles with the knot of his drawstring but finally undoes it. Looses his pants, steps out of them. Crouches down to peel off his socks. Down to nothing but his underwear, he stands and looks at them with bleary eyes like there's nothing more he can do.

"Go! Go! Go!" "Take it off!" "Keep going!" "Take it off, or I'll cut it off!"

The kid hesitates, but they keep screaming till finally he breaks. He pulls down his underwear and stands naked.

"That's it? That's all you got? You call that a cock?" "You like doing that, don't you? You like whipping it out for us?" He covers himself with his hands. "No, keep 'em up!" "You gonna play with yourself now?" "Shake it, faggot! Make it wiggle!"

"No, wrap it up," Camo says, and a gray object flies in from offscreen to pelt the kid. The roll of duct tape. "Wrap that around your nuts and rip out your bush. Go on, wax yourself, bitch."

The kid looks at the tape and Camo like he doesn't understand.

"You heard me! Fuckin' do it!" Camo shouts. *"Do it!"* The others laugh as the kid flinches, reaches down for the roll. As he peels off a length of tape and clumsily wraps his nuts, pasting down on his pubic hair.

"Do it! Do it! Do it!" they chant. "Do it! Do it! Do it!" till he does it. He tears off the tape as fast and hard as he can, red-faced and screaming into his gag.

Judd hits a key, pauses the video. He takes off his glasses, rubs his eyes. "I can't watch anymore," he says, and starts to turn away.

I grab his arm to stop him. "Why not, Judd? It's just another movie, isn't it? Or is it different when the person on that screen's sitting next to you? Well, don't worry about that, Judd, because I'm not that kid. I'm not that quivering little pussy who never fights back. That's not me. I don't know who that little faggot is, but that's not me.

"I bet I know how it ends, though. They don't kill him. They should, but they don't. That's the one flaw in their plan. They should kill the cunt, but instead they throw him in a ditch. So he can crawl out, get a free ride to the hospital, a bunch of sympathy cards, his name in the paper. So he can tell detectives and DAs and ADAs all about it, so people can cheer when they convict the four fuckers. So people can pat him on the back and say, 'Congratulations, boy, you *survived*! Aren't you happy to be alive?' But you knew that already, didn't you? It's old news to you."

"Stop it, please," Judd says. "Would you please just stop?"

"No, you don't get that choice. That kid didn't get a choice.

That girl handcuffed to that bed didn't get a choice. So what entitles you to one? Because you're the audience? Because you get to sit on your ass and passively consume other people's pain?

"Let me tell you about choice, Judd. When somebody puts a knife to your throat and tells you to get in a car trunk, you do it. You don't know where you're going or what'll happen. You're so scared, you're pissing yourself, but you do it. When you get thrown down and get kicked and spat on, do you whip out your kung fu and beat everybody's ass? No, you take it. You curl up in a ball like a little pussy faggot, and you take it. Let's see what else you take."

I hit the key to resume the video.

"Watch the time," Graybeard says offscreen. "Gotta keep going."

The kid's on the floor. Camo and Handy carry him to the disc, drop him so he's kneeling on it. One holds back the kid's hands while the other loops a chain around his wrists and ankles, through the disc's handles. Handy takes a dog collar from the worktable, buckles it tight around the kid's neck. When they're done, the kid is bent backward facing the ceiling. His hands and feet are chain-bound together, pinned under his ass, locked to a handle. Another chain hangs from the dog collar.

"Get in there," Graybeard tells Yellow. "Get closer."

"Get where you can see this," Camo says, and pulls the knife from the sheath on his belt.

Yellow lowers the camera, positions it for a clear view of Camo cutting off the kid's ponytail. They're screaming again, "Awwww!" "Cut it off!" "Rip it out!" "Awww, poor baby!" as Camo saws away with his blade, as the kid keeps his eyes closed and cries.

Somebody hands Camo the clippers already buzzing. He rakes the metal teeth upside the kid's head, zigzags his scalp. They're laughing and whistling as the hair falls, "Ohhh!" "Going, going, gone!" "Look how cute you are now, bitch!" Camo flicks a few tufts in the kid's face and scrapes the clippers on raw skin.

Yellow moves in for a close-up of the kid, who opens his eyes. They fix on a point offscreen and never blink, even with all the noise. They're not looking at the people doing this or searching for an escape. They stare at nothing and contain nothing, as empty as the eyes of a corpse. In fact, if you paused the video right now and showed it to anyone, they'd say he was dead. And they'd be right.

Camo finishes up with the clippers and says, "Listen, I'm taking this tape off. Spit out the pad and don't even try to scream. Got it?"

No response from the kid, so Camo slaps him across the face. And again till the kid bobs his head yes, got it. Camo rips off the tape, and the kid spits out the hairy lump of a steel wool pad. Blue slime gushes from his mouth as he coughs up soap and spit. As he sucks in breath and retches it out.

"You got the pipe?" Camo says.

The camera pulls back to show Handy coming over from the worktable, holding a wrench and a short cut of plastic pipe. He crouches between Camo and the kid and says, "Open up, bitch. Open your mouth wide or I'll knock your teeth in."

The kid closes his eyes and obeys. Handy lodges in the pipe lengthwise and hammers it down with the wrench. The kid whimpers with each hit, the pipe grinding against his teeth, burrowing to his throat. His lips spasm around the plastic, his Adam's apple bulges like it wants to burst the skin.

Handy runs the dog collar chain through the handles on the disc, stretching the kid backward by the neck, farther till his head and shoulders touch the wood. Contorted in a reverse-fetal position, jaw locked open, chin tilted skyward, the kid lies there. Reduced to nothing but a limp cumtrap.

"Places, everybody," Graybeard says, clapping as he shuffles past the camera. "That means you, too. Put that on the tripod and get in your place."

Yellow mounts the camera, elevated and angled so it shows the kid in the center of the screen. The four stand around the disc, each visible and distinct, each to his chalk X. Handy leans to the wall, hits a switch, and the disc spins.

"Everybody ready?" Graybeard says, and they all say yeah. "On your marks. Get set. Go!"

Laughing and shouting, they drop their pants and underwear. All four of them start jerking off, edging close to the disc for the best possible shot. All aiming for the kid's face, better yet his mouth, as he spins around below them.

Judd turns off the monitor. He tosses his glasses on the desk, holds his face in his hands. Between us there's silence and the end. And does it matter? You lose eight years guarding an open secret, a dozen on a false friendship. You lose Job 2 in the morning, Job 1 by noon. You lose long after the cum wets your face and you swallow the bull's-eye shot in your mouth. You break down, spend your days wishing you had the balls to blow your brains out, but all you do is lose.

I go to the cot, get my duffel, stuff in some clothes. Jeepers, lazy sack that he is, barely wakes from his nap when I pick him up and pitch him in, too. Zip it and head for the door.

Judd wheels around from the Wall and says, "Hey, don't— please, don't think I meant to—I don't know what to say."

"Because there's nothing to say. There's nothing, Judd."

"You're not gonna call the cops, are you?"

I throw open the door and walk out. Let him wait, let him worry. Let his fear torture him till he begs it to stop, then let it torture him some more.

19

The planks of Lou's porch creak under my feet, and I don't care if they break. Not with the day I've had. Rolled-up newspapers around the door suggest that nobody's been here since my last visit. I check the mailbox and touch only the same empty, rusty space as before. But of course. Eugene gets the mail, like Lou said.

In the vestibule, I unzip the duffel to release Jeepers. Poor guy emerges wide-eyed and startled, then creeps around in that cautious way cats do when they've been transported somewhere new. He looks at the towering stacks of old newspapers, the electronic junkpiles in the living room, the foreboding stairs, then looks at me with a pleading meow.

"Don't worry, we're not staying long. It's just a stopgap."

I head to the kitchen, and nothing has changed here, either. The same whiskey bottles, the same crusty dishware, the same crap-heaped litter box. I search for something to hold water and settle for a grimy bowl with a few dead roaches in it. The faucet handle turns with a screech, the pipes rumble so loud it sounds like somebody's trapped in the wall, trying to batter his way out with his fists. With a spit and a hiss, the spigot lets out a brown stream. Once the water runs relatively clear, I fill the bowl for the cat.

Jeepers doesn't even sniff the offering and follows me upstairs like he's scared to be alone. I bypass the immaculate bedroom for Lou's and check the drawer. The money's still there, so that's something. Knowing I could take it. Admit defeat, accept failure, sell out, avoid the old man till he dies. Live off his money for a while and pretend I did something to earn it. Maybe I'm just tired, but these are starting to sound like attractive options.

So I lie down on the mattress among the dust, dog track programs, and Kashon's receipts. As I fade, the last thing I see is one of those pink slips on the floor, marked up with Lou's scribble and topped with the company logo. ELIAS KASHON INC. between cornucopias. The graphic reminds me of something else, but I don't know what. And before I can figure it out, I fall into the first real sleep I've had since the Comfort-8.

I'm stretched out on my back, naked and spinning upon a wooden disc. My head and shoulders lie flat upon it, my hands and ankles pinned under my ass. The disc slows to a stop, but I'm chainbound and can't get off. Lights glare down from above, frying my eyes, which I keep closed to keep intact. I can turn my head, though, enough to glimpse my surroundings.

The disc holds center stage in an auditorium, and an audience sits there watching me. Hundreds of bodies, no empty seats among them. Women, men, and children all wearing the same blank expression, all sharing the same grayish complexion. They have no eyes but pit-black holes in their skulls, and they move just enough to show they're alive. A tilt of the head, scratch of the chin, fist to the mouth to muffle a cough. All waiting in patient, expectant silence.

Footsteps approach from the wing, coming closer till the source of the sound stands over me and blocks out the light. I look up to see Mercy looking down without the usual cool. If anything, she seems embarrassed as she drops a white towel on the disc.

"For goodness' sake, take it," she says.

The chain slips off my wrists and ankles. I maneuver to sit upright, gaining my bearings. Then manage to stand beside her, towel draped around my waist.

She surveys the audience, face by face, with an air of disappointment. "I told you this would happen. I said they'd catch you if you kept looking for her."

"You said they'd catch me if I got close. So I must be close."

"Haven't you had enough? You spent years hiding from those bastards, and I led you back to them."

"And it didn't kill me, did it?"

She turns to me, her eyes darkening. "Maybe I underestimated you. But don't push it, sweetie."

"Or you'll do what?"

"Whatever I have to do to win. That's the crucial difference between us. You don't like to lose; I don't lose."

"Then why call yourself a fallen goddess? You must've lost one fight or another to end up here, pissing around with scum like me."

"You talk tough for a boy in a towel who was chained up a second ago. It's easy to be so tough in your dreams. Too bad we know what you really are. Me, you, all of them. Look at them," she says, turning to the audience. "What do you see in their eyes? Love, admiration, respect? No. They want to humiliate you. They want to see you suffer. They might smile and applaud, but in their hearts they have nothing but contempt for you. For your weakness, your cowardice, your every imperfection."

Mercy swipes the towel off me, and the audience roars with

laughter. A mob of gray faces up to the rafters, pointing and laughing, clapping and laughing, whistling and laughing, quaking this cavernous theater with a sudden crush of noise.

She walks away with the towel, and I can't move to follow her. My feet and hands are leaden. I can't do anything but face the crowd and take the laughter, take the abuse, and try not to cry or cave to the shame. And still they laugh even as tears of blood drip down their cheeks.

And the more they laugh, the more blood glistens from their eye sockets. In the front row, a man's jaw drops loose from his skull, the bone dangling by ligaments. A woman's throat bubbles and breaks open with maggots. A little boy's scalp splits down the middle and peels away, exposing his skull. From front to back, the wave of decay infects them, but they laugh and keep laughing like nothing's happening as they shed skin and spurt pus. As their bodies slump over, as one falls off the balcony and splatters onto the aisle below, they laugh.

Slowly I pull myself from the spot, and I do mean slowly. My limbs weigh heavy, my feet feel like they're squishing in mud, but I plod toward the wing. As I cross into shadow, escaping the sightlines of the audience, their noise ends as abruptly as it began. For a moment I move in total darkness, my body lightening to normal.

The darkness cuts to light, and I'm standing in the locker room of Cooper Rink. Naked still, but my gear's laid out on the bench. Everything except the mask. I suit up, glad for the clothes, and head for the only door among lockers and showers.

It opens to a winter night and a clearing among woods. Pieces of the rink remain, scattered as if Cooper were bombed and the forest overgrew its ruins. No walls or roof, but weathered boards with panes of cracked glass, bleachers covered with dead leaves, a scoreboard stuck sideways in the earth. Tips of tree branches tickle the stars with every wind. Blue-black clouds creep over the face of the full moon. Snowfall glitters in the spectral light, lands on a sheet of ice that sprawls from my blades to Mercy's lone, distant figure.

I skate toward her, crossing a blue line, center ice, blue line. She's not wearing a coat, only her black dress and gloves, but she doesn't shudder even as her breath freezes. Nor does the snowfall seem to touch her. She acknowledges me with a glance and tired sadness in her eyes.

I follow her gaze down to the ice between us. Something's moving under the surface. At first I think it's some kind of fish or an otter. But then I see tiny fingers and tell myself no. It can't be—though I know it is, I refuse to believe—it can't be, but it is—a baby's eyes, a baby's gaping mouth. Her skin's turning blue, her little body thrashes against the ice.

I drop to my knees, throw off my gloves, wipe aside the snow with my hands.

She's clearer to see now. Her fingers just inches away. Her open mouth letting a freezing lake into her lungs. And yet her cry, a nerve-splitting wail, echoes through the woods.

"No no no," I whisper, clawing the ice. "No God please God no." There's no way to get to her, though she's so near. "No God don't do this. Don't do this!"

I hit the ice again and again, bashing my hands to pulp. Punching, splitting my knuckles, smearing blood and bits of skin on the surface. Fighting with all my strength, fighting harder and madder and nastier than I've ever fought for anything, and still no closer to saving her.

Another wail echoes from nowhere. So loud I cover my ears and scream myself hoarse to block it out, make it stop. But it

243

doesn't stop, and as hard as I close my eyes and tell myself to wake up, God damn it, wake up, I don't wake up.

Instead I hear the sound of sloshing water. And open my eyes to see Mercy kneeling, immersing her arms in a hole where there was ice. She lifts out the baby, who's alive and so warm she gives off steam. Mercy raises her overhead, basking her in the moonlight. In a guttural, forgotten language, Mercy chants an invocation. To who or what I don't know, but she throws herself into the words, voicing them with more passion than she ever showed onscreen.

She then pulls the white towel from a fold in her dress and bundles up the baby. And cradles her to her chest, looking down at me as I shake in a heap, clutching one mangled hand in the other.

"Now you see how powerless you are," she says. "You see the choice I had to make and why I still protect her. Would you rather I let her drown?"

"That's a hell of a way to prove your point!"

"Because you're stubborn! Louie was no dummy to pick you, I'll say that for him. You're stubborn, hungry, and making this harder than it has to be. But I'm telling you to stop. Just stop, and no one will get hurt any more."

"Since when do you care about hurting anyone? If you're so protective, where were you when she broke down in her dressing room? Where was your power then?"

"How dare you question what you can't begin to understand?"

"Because we're in my head. This is my dream, and I can question whatever the hell I want. Maybe I can't do magic tricks, but I know you're getting desperate. And you're scared of something if you have to stoop so low to bully me."

"You sniveling dog. I could strike you down with a bat of my lash."

"Then do it already. Do it!"

"Don't tempt me!"

Seeing her rattled, no longer her poised self, I stand and move closer to her. "You're off your game, Mercy. Your temper's showing. Just because you rescued that baby doesn't mean you should keep her. Maybe you shouldn't even be holding her, not when you're making death threats."

She backs off a step, blue eyes widening. "How *dare* you?! I gave her everything a woman could want. It's not my fault she couldn't handle it. And if she devastated a few saps along the way, so be it. That's the price of my love."

"Some love. You made her a monster in your own image."

Mercy hauls off and slaps me. It stings, but no worse than a slap from anyone else. I edge in closer so we're nose to nose. She squeezes the bundle against herself so hard she could be suffocating the baby, who doesn't move or make a noise.

"What good did you do her? Lou loved her, and she loved him, too, and you tore them apart. For what? So she could waste her life hiding from the world? No wonder you got demoted."

She belts me again, this time with a backhand.

"Knocked off your pedestal. Stripped of your status. Thrown down like a common, gutter-sucking bitch."

Mercy goes for a third slap, and I raise my hand to block it. Then grab her other wrist and wrench it toward me. She looses her grip on the bundle, and I rip it away from her.

But once I touch the bundle, I know there's no longer a baby in it. I unwrap the towel, and a mess of produce spills out onto the ice. Squash, pears, apples, black and red grapes, ears of corn, all falling till there's nothing in my hands but an empty horn of wicker. I stand there holding it, confused, then look at Mercy.

"Congratulations. You got what you wanted. I trust you'll

245

pursue this to the end," she says with a bitter smile and starts away.

"No kiss this time?"

She ignores me and vanishes into the woods, a curtain of moonlit snow falling behind her.

I wake up sometime after nightfall, sweating, my heart hopping faster than a jackrabbit. Blindly I stumble from the mattress to the wall and hit the light switch. Kashon's receipts litter the floor, as always, and I grab one. ELIAS KASHON INC. between cornucopias.

Of course I remember the dream. More important, I also remember a time when I glimpsed something but wasn't sure what. And now I'm starting to think that something was a cornucopia. Or two, to be exact, on either side of the Kashon name.

Jeepers wakes from his nap, and we stare at each other.

If I'm right, if I really did glimpse the logo where I think I did, then that's huge. It might even be the break I need, and damn straight I'll pursue it to the end. But first I need to know if I'm right, and I can find out tonight.

Jeeps keeps watching me while I dig the videodisc from the duffel, maybe wondering what I'm so wired about. I leave him with a chin rub and a warning to watch out for the rats, considering what they did to Lou's last cat. And with that, I hurry out of the house.

Into the late-May night I run, onto Wellsbrook's cobblestones silver with streetlight. Past darkened houses hiding sleepers and stories we'll never know, windows flickering with TV's lonely, soul-eroding glow. Through an alley to flights of concrete steps, the kind you can find throughout this town so full of hills, steps named like streets and maintained by the City, which means glass

246

crunching and edges crumbling under my feet, overgrown weeds grazing my limbs. Down, down to West Liberty Avenue, the border between Brookline and Beechview, four lanes choked with car dealers, fast food, gas stations, and pollution-spewing traffic. Across and onward, every footfall a jolt, every breath a rush, every second a loss of Time.

Judd wheels around in his chair, shocked as I barge into the basement. I charge toward him, shove the chair aside. He topples to the floor with a yelp. Balled up and shielding his head, he soon realizes that I haven't come to kill him. But he doesn't flee, doesn't get back up. He just kind of lies there on the floor, hesitant to do anything but watch me load the disc.

The video begins as it did on Pollard's screen. The opening blur, the camera focusing on the desk and mirror. Her makeup and hairbrushes cluttered about, the torn envelope and folded letter.

Mercy appears, seats herself before the mirror. Looking tired and worried, even more pale than usual. She picks up the letter, read it, turns it over, and that's where I pause the footage.

I drag the cursor over the letter, drawing a box around it, highlighting it. Then the zoom-and-render combination. One keyboard command magnifies the letter, blows it up till it's a pixelated splotch filling the screen. Another command, and a red line moves back and forth across the screen like a windshield wiper.

With each pass of the line, the splotch clears up a little, and my heart beats even harder than before. My nerves tense, breaths shorten till I'm practically panting. I can taste the satin she jammed in my mouth, that curdled into steel wool and blue soap. The little wires burrowing, the foam collecting in my throat, coating my tongue, and the line stops.

As clear as the Wall can make it, there's a close-up of the letter. Its text is still too small to decipher, but I knew my eyes

247

caught something familiar at Pollard's. And now that I'm staring at it, I'll be damned. The letterhead contains the Kashon logo, cornucopias and all.

I pull the receipt slip from my pocket and hold it up to the screen. "Tell me something. Am I crazy, or do these match?"

Of course they do. I see it, I know it. But I just need to hear someone else say it.

Judd clambers up to his feet, squints at the screen through his glasses. "You're not crazy."

"I'm not crazy." I wander over to the cot and collapse on it, holding my face in my hands. "I'm not crazy."

If Lou's telling the truth, if he really had no contact with Mercy after she dumped him, then there's only one other person who'd send a letter with that logo: Eugene. His big brother. The overprotective asshole who gave Lou the house and the job to keep him off the street. Who, like Dad said, subsidizes Lou and even receives his mail.

Could Eugene's controlling the mail explain what happened? Is it possible that Eugene intercepted a letter from Mercy to Lou and sent her a nasty response? Yes, it's possible, and it points to the core questions of what he knows and what he's done. And if he really does hold some key information, now I have to persuade him to give it up. Which won't be easy, seeing as how we've gotten along so far.

"So, I guess I have to ask," Judd says. "Why's Mercy Carnahan reading a letter from Elias Kashon Inc.?"

"I don't know. But if I don't find out soon, my skull's gonna explode."

Within hours, I step off the bus and into the Strip. Dawn hasn't broken yet, but dozens of Mack trucks still crowd the terminal on

248

Smallman, headlights slicing the darkness in a commotion of engines and forklifts, clacking pallets, guys stacking boxes and shouting and laughing. I walk past this, keeping to the sidewalk opposite the dock, crossing Eighteenth and Nineteenth, toward St. Stan's looming ahead at Twenty-first, till I end up in the church lot. Where I take a seat on a concrete slab, positioned to watch Kashon's.

Nothing doing, not a soul to be seen till a biblical-looking bum with a waist-length white beard comes staggering down the nearby alley. He stops alongside a garage, unzips, and pisses on some garbage cans. Then continues on his way, slurring the Motown song "My Girl" at top volume.

More time passes, and finally the black Caddy cruises into Kashon's lot. Eugene climbs out and unlocks the warehouse doors, and that's my cue to move. He's turning on the lights as I walk in after him and stop on the threshold of his office.

Stale air stifles the room, its walls ingrained with the soot of the steel era. An electric typewriter, manual adding machine, and rotary phone share the desk, its drawers likely stocked with carbon paper. In the corner sits a gunmetal file cabinet, yellowing news clippings stuck to its broad side with magnets. Art Rooney holding a Lombardi trophy sometime in the '70s. An article headlined "Kashon Celebrates Sixth Decade in Strip," another "Watermelon King Continues Undisputed Reign." A plastic Santa hangs in the window, waving to the boxcars stranded out back; it's the kind of decoration that looks like a bunch of pasta noodles fused together and painted, a style long extinct, never mind that Christmas came and went five months ago.

Eugene stands in the middle of this unwelcoming space, staring at me under the brim of his fedora. He takes it off, then his coat, drops them both on a chair.

"Let me guess," he says. "You're looking for a lost love."

"That's one way to put it."

"Haley told me you talked to him. I figured you'd want to pester me, too, but I doubted you'd have the nerve to show your face here again."

"Yeah, well, I worked up the nerve. Look, I just want to know whatever you can tell me. I'm trying to do something nice for your brother, and I'm asking for your help."

"Something nice? You think finding her would be *nice*? You don't even know what you're looking for. And if you think Lou's dying now, let me tell you. He's been dead since the day he met her. You'd know what I mean if you grew up with him.

"Tommy was my brother, too, and I loved him, but he never shied from trouble. God knows he didn't deserve what he got—I still think the cops had a hand in it—but he always threw himself into one mess or another. Getting drunk, fighting, stealing women. Me, I wasn't no hell-raiser, but I was never full of potential. All I cared about was making money so I could buy my own car.

"But Lou, he was the one who was gonna make the old man proud. He had a brilliant mind, could ace whatever they threw at him in school. Always tinkering with gadgets, always wanting to know how things worked, everything from jet engines to TVs to space rockets. He was gonna go to college when he got back from the service and be an engineer at Westinghouse. That was his plan, and I have no doubt he would've done it.

"But instead he met her, and that was that. Nobody could've been more wrong for him. He needed somebody fun, somebody with some bounce. But her, she was just a weird mope. Never talked much, and when she did, she had nothing to say. Being an actress was perfect for her. It gave her the chance to borrow made-up personalities since she had none of her own.

"I knew it was doomed as soon as I met her, but obviously nobody listened to me. The old man thought she was pretty, Mom thought she was sweet, and that was enough for them. I was honest with Lou, and he didn't speak to me for three months even though we shared the same room. So I backed off, even when they got engaged. And we all know how that went.

"And that's it. That's all I got. Now go do whatever you want with that," Eugene says, and goes to the watercooler by the window, pours himself a paper coneful.

"Thanks. But there's something else. You've been getting Lou's mail since he came back from the service."

"Yeah. So?"

"I happened to come across a film of Agnes in her dressing room when she was on Broadway. She's reading a letter she just opened. When you pause the footage and blow it up, you can see the letter has the Kashon's letterhead on it. And when she reads this letter from Kashon's, it upsets her, which seems to be its intent.

"Lou says he had no contact with her after she dumped him. None at all. So if you're the one who's been controlling his mail all this time, then no, we're not done talking."

Eugene stands there looking stunned. He forces down a gulp that shakes his wattles. Quickly he downs the water, crumples the cone, and pitches it to the wastebasket. It misses, bouncing off the rim and to the floor. He doesn't bother to pick it up.

"You got any brothers? Any sisters, even?" he says.

"No."

"Then you can't understand what it's like. To lose one when you're a kid, then watch another one become a total fuckin' wreck. All he did was drink and sleep when he got back from the war. Wouldn't say a word to me or anybody else. The old man let him stay home and hang around here out of pity.

251

"But then the old man died, and Mom died, and that left nobody but me to take care of him. I kept waiting for him to snap out of it, to get back to normal, but he never did. I didn't know what else to do for him. Today you'd just make him go to Alcoholics Anonymous or send him to a shrink for being shell-shocked. But back then, nobody did that shit. If you were a man, you sucked it up. You kept your devils inside and didn't bitch about it. That's what I thought he was trying to do, and I respected him for it.

"If Lou was falling apart, we buried it, we ignored it, never talked about it. Yeah, maybe there were times I thought he needed more help than I could give. But when you know somebody your whole life, there's always tomorrow to work things out. Always a someday for the big heart-to-heart talk. But you never do it 'cause it's easier to get used to your brother's problems, and so you let them fester. And they keep festering, and you keep putting off someday, and there goes a year. And another and another.

"And that's how we got along, the both of us still living at that house. Every day like the last until I picked up the mail and found a letter from guess-who. While her fake name's still in lights and her painted face still plastered everywhere you look. So what do you think I should've done? Think I should've shown it to him? After what she did to him, and the shape he was in, are you gonna tell me it was a mistake to keep it from him?

"No, I didn't take any chances. I got married and moved out soon after, but I took Lou's address and number with me. If she was gonna try to talk to him, she'd have to go through me first. I already watched her castrate him once. No way was I gonna stand back and let her do it again.

"She didn't give up so easy, either. I got more letters as her movie career wound down, then a lot more before her big Broadway debut. Got a rash of hang-up calls, too, but never her voice. I tried to blow it off at first, but the letters kept coming and coming till it got so ridiculous I had to answer. So I wrote back as Lou and told her to fuck off. That shut her up for a while; I like to think it helped her bomb, too. Send her scurrying off the stage like she did."

"And she stopped after that?" I say.

"You kidding? A headstrong broad like her? No, she showed up here in person, disguised in a big hat and blond wig. It was pathetic."

"When was this?!"

"Calm down, it was about fifteen years ago. She said her old man just died, so I guess she was coming around looking for sympathy. And she was out of luck because Lou wasn't here that day. He was over at the bar, getting shitfaced. So she had to deal with me instead."

"I take it you weren't nice to her."

"I was civil. It took a strenuous effort, but I didn't even raise my voice at her. She never knew I was running interference, and she thought she could trust me. Once I realized that, I even acted pretty nice to her. Listened to her talk for a while, making some sad noises about her past and her regrets. Then I stuck her good. I told her Lou left town after he wrote that mean letter to her, that he married a beautiful woman and had four beautiful kids. That he was an engineer for Westinghouse, traveling the world, and I didn't even know where he was living these days.

"And the whole time I was lying to her, as much as it hurt to whitewash Lou, it felt better to see the pain in her face. To watch those crystal-blue eyes of hers squinting like they were holding back tears. Justice, I was thinking with every word. Here's justice, babe. Nobody said it was pretty.

"So she stood there taking it till she couldn't take any more, then left a business card and asked me to give it to Lou if he ever turned up. She started to leave, and I stuck her again. Just as she was getting in her car, I told her, 'Oh, by the way. You ever come back here again, or try to talk to Lou again, I'm giving this card and your love letters to the press. Then we'll see what a recluse you are.'

"She looked at me like I just stabbed her. And she figured it out and asked if Lou ever got any of her letters, if he ever wrote to her, if anything I said about him was true.

"I smiled and said, 'Guess you'll never know unless you give up your mystique. It's up to you.' Twisting the knife. Her face got quivery like she couldn't control it, and she ducked in the car and had her driver whisk her away. And that was the last of her. That was the choice she had and the choice she made."

"You proud of yourself, Eugene? Still glad you got back at her?"

"Not really, but I'd do it again. I stood up for my brother. You think I was wrong?"

"I don't care. I just want that card."

"Sure you do," he says, and slouches against the desk, his old body tired of standing. "And why should I give it to you? Did you hear a single thing I said?"

"I'm not here to argue with you. I can't say you were wrong because I don't know. She made a choice, you made a choice, and meanwhile Lou's still in the dark, pining away for her. What about his choice? Doesn't he deserve another chance to see her? It's his dying wish, for God's sake."

"Don't try to work my heartstrings. I've had years to think

about it. Years to wonder if I did the right thing, years of guilt and fear that Lou would find out what I hid from him. Christ, I don't even know why I'm telling this to you, of all people."

"Because I can help. I can make this work for everyone. You tell me where she is, I'll bring her to Lou, and he'll die happy instead of miserable. And he'll never know about you and her. I think she'd agree to that."

"Last time I trusted you, you fucked me over."

"I did what I thought was right. What I thought was best for Lou. You should understand that better than anyone."

Eugene looks down to the floor, thinks it over. For minutes, there's silence. He leans forward by degrees, slumping his shoulders and caving his chest. The overhead light shines through his comb-over. When he looks up, his brown eyes bear the glaze of defeat.

"I'd ring up the number every so often, just to see who'd answer. Last time I tried, maybe five years ago, it was disconnected."

"If you got an address, I'll take it. I'll take anything."

He deflates further with another breath. And just as I think we're in for another silence, he moves around to the other side of the desk. Kneels down, reaches into the underside, and scrapes its metal with his nails. Pushes himself back up with an old man's grunt, holding a card winged with ripped tape.

"I just want to know one thing," he says, approaching me. "What's in this for you?"

"Nothing but my word."

"You sure that's all it is?"

"That's all I got."

"Then take it. Take it! Get it off my hands!" Eugene says, and hands me the card.

Nobody's name on it, but it reads SWAN HOLLOW, BED & BREAKFAST with a little picture of a lakefront cottage. 211 DOROTHEA DRIVE, ROPERSDALE, PA.

Scoooooore!

20

From Kashon's I head to the Steel City Novelty Co., walking right through my dread. The bells on the door handle startle Dad, who's hunched over the counter with his coffee. Once he sees me, he puts on his best nonchalant face and says, "Twice in a decade? What's the occasion?"

"I need to borrow the car. I'm in the middle of something crazy you'd never believe. I'll explain it all later, I swear."

"Why aren't you at work?"

"I got fired."

"What?! What'd you do?!"

"It's not worth going over now. I'll explain it later."

"Let me get this straight. You don't show up here for however many years until a couple weeks ago. Then you get fired, but you can't say why. And now you show up again, asking for the car, and you can't say why. Is that right?"

Before I can answer, a middle-aged woman and her teenage daughter show up at the door. Dad lets the jingle subside and says, "I'm sorry, ma'am, we're not open yet."

"But your sign—"

"I know, and I apologize. We'll be open in a half hour." He

absorbs her annoyed retreat and looks at me. "And now you cost me a customer."

Dad goes to the door and flips the sign so it says CLOSED to the street. Then stands there watching the morning traffic with his hands in his pockets. Not knowing what else to do, I wander over to the bin of "Creepy Crawlies!" full of spiders, centipedes, and beetles with jagged pincer jaws. I root through the rubber bugs, stretching the silence, trying to find the words and nerve to speak.

And so here we are. Dad looking outside, me poking around in a bin. A father and son who never had much use for affection, even when times were good, still stuck in the same pit of regret. Still evading the same unspoken pain, scratching the same scabs.

I can't even face him, nor trust my voice to hold out, but I also can't take the sameness anymore. So I say, "Look, I know I've been an asshole, and I don't mean just lately. But let's be clear about something. I wasn't avoiding you just because of that night. It was never just anger; it was shame more than anything. Shame over who I am and what I've failed to be. I mean, let's face it, I haven't amounted to much. Avoiding you seemed like a reasonable way to deal with it."

"You can have the car."

"It's not about the car. Listen to me, please. What I'm trying to say is, eight years is a long time. And I've spent too much of it feeling sorry for myself and pretending I'm not your son. I want to be your son again. If you'll have me."

For a while Dad keeps looking outside, so motionless I wonder if he even heard me. When he finally does turn around, his glassy stare knocks mine down to the bin. Slowly he approaches till he stands right beside me, and I have no choice but to face him.

"What do you think I've been trying to tell you all this time?" he says.

"I don't know."

"You don't know? *You don't know?*" Dad grabs a rubber spider from the bin and bounces it off my head. "You're a jag-off. Did you know that?"

His wrinkly face is caught between laughter and tears, and the sight's enough to choke me up. There's nothing to say anymore, not when he pulls me in for a hug, and all I can do is hug him back. And close my eyes and feel the old dread passing, dying with years wasted in hiding.

I follow him to the back room cramped with overstock, a morgue of unsold Sea-Monkeys and Venus flytraps, motorized remote-control shark fins (the box shows a bunch of duped swimmers, splashing toward shore in a mass panic), "Just Add Water" dinosaurs that grow from pea-sized to potato-sized when submerged overnight. Oblivious to these marvels, Dad walks past them and opens the door to the back alley.

His gray LeSabre fills its customary space between the Dumpster and loading dock. Dad bought the car when I was in junior high, and it shows. Nicks and dents pockmark its body, rust colors its rear fender. Some trim hangs loose off the passenger's door, and a chink in the windshield threatens to bloom to a wider crack.

"I know it's looked better," he says, reading my mind. "But it still runs."

"Thanks. I owe you big for this. You know what I'll do? I'll take you out to eat when I get back, wherever you want."

"With what money? You have no job."

"But I got one hell of a prospect. You'll see."

"Yeah, yeah. Just do what you gotta do and get back here okay."

As I back out of the space, Dad lifts his hand in a tired wave. I return the gesture and go, putting distance between us. I glimpse him once more in the rearview, lingering in the alley with an old man's stoop, bent with the weight of another day's work, dwindling down till he's gone.

Did you ever go somewhere you haven't been in years only to have the place dump a bunch of memories on you? One doesn't usually think of a car as a place, I guess. But while driving the boring stretch of I-79 North, I don't feel like I'm moving so much as stuck in a see-through box. And everything within that box is a reminder, everything from the clock radio's turquoise digits to the silver knob of the cigarette lighter to the bumps of the steering wheel's grips.

I learned to drive in this car ten years ago, back when I was a high school sophomore. Dad took me to Smallman one Sunday morning and let me take the wheel. The street was just about empty, but he ended up clutching the dash anyway, screaming for Jesus after I ran a few stop signs.

By junior year, I was driving all the time, most notably to and from Cooper Rink. (In fact, anyone stalking me then would've seen me driving this car onto Old Watermill Road after every practice and game. *This ain't the usual car. Where's the usual car?*) After school and working my seventy-house paper route, I'd report to the ice to meet Coach, the only other person in the building for our routine.

I'll say this for Coach: he made good on his promise to grind me up. I lost five pounds on the first day alone doing nothing but skating. ("At least you're honest. You weren't lying when you said you could barely skate.") Laps around the rink, around and around and back and forth, my feet drenched in sweat. Skated so much my legs were still churning when I lay in bed. And when I woke up the next morning, I was so sore I practically crawled to school, but I still went. Still delivered my papers afterward, still returned to the rink for more.

"Tonight you're sleeping like that. And tomorrow you'll do your paper route in it, too. That's a direct order," Coach had said the first time I suited up. There I was on the ice, bulked up and weighed down with leg pads, blocker, catcher, arm and body protector, jock and padded shorts, and mask, holding the stick and trying not to fall, and he said, "I'm serious. Being comfortable in your gear's not enough. You need to become unconscious of it."

"You're telling me to deliver seventy papers like this and not get laughed off the block?"

"If you're worried about getting laughed at, you're not long for this game, son."

"But it's like eighty degrees outside. I gotta walk up and down steps."

"Passing out's one way to become unconscious. Don't look at me like that. Stop bitching and start moving. Give me three laps," he said, and blew that damn whistle.

Don't ask how many days we worked on the stance, Coach chiseling the phrase "spartan economy" into my skull, meaning no wasted movement. Chest up, glovehand out, stick on the ice, knees flexed, weight on the balls of your feet far enough apart but not too far apart, skates parallel, and square yourself to the shooter. Got it? Now get down on the ice, on your back, and jump into your stance when you hear the whistle. Now skate and stop and hit your stance when you hear the whistle. Too slow? Take a lap.

Going down in the butterfly, recovering. Going down, on-ice recovery. T-pushes and shuffles, C-cuts and telescoping, covering the load zone and all five holes, and no, I didn't know what these

261

weird phrases meant before Coach showed me. But I kept at it like a zealot, six days a week all spring and summer. Dropping to my knees, getting back to my stance. Dropping, sliding to either side to cover. Aiming the lead leg, pushing with the drive leg, and squaring up in one swift move. Or moving side to side by degrees as the play came closer. Cutting arcs forward and back with my toes, drifting forward or back by spreading or closing my legs. And this was all before Coach brought in Durdovitch, Kelly, and Conlan to start taking shots, to resume our gym class magic on the ice.

Throughout all this craziness, I kept thinking I could walk away. Kept telling myself I had time to admit I'd been miscast. Other kids worked at these skills for years, from the time they were toddlers. So how the hell could I do it in months? But then I picked up everything so fast and did so well in practice, and earned enough praise from the other Falcons, that I didn't want to stop. Doubt and fear belonged to the old Dexter Bolzjak, that weak loser content to lock himself in his room and wallow in his loneliness.

So went my mental tug-of-war up to the season opener. We took the ice with Deep Purple's "Space Truckin'" blaring from the PA. Coach requested this for every home game, believing the song was an ominous, badass intro guaranteed to psyche up team and crowd alike. The stands were mostly empty, though, leaving the heavy, distorted sound to sink in a bog of cacophony. Coach didn't care. He lurked behind the bench, nodding to the beat while everyone else ignored or endured it.

Meanwhile I went to my net, so nervous I was shaking. I spotted Mom and Dad easily enough in the sparse audience, and they had no idea how close I was to quitting. The other Falcons, no idea. Our opponents the West Liberty Snow Dogs, no idea. And if Coach knew about the vacuum in my guts, the jitters in my limbs, the temptation I had to skate over to him and say, "Sorry, I can't do this," he wasn't letting it worry him, not during "Space Truckin'."

But then the music stopped. The Falcons and Snow Dogs lined up for the face-off, the ref dropped the puck, and now finally and forever it was too late to walk away.

The stickblades clacked and chipped the puck back to the Snow Dogs, who came charging in their blue-and-white unis. Their left winger took it all the way up the boards, dumped it behind the net. The puck deflected back to the slot, where their center was ready. He blasted it, but I stopped it. Took it in the chest, let it drop into my glove.

Whistle. The people in the stands cheered. I mean clapping and whooing and stomping the bleachers. The noise froze me at first. I didn't even think to give the puck to the ref, who had to dig it out of my glove, asking if I was okay.

Another face-off, and the Snow Dogs came back again. From Center to Right to Center, slap shot. I dropped, and the puck thunked off my leg pad. Slid out to their left winger, who came barreling over the blue line and wristed it. And I saw it, never lost it, eyes locked upon it as I knocked it away.

And the people cheered again, more sustained than before. Scattered here and there, some of them even rose for an ovation. Then more jumped up when Motrick, our lanky second-line center, took it to the net and beat the Snow Dog goalie. The red bulb lit up, the scoreboard registered a "1" next to HOME, and they went nuts up in the stands.

The score was 4–0 when the game ended. Durdovitch and the rest mobbed me with congrats and hugs and headbutts, and none of it felt real. I was happy, I guess, but more relieved than anything, whispering "I'm not a piece of shit" for the rest of that night. From the rink to my bed. "I'm not a piece of shit. Thank you, God, I'm not a piece of shit."

Next week, the Cougars. We won, 3–1, though I gave up a softie off a rebound. Still not bad, since it took them thirty-eight shots to get one past me. Otherwise I refused to cost the team a game. Ask the Apaches (who we beat 6–0), the Highlanders (2–0), the Sabertooths (7–3, not my best but good enough), the Eagle Owls (5–2), the Grizzlies (1–0), and the Snow Dogs (4–0) after a rematch.

They came in waves, flicking wristers and backhanders, trying wraparounds, firing heavy slappers, and I stopped them all. Just put myself out there and performed, fighting off the nerves, breaking away to a place where I was someone better. Someone strong, confident, and worth your while. Where I could spring a hundred people to their feet and keep them screaming, send them home knowing they saw a show. And where no one—not a single soul in the barn—would ever guess I was a fraud.

Not that everyone was a fan. Being on the team didn't get me a girlfriend or membership in a clique, and just as well. I was too withdrawn, too morose, wouldn't have been much fun anyway. And of course I got booed and heckled at away games, but that was to be expected. What I wasn't ready for was one particular reaction I got away from the ice. And I don't mean the four fuckers.

I'm talking about another night midway through the season. It was in January, close to Dad's birthday. I drove this car to the mall to buy him a new sander from Sears and realized I was a few bucks short. Lacking a debit or credit card, I figured I'd catch Mom to borrow the difference.

I walked into Kaufmann's, the department store where she

worked the perfume booth part-time. Mom wasn't around, but two of her coworkers were. The younger one was in her twenties, not long out of college. The older one (name tag: LINDA) was in her fifties with blue eyes, wet yellow ringlets pasted to her brow, and pants hiked up over her gut. Since it was a slow night, they noticed me lingering around.

"You waiting for your mother?" Linda said.

"Yeah. How'd you know?"

"I know you're Samantha's girl. Oh, I'm sorry. I meant *boy*. I couldn't tell with your pretty hair."

"She duc back soon?"

Linda looked to her coworker, who seemed embarrassed. "Isn't he pretty, with all his pretty hair? Oh, and those ripped jeans. What a class act!"

At that point, I should've just walked away. Or, at the most, said fuck you and walked away. But instead I just stood there, blindsided by this lady's tone.

"You see the article about him in the *Post*? They called him a phenom, said he was a special talent. Talked him up like his mommy does," Linda said, and looked back to me. "You know, my husband was a Marine. He got three Purple Hearts in Vietnam. You know what he said when he saw your picture in the paper? He said you're a faggot. A little queer that wouldn't last five minutes in basic training."

"Shhh! Linda!" the coworker said with a blush.

"I just—I just can't take it anymore," Linda said, her face scrunched up in disgust. "First we get a pot-smoking draft-dodger for president, letting all his faggot friends in the military. And now *this*, kids walking around like *this*. It's like the sixties all over again. It makes me sick. The whole country's going soft, and nobody cares!"

That's when I started away, but Linda wasn't done yet.

"You want to know where your mommy is? She's down at Halloran's, getting liquored up. That's where she takes her breaks. Why don't you go see her?"

On the way downstairs, I wasn't even pissed yet. I was more stunned, wondering why anyone would care so much about what I looked like or what some article said. And as nasty as Linda was, what was I supposed to do? Engage in a sociopolitical debate? Spit in her face? No, best to just walk away and pretend it didn't affect me.

I stopped on the threshold of Halloran's, a self-described "traditional Irish pub" with a shamrock in the "O" of its logo. The joint pushed its theme with pictures of Dublin on the walls and gas logs burning in a hearth. Flamelight glimmered off the bottles and mirror behind the bar, and a brass plaque (NONE BUT THE FINEST GUINNESS PORTER SOLD HERE) mounted above. Couples sat around gorging on burgers and fries, grease dribbling down their chins, while traditional Irish icon Phil Collins played on the jukebox. "Do You Remember?" I think it was, in all its sapping gravity.

Mom was seated at the bar, her back to me, conspicuous by her copper-colored hair. A blond guy in a suit slouched alongside her. One hand on his bottle, the other on her thigh, stroking it, fingers catching the hem of her skirt with each pass. He looked about ten years younger than her, leaning close to her, talking her up with spittle-wet lips. In the mirror I saw her smiling like she was charmed. In the flesh I saw her reach down and lay her hand upon his. Not stopping him, letting him touch her as much as he wanted.

She finished her drink, gave him a gaze that said, "Just wait till I get off work." Feeling pretty good about himself, the guy eased off and sipped his beer. But he still kept his hand on her, as if to reassure her that yeah, after work sounds perfect.

Within a few minutes, the bartender noticed me hanging around the doorway, doing nothing but watching Mom and the guy. He gave them a heads-up. The guy turned around first, and I ignored him.

Then Mom turned around, and her face lost everything it showed a moment ago. All her desire, all her flirty naughtiness, gone. The life drained out of her skin, left her pale and braced for an attack. And the longer we locked stares, the more her shock gave way to shame. She was the one who blinked, who looked away first. And when she brought her eyes back to mine, they betrayed weakness. Like I could've made her cry if I'd just kept standing there.

But I couldn't, not for another second. Seeing them together made me want to break the guy's bottle over his head and slice his face. As for her, I didn't even want to think about what she deserved. Or about her as a person, Dad as a man, what the three of us were supposed to mean to each other.

Nope, didn't want to think about it. I walked away and left her on her bar stool with her smug dick. Went outside, got in this car, and screeched the tires out of the lot.

She didn't come home till after midnight. I was in my room, watching Letterman while Dad snored down the hall. Car door, front door, footsteps, I listened and tried to be detached. And yet I tensed up when she knocked, felt my blood getting riled when she walked in.

She closed the door behind her, gently to avoid waking Dad, and sat beside me. Neither of us said anything for a while, just took turns looking at the TV or piles of clothes on the floor. Even then I wasn't one for awkward silences, and so I blundered in first.

"That Linda you work with. She's a real cunt."

Normally that would've triggered a red-faced outburst, but this was hardly a normal night. Mom still bristled but took a breath, measured her response. "We never got along, but she's been giving me all kinds of grief lately. Her son's the star player for the Highlanders. She didn't take it too well when you shut him out."

"Whatever. Fuck her and her piss-colored perm."

"Is she the one you're really mad at?" Mom said.

I looked at her for the first time since the bar, into her eyes bleary from tears or booze. Her Cleopatra makeup was starting to break down, melting into her crow's-feet. Before I could stop it, the phrase "old whore" came to mind. Flew right past my catcher and hit the net. Score.

"I know you won't believe this, but me and—"

"No, don't. Don't give him a name. I don't want to know it. I don't want to think of him as a person. Because he's not. He's shit, and that's all he'll ever be."

"Don't you think you're jumping to conclusions?"

"Look at me and tell me I'm wrong."

She looked at the TV instead, its glow reflected in her eyes. "Keep your voice down," was all she could say.

"So Dad doesn't know."

"Of course not. What do you think?"

"How could you be so open about it? Right out in public like that?"

"You do anything long enough, you get complacent. Not that that's an excuse."

"Were you ever gonna tell him?"

"I was going to wait until you went off to college. And then, yeah, I was planning to leave him."

I let that one sink in while Letterman and Goldie Hawn giggled about her latest movie. After a minute of their banter, I got off the bed, turned off the TV with the remote. Then I fired the remote at the wall as hard as I could. Mom flinched when it shattered, its batteries bouncing loose.

Dad's snoring continued, faint but unabated.

"And you want me to keep this secret for you? Because I don't think I can."

She thought about it, then stood up from the bed. "No. I can't ask you to do that. But there is one thing I want from you. Remember that I love you. And that I'll always love you, no matter what. Please remember that."

"The same way you love Dad?"

"Dexter, please—"

"You know something? Since I got home tonight, I've been thinking about a speech somebody gave a few years ago, right in this same room. Something about how sad it is that everybody's so distrustful of each other. How we all have this horrible impulse to hurt and degrade each other, and how we should try to fight it. When she said all that, I'll admit, I thought it was bullshit. But as time went by, I started to believe there might be some truth to it. After all, I believed in her, who gave such beautiful advice. Who I loved and trusted as much as I could ever love or trust anyone.

"And now? Now I know there was no truth to it or anything else she said. It was always a lie. And that person, who I loved and trusted, she doesn't exist anymore. Maybe she never did."

We locked stares again. Fresh tears appeared in her eyes, and this time I was the one who looked away first. For all those hours of splatter I'd watched, all those fake stabbings and slashes and blown-open skulls, all that elaborate, choreographed maiming

269

and pain, it turned out I didn't have the stomach for the real thing. This was violence, the kind that leaves scars beyond the years. Knowing you hit someone harder with words than you ever could with your hands, how what she deserved no longer mattered once you struck her, and how there's no taking it back. No rewinding it, no undoing it. No, once she left the room crying, I lost her and she lost me, and that's not something you ever get over.

Samantha broke the news to Marv within a week, while I was at a practice. So I missed the explosion but came home to the aftermath: him in his recliner, scowling at the TV, broken knickknacks and dishes all over the floor, her gone for that night and every one after. She still came to the games, though, out of guilt or some ghost of motherly duty. And they still sat together, always in the same spot near the aisle, about a dozen bleachers up. I don't know why they bothered, but they did. Game nights seemed like the last scrap of civility left between them, a shared habit that neither was willing to break. At least not yet.

Meanwhile the word had spread about how good the team was, and our crowds grew by the game. That *Post* article had generated attention, too. After they hyped me and ran a picture of me unmasked, I became "Goalchick" to louder, larger clusters of hostiles. (Not to mention the four fuckers, who'd started to monitor my comings and goings from the rink, where I'd park, my route home, where Marv and Samantha were on game and practice nights.) And by the end of February, when we took the ice against the Orcas, that was one thunderous sound coming down from the stands, seismic enough to crush "Space Truckin'."

My guys lined up with their guys, the ref dropped the puck, and I put on my show. I'd never seen the puck better, never moved better. Like Coach said, I had the juice gushing in my veins and would never have it again. Five hundred people packed the rink that night, and I made them jump and whoop and ooh and ahh. When I felt like showboating, I even ripped off Patrick Roy's Statue of Liberty move, catching the puck and sweeping my hand skyward. Playing to the rafters, basking in camera flashes, listening to my fans chant my name.

And none of it mattered. Not with Samantha and Marv sitting there trying to look happy. Not when I knew how miserable they were inside, how powerless I was to help them. What's the point? I kept thinking. What's the point of playing a fuckin' game when your family's falling apart? When you can't look at the people you love without seeing them at their worst, weakest, and most deceitful?

You need to leave, I thought. Both of you. Just go home, go away. Stop pretending all three of us wouldn't be better off if you'd never met. You can't hide it from me, the dying-marriage despair eating away at you. Besides, there's a greater fake in this building, and you're cheering for him. Shot, save. Shot, save. Shot, save. That's it, people. Cheer. Scream. Stand and clap with the buzzer when the scoreboard hits 00:00, Us 4, Them 3. Laugh it up, Marv and Samantha. Smile like there's something to celebrate here.

In other words, they'd become a distraction. By the time of the playoffs, they decided to alternate. One attended while the other went elsewhere, culminating in the mix-up that kept them both away for the state championship. But you know what? I asked for it. As much as their absence rattled me that night, and as sure as I'm driving to the same Ropersdale that sent its Blizzards to bury me and my myth, I asked for it. It only took eight years, but I think I can admit that now, that I called upon calamity. And man, did it answer.

21

After 79 hits 80 and 80 hits 8, you get on Route 62 North to reach Ropersdale, or so my gas station map says. The road goes past modest houses, greasy spoons, and small shops biding their twilight in the age of corporate chains. Places named with wince-worthy puns (Lumber-One Timber, Big Bad Woof Dog Grooming) or brandishing cutesy ads you never see in the city. My favorite is the house doubling as a tombstone dealer, displaying an array of slabs on its lawn. It sits near a hairpin turn in the road, the site of God knows how many accidents, and a banner draped across its porch reads SLOW DOWN! OUR BUSINESS CAN WAIT!

Route 62 winds along a groove in the mountains, burrowing through stretches of woods. It meets the Allegheny and skirts the riverbank, sometimes so close to the water—nudged ever closer by the unyielding rock—that it bridges over to the opposite side, hits the same resistance, and bridges back again. But it presses onward, contorting with the river's curves, rising to ear-popping heights, declining to valleys shrouded with old growth and constant dusk.

I've been here before, I tell myself. Old Watermill Road. The same darkness, the same wicked bends and drop-offs that will

272

send you headlong into a trunk if you go too fast. The same placid beauty masking a threat, whether it's a car swerving around the next turn or a deer prancing into your front end. Whatever the similarities, I'm not stopping if I come upon another wreck. Whether it's a mannequin or real human body splayed along the road, I'm not stopping, not again, not so close to the end.

The river broadens for islands, slopes thick with woods and a pall of creeping mist. Stare into it for too long, and you start to see ghosts. Shadows of Iroquois or the tribes who chose the French over the Redcoats. All of them gone, slaughtered or forced to leave no matter how long they'd lived here. But the land still misses them, still bears their names and trails, still cradles their bones in its soil. It'll take a lot more strip malls and suburban sprawl to break such a bond, to chase the ghosts from their home, but give us time. Something tells me we'll get around to it someday.

The Allegheny hooks around to the right, and the road splits—62 follows the water while the bridge to Ropersdale lies straight ahead. So I've arrived, crossing over railroad tracks and a lumber mill. Past a parking lot full of off-duty flatbeds and trailers, into air pungent with the smell of sawdust.

Main Street offers a post office, library, bakery, war memorial. And there's your downtown. No wonder they were so fanatical about their Blizzards. Doesn't look like there's much else going on. Main turns residential for a steepled church, a middle school and ballfield. Quaint white-painted houses, yards with the telltale signs of kids—swing sets, basketball hoops, bikes—but none playing outside. Instead there's a tough guy in a Hummer tailgating me, pissed because I'm driving slow and clearly not from around these parts. He even gets fed up enough to roar past on the left. Normally that would annoy me, but right now I don't care, not when I see one house that stands out from the rest. And sure enough, it occupies the corner of Main and Dorothea Drive.

I'm not too knowledgeable about house styles, but I'd call it a Colonial. Its large porch wraps around the entire ground floor, sheltered by an overhang on all sides. Several posts support the overhang, giving the porch a caged look. Shrubs and a fence of spiked bars line the edge of the lawn, further obscuring the ground floor. The second story, more visible from the street, has narrow windows on either side of a central column. Rounded and spacious enough for its own windows, the column rises above the roof, capped with a turret that overlooks the block.

"Ostentatious" isn't the word for the house. If anything, it seems misplaced, like it belongs in New Orleans more than here. I'm guessing that sometime in the early 1900s, a local bigwig, maybe the mayor or mill owner, traveled down there, was wowed by the old plantation houses, and decided to build his own in the mountains of PA whether it belonged or not.

Once I pull onto Dorothea, I find that it's not a street so much as the house's private drive. I park behind the only other vehicle around, an old Chevy pickup from the '50s, and step out for a stretch. There's no movement about the house, no sign that anyone's home. The river runs close behind the place, branching off into a small pool about twenty yards away. A willow curtains off this recess, and through its weeping green I glimpse a few idling birds.

Not quite ready to brave the house, I wander to the willow and part its veil. Two mallards come paddling over right away, expecting to be fed. A goose hangs back, cautious at first, then makes its way toward me, too. In the far corner, a lone white swan cleans itself. Twisting its neck around in a torturous angle, wedging its bill under its wing and rubbing hard like there's a tough clump of mud lodged there.

I watch this bathing ritual, feeling the chill of the river wind, the house looming over my back. And look, I'm not a praying man. I never have been and doubt I ever will be. In fact, Doubting Thomas was always the Bible character who made the most sense to me. But taking this time to think about where I am and how I got here, I ask no particular deity that she's home. And if that's not asking too much, I ask no particular higher power for the guts and good sense to not fuck this up.

From the day Lou staggered up to me at Biggies, I've come too far and tried too hard. I've let down too many people, from my parents to Erin to Coach and who knows how many more. And I've lost too much and too many times to not win one for once.

The mallards and goose run out of patience and retreat back to where they were. The swan notices me and stops. It doesn't seem spooked, just interrupted and wondering why some weird guy is standing there staring at it. This feels like my cue to go, to take a breath and confront the task at hand. So I let the willow-curtain fall back into place, leave the birds to their peace.

At the front door, I push the button of an intercom buzzer.

Waiting, nothing.

No sound from the house, just distant cars and rustling trees, my heart drumming with growing doubt.

I hit the button again, and nothing again.

But then the intercom static-crackles to life, and a woman's voice says, "Who are you, and what do you want?"

I hold down the button, answer, "I'm a friend of Lou Kashon, and I got a message from him."

"Who's the message for?"

"If you know who Lou Kashon is, you know who the message is for."

Silence: a nauseous pause on which everything seems to teeter.

The door lock buzzes, though, and I'm permitted to enter.

I pass through a vestibule, into a living room where a spiral stairway corkscrews up to the second floor. An old German shepherd naps at the foot of the stairs, a sluggish heap of black and brown fur. His spiked collar suggests guard duty, but the poor guy's not up for it anymore. He wakes, looks at me with sad, rheumy eyes, and doesn't bother to move or make a sound.

To my left is a piano, a little girl-mannequin seated at the keys. She has blue eyes and a shiny black wig. Bangs, the back pulled up in pigtails like a child version of Mercy.

Dozens of masks cover the wall behind her, arranged in precise rows. Each a sexless, raceless, ageless face marked with a different blemish. From left to right, the blemishes start slight but grow more severe. Black eyes and bruises at first. Then scars, gashes, bullet holes. Down to burns and decay, each face further stripped till the last mask on the bottom row is nothing but a skull.

A rabbit-eared TV flickers on the far side of the room, playing black-and-white footage I recognize as *Lady of the Dark Pleasure*. Another mannequin sits on a sofa facing the screen, a potbellied bald guy in a wife beater holding a beer. The TV reflects in his eyes, which seem to be watching me instead, fixed on me no matter where I stand.

From a hidden speaker, the woman's voice says, "Come on up. I'm waiting."

And before I can even look for the speaker, the girl-mannequin tilts forward with an electric hum. Her hands rise and fall, never touching the keys, but a low, synthesized drone blares out from more hidden speakers. The dirge rattles me by force, dropping lower and impossibly lower, each chord sustained to punish the

276

nerves. A voice joins the sonic barrage, raspy and female, chanting the same language Mercy prayed to the moon.

I step over the dog, who lies still despite the noise, and climb the spiral. The dirge continues upstairs from still more speakers. I reach the second-floor hallway, which curves around in a complete circle, baseboard and molding warped to match. Four open doors face each other, evenly spaced along the loop.

Trying the nearest one first, I enter what used to be a bedroom. The bed's still there, but sawed in half and spread apart. An open coffin fills the gap between the halves, a handcrafted box of wood painted black. Within the coffin lies a dummy in a straitjacket, its face eyeless and gray, a web of pearly slime around its mouth. Its body writhes hard and nonstop, rap-tap-tapping the wood, powered by a hidden current.

Two more dummies lie tucked away and sleeping, each to its own bed-half. They're androgynous twins with curly blond hair, cherub cheeks, and sweet-dream smiles. And yet coils of razor wire tear up from their crotches, shredding the blankets, thrusting to the ceiling like metal geysers. Bloodred paint slathers the coils and meaty chunks flecked all over them, wads of cloth posing as minced flesh.

I back away, back to the hallway and the dirge, the path leading to the next room.

The space, and I mean the whole damn room, is frozen underwater. I know it can't be, but there it is: a solid volume of ice, objects suspended within it. A red four-wheeled wagon, a tree branch, an unhinged door, a car tire, all floating between floor and ceiling.

Once absorbing that initial wallop, I venture into the illusion. A tunnel runs from the doorway to the center of the room, an opening that draws you in, immersing you in the freeze. When you reach the center, you find yourself trapped in a cylinder, a nook so tight you can't extend your arms. The only way out is the way you came in, but you can't even see that passage anymore. You only sense the ice around you and over you, enclosing you, constricting your breath.

I don't know how she did it, how she sculpted and treated so much glass to make it look like ice. Or what she did to make the objects float, since I see no wires. And turning, I find more rot in this transparent crypt the longer I stay within it. The corpse of a man levitates in the corner, upright and chained to a cinder-block anchor. Another body hovers closer to the center, a little boy in overalls, his skin bluish, eyes bloated to saucers. A woman lies facedown near the floor, fish nibbling the skin from her fingertips.

To the hallway again, the dirge again, that voice again, imploring something to arise from its slumber. An ancient, malevolent creature that would rip through your viscera and suck your marrow, lusting for a taste of your soul.

"Jesus Christ," I whisper when I look in the next room. Just as the last one takes you under frozen water, this one puts you right in the middle of an explosion. And judging by the mess strewn about, the explosion is a shotgun blast to someone's head.

To enter the room, you step over a row of wooden teeth, onto a plump carpet of tongue. Bloodred paint and pulp splatter the walls. Brain fragments and skull shards hang weightless in space, everywhere and forever airborne. At least a hundred pieces, all dangling from wires connected to a blanket of scalp overhead. The largest piece, a basketball-sized eye, trails a length of pink nerve-cord to the floor.

I touch the eyeball, and all the other pieces move with it, brushing against me as the scalp rotates. This mobile fills the whole room, brings you to the frozen instant of a head-shot, tempts you to handle the flying debris of a shattered mind. Which I do, and its textures—glass eye, spongy brains, burlap skin, ceramic skull—feel more pleasing than I should admit.

But determined to stay focused, I retreat through the bloody jumble and step back over the teeth. Back to the hallway once more, and the dirge, toward the last open door.

A gigantic maggot curls from wall to opposite wall of the room, blocking out the windows with rubbery bulk. Its belly has ruptured, hemorrhaging earth and half-digested corpses. Skulls and shoulder blades, rib cage and pelvis, all mired in the muck. Scattered limbs, a lone skeletal hand raised and grasping for nothing.

Agnes stands ankle-deep in the sludge, her back to the door. She's taller and thinner than I would've guessed, wearing a flannel with rolled-up sleeves, dirty jeans, and hiking boots. Braided white hair halfway down to her waist, hands muddied with her work, rag slung over her shoulder. As if sensing someone behind her, she picks up a remote from a nearby step stool and shuts down the dirge. Then turns around, wiping her hands with the rag.

"So you're the messenger. Come. Tell your tale."

I can't move from the doorway. Her face has aged, but her eyes are the same. Blue like I knew they were when I studied them on the Wall, frame by frame. She still has her bangs, still cocks an eyebrow and smirks at my hesitance.

"Sweetie, it's okay. I'm not famous anymore. And I'm too old to hurt you, don't you think?"

"For not being famous anymore, you weren't easy to find."

"But you did. Care to explain how?"

"It's a long, ugly story not worth telling now."

"I have time. You never told me your name, by the way."

"Dexter. And I can't believe you trust me enough to just invite me in."

"I don't trust you. But I'm not afraid of you, either. And I'm curious to hear what you have to say. So please . . ." She gestures for me to go on and spill it.

"Me and Lou worked a couple blocks from each other in Pittsburgh. He knew my dad, which led to him recruiting me to find you. He told me about the two of you, said he wanted to talk to you one last time. And I do mean 'last' because he's dying. He's got cancer through and through, and he's barely clinging to life at this point. Foolishly, then, I promised him I wouldn't just find you but bring you to him in person. And so here I am."

Agnes stares at me, and I meet her gaze. She looks shocked, jarred from any comfort she'd enjoyed earlier. Then her face reddens, and with a tremor in her voice, she says, "If this is some kind of sick joke, you'd better leave right now."

"It's no joke. Don't believe me? Want more details? You wrote Lou a letter when you were in high school. You thanked him for helping you with your Halloween dance. You were in a panic because you were supposed to do the decorating, but you blew it off till the last minute because you were so wrapped up in your studies. So by a lucky break you went to the Strip and met Lou at Kashon's, and he came through with a truckload of pumpkins.

"Lou still has that letter in a drawer in his house. He let me see it to prove he really knew you. You want more proof?" I take the business card from my pocket. "I got this from his brother Eugene this morning. The trail I followed led to him, and I got him to talk about your last visit there. If you want to know everything else I did and found, I'll tell you everything. You know yourself, it's a three-hour trip to Pittsburgh."

"Stop it! Damn it, stop it!" she says, and takes a breath. Then another, deeper one to collect herself and regain her composure. "This is a hell of a thing to throw at somebody. After so many years, a *hell* of a thing. How am I supposed to believe you? How do I know you didn't dig all this up so you could use it to—"

"Sell you out? Lead you to a bunch of cameras? Agnes, I'm the last person on this planet who'd do that to you. I understand why you wouldn't trust me. I wouldn't, either, if I were you. But you can call the hospital. He's at St. Francis, Room 226. I think it would be better—would mean a lot more—if you showed up in person and surprised him. But if you'd rather call, then call."

"You have anything else to say?"

"If you won't come with me, and you won't call the hospital, then call the police and have them arrest me for trespassing. Because I can't leave this house without knowing I've done everything I can do short of kidnapping you. I owe Lou that, and I owe myself that. Otherwise it's your call. You decide."

She searches my eyes, probing for any sign of a lie. I don't blink or budge from the doorway. Slowly her anger lessens, and she looks away. To the floor, to me, and back to the floor, comprehending the situation while I wait and do nothing but wait.

Agnes watches Pennsylvania race past her window, having cleaned herself up and traded her at-home clothes for a dark blue dress. I tried to tell her how I found her but skipped so much of the unsavory stuff—the state of Lou's house, the money, the trip to the hospital, Pollard's film, Endicott, *Shots on Goal*—that there wasn't much story left. She seemed to suspect she was getting a heavily edited version but didn't press me. Maybe she's waiting till later, maybe she's overwhelmed or too tired, I don't know. But we continue onward in a long, uncomfortable lull.

I wouldn't call Agnes hostile, just not easy to talk to. That she even chose to get in the car was amazing enough, and I feel like I'd better watch every word to avoid changing her mind. Plus there's the fact that this is Mercy Carnahan, La Devila herself, sitting right there next to me. What can I possibly say that she hasn't heard before, that wouldn't sound trite or downright stupid?

"So, um, I like all the art stuff in your place," I say, and cringe at the pause that follows.

"Thanks," she says, still looking out the window. "But liking something doesn't mean a damn thing. You like puppies and candy, I like ice cream and Waikiki Beach, and who cares? 'Does it breathe?' is the question. Does it take you somewhere you don't often go? Does it challenge your perspective? Does it open you to what's possible, does it reach you, does it affect you?" She turns to me. "Does it breathe?"

"Oh, it breathes all right. But you'll have to forgive me for being caught off guard. I was expecting a bed-and-breakfast."

"It *was* one when I gave Eugene that card. But that was a long time and a lot of laundry ago. Washing dishes, cooking for people, then hearing them complain anyway? It turned out I wasn't the customer-service type. Should've known that going in, I suppose."

"Speaking of pleasing people, there's something I wanted to ask you about. That Christmas pageant when you were little. When you played a sugarplum and danced till you passed out. If it really happened, I guess I'm wondering what kind of kid would push herself like that."

"It had nothing to do with pleasing people. It was a defense. A refuge, that's all."

"A defense against what?"

"Life. The ugliness of it, the day-to-day depression of it. The sickness that plagued my mother. The cruelty of kids who'd mock her in school with cuckoo noises and drawings of her howling at the moon. The way they'd tease me, calling me 'Agnes Madness,' 'Agnes Crackpotski.' The parents who encouraged them by telling them my mother was crazy. Or the ones who wouldn't let their kids play with me because of the gossip they'd heard.

"I dealt with it the best way I could, by escaping. My father took me to a few Saturday matinees, and once I saw Clara Bow, that did it. And then Louise Brooks, too. From then on, I spent all day, every day in the barn—pretending it was a ballroom, queen's castle, luxury liner—hamming it up in my own make-believe movies. When I wanted a live theater audience, I'd sing for the horses and dance for the pigs. I'd stay up past bedtime, writing love letters to Clara and Louise, designing costumes I thought they should wear. Not knowing their careers were over by then. I even got the spanking of a lifetime when I chopped off my hair, trying to give myself a bob like Brooks.

"On the night of that pageant, I was a nervous mouse of a thing, sweating in a baggy purple costume Mama had thrown together from an old horse blanket. Waiting backstage, looking like a squashed grape while the other sugarplum girls looked so lovely in their frilly pink tutus. Huddled in their group, laughing at me and Mama, doing their cuckoo noises.

"And right about then, I felt her within me for the first time. Heard her voice whispering, telling me to go out there and tear the house down. To dance like no one else was around, dance away the pain and humiliation, dance like dancing could save you from this life. I heard her as plain as you're hearing me now, and nobody noticed. Nobody else heard the voice."

"And that didn't scare you?" I ask.

"Of course it did. But she knew me. That was the thing. She

understood me, she cared. She came to me when I was weak and afraid, when I was a coward, and she gave me strength.

"So then Miss Oxby played our cue, and we went out onstage. I couldn't find my parents in the audience, only a crowd of strangers. Their faces were shadowy and gray, their eyes black and empty, and they were laughing like their kids. Staring and laughing at the weird girl whose crazy mother couldn't even sew a costume.

"The other girls started the routine, and I did what the voice said. Threw myself out front and danced like I danced for the pigs at home. Nobody knew what to do, and I didn't care. I went off to another plane, kicking like a real little flapper. Freed myself from Agnes and became the vessel of the voice, the brightest star in the universe, let alone Harmony.

"You should've seen those faces change! From shadowy to rosy, from mocking to adoring, their eyes sparking from dark pits to lusty color. I had them hooked, all of them smiling like I was their own cutie-pie darling. The longer I went and the faster I moved, the more they loved it, whooping and hollering and calling for more.

"And I looked at them, and thought, 'Go to hell, you phonies. All you ever did was hurt me and my mama and let your kids do the same. So now I'm tearing your angel-babies apart and dancing on the scraps. Love me, want me, keep wishing I was yours. But touch me and I'll bite out your throat, spit your own blood in your face.'

"I must've passed out then, because the next thing I remember is waking up in the principal's office with a wet towel on my head. My parents and the principal standing over me, Daddy saying, 'Oh, mercy, mercy.' Sounds crazy, doesn't it?"

"Not to me, it doesn't," I say. "Though I wish it did."

"As you know, that wasn't the last of it," Agnes says. "After the pageant, I felt her in me all the time. I imagined what she'd look like, how she'd walk, move, smoke a cigarette. I'd spend hours at the mirror, making the faces she'd make, talking the way she talked.

"And she always had something to say. When the Academy offered a full scholarship, and I fretted over leaving home, she said, 'You kidding, sis? Ditch this jerkwater burg. Yeah, your folks are decent people, but do you want to end up like them? Get out before your mama grinds you down like she ground down your pop. If you really want to help them, get out and send home some fat checks once you hit big. But make sure you get out.'

"When I met Louis, I argued with her every day. She was against our dating, engagement, everything, and I'd resisted her. But then Stanley Frisch came calling, and she pounced, saying, 'Here's what you've always wanted, sis! What you've dreamt about since those days in the barn, your one and only shot. Are you gonna take it or trap yourself in a kitchen? Do you want the power and glory or a bunch of dirty diapers? Yeah, Louie's a swell guy, but you'll have others. And he'll find somebody else, too, I promise. It might sting now, but you'll both be happier over time, you'll see.'

"So I rolled up to that restaurant, and you know the rest. I can't deny what I did, and I can't make excuses. I can only tell you how it was. I had a choice—get married or be her—and I chose her."

"And you're not her anymore?"

"I couldn't be if I tried. She bailed. She left me like she came to me, while I was waiting backstage. I assume you've read about *The Crimson Kiss*? As much as they've written about it, nobody ever got the story right because nobody knew the most important part. Just before I made my entrance, she said, 'Time's up, sis.

285

Hope you had fun. And remember, you were never anything without me.'

"I walked out there to a standing ovation, but I wasn't on Broadway. I was back in Butler Elementary in a baggy purple costume, jelly-legged before a crowd of shadowy faces. It didn't matter how many movies I'd made or how big my name was. Once the applause stopped, I felt nothing but a gaping void inside, and all I could do was walk away. You could say it was karma, divine retribution, my just desserts. But don't worry about Mercy. She's still young, pretty, and famous. And I suppose she always will be."

"If she betrayed you like that, why are you still protecting her?" I ask. "Why don't you hold a press conference, show the world you're alive and doing fine without her?"

"I could never do such a thing, Dexter. You might see that as a failing, and you might be right. But what I see is the telegram from the studio saying that Mama had killed herself. Alone in a psychiatric hospital while I was across the country, filming an asinine movie. I'd sent those fat checks like Mercy said, put Mama in the best facility in the state. But I hadn't seen her since I left home, and I never would again.

"For twenty-seven years, I was too busy hiding from cameras and tabloid hacks to see my father. When Daddy fell sick and I finally made a top-secret visit to the hospital, he was too far gone to recognize me. And today you come to me with this news about Louis. If he curses me out, you could hardly blame him.

"And these are the people I loved! I couldn't have treated them so badly for nothing. I have to believe in Mercy Carnahan, and I have to protect her even now. Do you think I chose a false goddess? That I devoted my life to a gimmick? I don't think so; I can't afford to think so.

286

"No, I chose a code. And according to that code, you always leave 'em wanting more. Maybe I took it too far, but nobody can say I didn't live it. And that has to be worth something, to live by the code you choose. It has to be."

"Fair enough," I say. "But there's another way to look at it. Maybe she never really left you because you're one and the same person, and you always were. Which means you're still following her orders right this very second."

"Well, that was the risk you took when you chose to hunt me down. Wasn't it?"

I look at her, and she's already looking at me. With malice or fondness in her eyes, I can't tell which, she reaches over and pats my knee.

"But enough about me, sweetie. What's your story? Surely you had a life before Louis."

We pull into the hospital lot, and I find a spot near the doors. For a moment we just sit there, caught in an odd space where we both know what to do, but neither is willing to make the move. I give her time, careful not to push her more than I already have. In the silence, a bug crawls across the windshield, pausing on the splotched trace of another. It wags its antennae, detecting something troublesome, but then continues on while I keep hoping like hell she doesn't back out now.

"So this is where we end up," Agnes says, and looks down to her hands on her lap. She turns them over, her palms wet with sweat. "You know, it's been so long since I've seen him. Is it weak to admit I'm afraid?"

"You'll be all right," I say, but she doesn't hear me. Instead she watches the doors, breathes, and drifts off in her thoughts. And I give her more time.

Then, when it seems she may never come back, I do what I can to comfort her. It's not much, but I reach down and take hold of her hand. Look her in the eye and say, "You will be all right. Just be yourself."

Agnes wakes, startled by my touch. But she doesn't pull free. She squeezes my hand, gazing at me with a fragile smile. The same she gave when she first saw Lou, I imagine, and now I can't fault him or anyone else for falling in love with her. And staying in love with her, dying haunted by her.

Hand in hand we stand together in the elevator. The doors open, show us out to Lou's floor. By now I'm all jangled nerves myself, my own breaths shorter with every step toward 226.

I stop near the door and say, "How about this. I'll go in first. Talk to him a little, lure him into thinking it's a normal visit. And then you come in and wow him."

Agnes says okay, and I go ahead.

"So, Lou, I was out messing around, and—"

A nurse's aide flinches, faces me with an armful of pillows. She's changing an empty bed. Me, her, the bed, and that's it. That's all.

"Excuse me?" she says.

"Lou. Where's Lou?"

"I'm sorry, sir. You must not have heard yet. He passed this morning, around six or seven. I'm—I'm really sorry. The receptionist outside can help you more than I can," she says, and not knowing what else to say, leaves the room with her pillows.

I start to go dizzy. Out of breath, as if I just got sucker-punched in the gut. Holding on to the wall, trying not to fall, never so hollow or lost.

And then Agnes enters, bright-eyed and beaming.

22

Agnes couldn't have been more gracious. It's okay, she insisted. She'd call a cab, spend the night at the William Penn downtown, arrange her way home tomorrow. I'd already driven upstate and back once. No reason to do it again, especially so soon after the news. No, sweetie. Best that you go home and rest. She knows this town. Don't you worry about her.

We agreed that I'd go through Lou's house, send anything he would've wanted her to have. And there wasn't much else to say before she left. I waited with her till the cab came, walked her to the door. A hug. Two souls brought together and torn apart under twisted circumstances. No tears shed, no lessons learned. Just the brutal truth of death. Maybe one day our too-brief meeting will make more sense, and I'll know what to feel about her. But then, when she climbed in the cab and it pulled away, I was too numb to even wave good-bye.

So. That happened.

Took the car back to Dad's and crashed on his couch for the night. Dreamt of an empty hospital bed with pristine sheets and pillows, of Agnes walking in again and again and always with the same expectant smile. Every time, she stopped and began to realize what happened, then she'd vanish and come beaming in again anyway.

Dad woke me around dawn, asked if I still needed the car. I said yeah, thinking there's one last bit of business to square away: retrieve Jeepers and the money. Lou would've wanted it that way, I think. He said as much when I last saw him.

I park on Wellsbrook a few hours later, walk around to the rear door. The neighboring backyard rises slightly and levels off to a concrete driveway. I see Francesca there, crouching in net and fully equipped, from mask to Rollerblades. She's facing a metal box propped up on four tires in Lou's yard. A black tube sticks up from the top of the box, and an extension cord stretches from its backside to her house.

The tube clicks, and the box ejects a puck. It sails wide of the net and lands somewhere in her other neighbor's yard. Click, puck loads and goes flying, this time toward her shoulder. She jerks back with the hit, and the puck rolls in for a score. Before she resets her stance, the machine fires off another to the lower corner. And another score. She never even saw that one.

The machine doesn't care and doesn't wait. Click, shot. Dings in off the post. Click, shot. Banks off her blocker, trickles in behind her. Click, shot. She stops it by going down in a butterfly but might've hurt her knee, slow to recover as the next shot whizzes into the twine. And lands in a pile of other pucks.

Francesca notices me watching her and tries to reset. Click, shot. The puck hits her right in the mask. It never does cross the goal line, but she's had enough. She throws down her stick and tears off her helmet.

"That's it. That is it!" she says, and the machine seems to agree. It clicks, but nothing comes out. No more pucks to shoot, nothing to do but sit there humming and drawing power.

Francesca comes hobbling toward me, as upset as the last time we met. "So you're gonna rip on me, too, huh? Tell me how much I suck? I tried to play with the kids at the park, and they all called me 'Fat-cesca.' I hate it! I hate them!"

I don't know what to say to any of this, so I don't even try.

"So, am I really fat?" she says, staring at me through her raccoon makeup, intent on getting an honest answer.

"You are kind of chubby."

"Oh, *thanks*! You look like crap yourself, you know. Like a hungover bum who hasn't slept or showered in a week. So there."

"I'm not here to argue. I'm getting my stuff from Mr. Kashon's, and that's all. He died yesterday morning, you know."

"I know. My dad saw it in the paper. Sucks."

"And this will be the last time we ever see each other. So let's not fight, okay?"

"You're really not gonna help me?"

"I'm trying to help you right now. Listen to me. If you don't love to play hockey, then don't play hockey. You don't have to prove yourself to me or anybody else. You're a good kid just the way you are. You have a beautiful spirit, and you're worth something. Don't let anybody tell you otherwise."

"No, I'm fat, ugly, and dorky. That's what everybody says."

"You're a smart, funny girl, and you're very pretty. Look, if I were your age, your old man would have a shotgun shell with my name on it. And I'm sure there's at least one kid at school who likes you."

"Doubt it."

"I don't, and I'll give you a hint about finding him. He's probably creepy, weird, and awkward. You might catch him watching you from a distance, but he's too shy to approach you. Give that kid a chance. You might make each other happy for a while."

"Whatever," she says with a despondent shrug. Then, before I can start away, "Hey, wait. You still owe me a favor, remember? For helping you with Mr. Kashon."

Francesca moves in so close we're almost touching. Closes her eyes, lifts her chin, and puckers up. What the hell, I figure, and kiss her. It's nothing extravagant, just a kiss on the lips. It may be her first, and it'll surely be our last. When I step back, she's blushing. Eyes still closed, smiling with her fang showing. I whisper a good-bye and head for the door.

"Wait, wait! One more thing. Do you know that lady who stopped by Mr. Kashon's last night?"

"What lady?"

"You'd know if you saw her. She came after midnight, pulled up in the alley in a fancy old-timey car. Since it was dark and I was looking through my window, I couldn't see her face that good. But she looked totally glammed out. Like with the gloves up to her elbows and long black hair and snowy pale skin. Like she was a fashion model or something. Just thought maybe you knew her, since you've been hanging around Mr. Kashon's."

I stare at her, unable to speak. Thinking, and calculating, and knowing she has no reason to lie or recognize who she saw.

My silence makes her uneasy, and she adds, "Or maybe it was just a stupid dream. Never mind."

I smile as best I can and say, "It was a dream."

Francesca doesn't quite buy it but returns my smile anyway, lingering to watch me leave.

Once inside the house, I hurry through the kitchen and hallway, sideways between the stacks of yellowing paper. Up the steps, by now immune to the creaking wood underfoot, the stale air, the layers of dust on every surface. Into the bedroom where I left

Jeepers and my duffel, where Lou first told me her name and showed me what I'd win for finding her.

I kick aside bottles and fallen plaster, kneel before the dresser. Open the drawer, and the money's gone. All of it, every single dollar, gone along with my duffel.

That's not to say the drawer's empty. Instead of the money there's one shaking Jeepers, his fur all fizzed, eyes bugging out of his skull, black ribbon tied around his neck in a loopy bow. There's also a folded note.

I take it out, open it to her familiar cursive. One read, and I feel the need to sit. Jeepers hops onto the mattress, still shaking, and burrows under my arm like he's cowering from something. I pet him gently, trying to soothe him while reading it again. Nope, still don't believe it. It's not till the third read when the full brunt of the note comes down. And it's heavy enough to lay me flat on my back, wrecked and sunk in a swamp of possibilities.

In case you're wondering, it reads:

Sweetie,
Hope I wasn't too rough with your pussy.
So well-played, such a shame one of us had to lose. Don't you wilt just yet, though. I didn't lie when I said I was fond of you, and to prove it, I leave you to your time. Time to dwell on your failures and mistakes, to remember everyone you've disappointed, to ponder the passages and slippages of Time itself, to spend until you have none left. It's all you have and always less than it was, but it's all yours.

Forever Your Love,
Mercy